A WILLOW CREEK CHRISTMAS

LILY GRAISON

A Willow Creek Christmas
A Willow Creek Series Romance Novel

ISBN-13: 978-0615932729
ISBN-10: 061593272X

Cover design: Clarise Tan
http://www.ctcovercreations.com

Visit Lily's website at www.lilygraison.com

A WILLOW CREEK CHRISTMAS

CHAPTER ONE

Noah yanked on the horses reins, barely getting the wagon stopped before he yelled, "Hell's fire, woman. Watch where you're going!" The idiotic woman who stepped into the road in front of him turned her large blue eyes, wide with alarm, his way, her mouth open as she gasped in fright. She stared at him for long moments then blinked, clutching the shawl around her shoulders tighter before running across the street and disappearing between two buildings.

He watched her go, shook his head in disgust, then got the horse moving again, steering him toward the Willow Creek mercantile. Pulling to a stop alongside the wooden sidewalk, he glanced inside the store. Then grimaced. Packed with customers as usual.

Securing the brake, he hopped to the ground, rounded the wagon and hurried inside the store. He glanced toward the group of school age kids when one said, "Look Alex, Willow Creek's resident monster is out before dark." The sound of their giggles were loud inside the building, and he noticed Holden Avery's daughter, Alexandra, shove an elbow into a boy's stomach. Noah threw them a glare, holding the boy's gaze until the youth paled and made a beeline for the back of the store.

The word monster played on repeat inside Noah's head as he tried to ignore those openly staring at him. They'd heard the kid too, and by the looks on their faces, agreed with the snot-nosed little brat.

As always, he kept his head down, walked to the counter, then waited for Morgan Avery, town marshal in Willow Creek, to conclude his business.

The whispers in the room grew, each uttered breath echoing in Noah's head. They were staring at him, he could feel their gazes like hot pokers in his back. He remembered now why he loathed coming to town.

Morgan turned to leave, spotted him, and stopped. Noah sighed. He'd hoped the man would keep on walking but like the rest of that Avery bunch, they made a habit of thinking he wanted to talk with them.

"Noah. It's good to see you." Morgan pushed the front of his hat up. "How you been faring so far from town by yourself?"

"Fine." Morgan looked as if he were waiting for him to say more but as far as Noah was concerned, he'd answered the marshal's question.

"Do you need any help getting your place ready for winter?"

"Nope."

Morgan smiled. "Anybody ever accuse you of talking too much?"

"No."

"Didn't think so." The marshal shook his head, still grinning, then said his goodbyes, much to Noah's relief.

The dour faced Mrs. Jenkins muttered something under her breath as he approached the counter, then greeted him with a nod of her head as she stared at him over the rim of her glasses. In the two years he'd lived in Willow Creek, he didn't think the woman had ever spoken a word to him other than to tell him how much money he owed her. Which was fine by him. The less people he had to speak to, the better. He didn't settle here to make friends, anyway.

Noah held out the note he'd scribbled his list on to Mrs. Jenkins. She snatched it from his gloved hand as if he were about to reach out and grab her at any moment, to taint her in some foul way by being this close to him. He held back a sneer of disgust at her actions and looked away as she turned from the counter and proceeded to collect the things he'd requested.

The mercantile was full today. He hadn't been to town in nearly two months and the one day he decided to make the trip, he encountered more people than he'd seen in the past year.

He turned, browsing the tables near the counter, looking at nothing in particular when feminine laughter caught his attention. Against his better judgment, he glanced up.

Holden Avery and a woman he'd never seen before were looking his way. To his surprise, Holden lifted his hand and motioned him over. "Damn," he whispered under his breath before sighing. He should have known Holden Avery was nearby. He'd already seen the man's daughter.

He wasn't sure what it was about those Averys. They'd lent him a hand more than once since he moved to town, all without him asking a thing from them. He'd refused their help countless times, but they always insisted, doing whatever it took to make his life just a little bit easier. As much as it irked him, he figured the least they deserved was civility when they spoke to him, even if it galled him to do so.

He crossed the room and stopped a few feet away.

"Noah, I'd like to introduce you to Ms. Grace Kingston. Grace, this is Noah Lloyd." Holden glanced at the woman again and so did Noah. She was pretty with a head full of golden hair nestled under a hat with feather plumes and what looked like a bird's nest on one side. His gaze skated down her figure and back up. He'd seen dresses like the one she was wearing before. A lifetime ago, it seemed, back home in Charleston. He didn't know where she hailed from but she was too fancy for a dusty little town like Willow Creek. This lady was wealthy, her posture alone told him that, and he was sure she was just as snooty and highfalutin as those prissy debutantes he once knew.

She smiled at him and nodded her head ever so slightly. "It's a pleasure to make your acquaintance, Mr. Lloyd."

Noah didn't reply. He stared at her for a few moments before turning his attention back to Holden. The man smiled and shook his head.

"Ms. Kingston is looking for a husband. Seems she ran into a bit of trouble with the one she came out here for."

Noah raised an eyebrow at Holden's quiet statement. Why was he telling him about her problems? His gaze darted in her direction again. She was still smiling at him. An uneasy feeling settled in his gut before he felt a shock go through his system. Surely Holden Avery didn't think he—the town's most unlikable person—would be interested in taking in this fancy lady. To marry her?

He met the man's eyes, saw the expectant gleam shining back at him, and knew he did. He'd introduced him to Ms. Kingston in hopes of securing a husband for her.

Something dark and ugly reared its head as he stared at the two of them. Fire licked through his veins. His pulse quickened and he narrowed his eyes. "I don't want a wife," he said, his voice rough and scratchy to his own ears. "If you'll excuse me."

He nodded to Ms. Kingston, and turned, making his way back to the counter.

He felt his ears burning the moment Holden's words repeated themselves inside his head. *Ms. Kingston is looking for a husband.* And Holden asked him? Was Holden teasing him or had he really thought to play match-maker and hook this woman up with him?

He glanced at them out of the corner of his eye. They were talking quietly, laughing at something—probably him—and loathing filled him until his skin felt hot, the side of his face burning, the scar he'd lived with for so long seeming to come to life to remind him no one would look upon him and not be revolted. Especially a lady like Ms. Kingston.

A small voice in the back of his head whispered that she hadn't looked as if she'd been revolted. Maybe she would be okay with the way he looked.

Noah scoffed. She must be damn near desperate then. Either that or more polite than most women by pretending not to notice.

Mrs. Jenkins returned, the boxes of dry goods packed to the top, along with the special order he'd placed months ago. Noah paid her and heaved the first box from the counter and headed for the door without a word. It took three trips to get everything outside, but he breathed a sigh of relief when lifting the last box. It was heavy, the items Mrs. Jenkins put on top making it hard to see over. Knowing her dislike of him, she'd probably done it on purpose.

A squeal from a child distracted his thoughts. He turned his head in time to see one running his way, her blond locks obscuring her face. She ran into him, hitting him in just the right place on the back of his knee causing his leg to give out, the box tipping over and spilling its contents over the wooden sidewalk.

The girl bounced off his leg and ended up on her backside by his feet.

"Watch where you're going," he shouted.

The girl sat up, lifting one arm to fling her hair out of her face. She was young, no more than five or six, he noticed, and was a tiny little thing. Her clothes were threadbare and her face reminded him of a painting he saw once of a plump cheeked cherub. Of course, the cherub in the painting didn't have dirt smeared across its face, nor was its nose running, leaving a snotty trail clean to its lip.

Noah stared down at her, watching her bright-blue eyes

widen in alarm before tears started to gather. His own eyes widened then. Hell's fire, she was going to cry. He could tell by the way her face turned pink then red, her eyes filling with more tears as her lip protruded into a pout. The moment she opened her mouth, he braced himself.

She let out a wail loud enough to wake the dead and Noah cringed as he stared at her. He debated on helping her to her feet, or jumping into his wagon and leaving his purchased goods—and her—there on the sidewalk.

He looked down the street, noticed a few people turn to look his way, but saw no one this little urchin could belong to.

She cried hard while fat tears rolled down her cheeks, her wails drawing more attention by the second. Noah hunched his shoulders and reached for her, grabbing the front of her shabby dress and bunching the material in his fist before lifting her to her feet. He heard someone yell, "Sophie," and looked up.

A boy ran onto the sidewalk from between the mercantile and the telegraph office. He was older than the girl by a few years but his clothes were just as shabby. His face was cleaner but not by much. He turned his head and spotted the girl, relief evident on his face.

He ran to where they stood and Noah loosened his grip on the front of her dress. He watched them both, staring at the boy as he wrapped a bony arm around the girl's shoulders and held her awkwardly to his side. "Sorry, Mister." The boy looked up, his gaunt face ashen. "She got away from me when I wasn't lookin.'"

Noah didn't reply, just watched them until a feminine voice caught his attention. The woman who stepped in front of his wagon, and nearly got herself trampled in the process, approached at a fast clip. Their mother, he assumed. He gave her a look from head to toe as she approached them. She wasn't much to look at. Her clothes were tattered, her thin shawl ragged in places, a large hole in the material glared at him from her left shoulder. She turned bright-blue eyes his way and for the first time since leaving Charleston twelve years ago, Noah saw pain in someone else's eyes that nearly matched his own.

She gave him a slight smile, a nervous gesture he was sure, before she leaned down, tucking the children under her arms. "I'm sorry. They didn't mean any harm."

Noah stared at her, his gaze now fixed on her hair. It fell just below her jaw and hung in limp, dirty strands. He wasn't even sure of the color, nor had he ever seen a woman wear her hair so short. He instantly wondered why she did.

He looked back to her face. Her nose had the slightest upturn on the end, her eyes large and luminous, their color the purest cornflower-blue he'd ever seen. Pretty, if he cared to think about it, which he didn't. A quick glance down her body showed her to be waif thin, her clothes hanging off of her small frame. Just like the rags those kids were wearing, the woman's dress was stained and the stench of unwashed skin polluted the air around them and nearly took his breath.

She turned without another word, ushering the children away, and he watched them slip back between the buildings. Noah waited nearly five minutes—for what he had no idea—before shaking his head and picking everything up from the sidewalk and tossing it back into the box. Securing his goods, he climbed in the wagon and grabbed the reins.

The ride home was bumpy, the wagon jostling over the rutted road. The sky was darkening. It would snow soon. A storm was brewing, he could feel it in his bones.

Reaching his small cabin, he unloaded his provisions, tucked them away in the larder and unhitched his horse from the wagon. He tended the animals, ate a bowl of stew that had been simmering all day, and picked up his leather bound journal from the top of the desk. He unwrapped the special pencils he'd sent away for, found the small container holding the graphite lead to fill his pen and crossed the room to sit in the old rocker he'd found in the barn when he bought the place.

Opening the journal, he flipped through the pages until he found a space near the back and spent the next hour drawing the likeness of Ms. Grace Kingston, the lady Holden Avery had introduced him to in the mercantile. When he was satisfied with the drawing, he wrote her name under her likeness and dated it, blew across the page to remove any graphite dust and thumbed back through all the pages.

Everyone he'd ever encountered in Willow Creek could be found in the pages of his journal, along with the faces of people he'd known a lifetime ago, all of them staring back at him through small scenes of a life he barely remembered living.

Closing the book, he stared into the fire. The occasional crack and pop of the wood the only sounds to be heard other than the wind whistling against the outside walls.

Sighing, Noah folded his arms across his chest, leaned back and set the chair to rocking before glancing up at the clock. He had four full hours before dark. Four hours before he could escape into an oblivion of dreamless sleep.

Keri tried to soothe Sophie Ann, shushing her as they sat in the grove behind the mercantile. The small bench nestled under crooked, bare tree limbs was dry for once. She wiped Sophie's face and said, "Hush now. Stop your crying, love."

Sophie Ann sniffled, hiccuped once, and wailed again. "I got scared," she cried.

"I told you I'd be right back, now didn't I?"

She nodded. "Aaron said it would be dark soon and I don't want to be here at dark."

"I know, honey," Keri said, smoothing back Sophie's hair. "But it can't be helped. Not this time."

Keri gathered her little girl back into her arms, coddling her despite promising not to do so. She couldn't help it. Not after what they'd had to endure over the last six months. Watching them slowly grow thinner and listening to their grumbling bellies night after night was taking its toll. She wasn't sure how much longer they'd survive on their own—or survive, period—so if coddling them offered some small measure of comfort, she'd do it without a single regret.

Aaron slid in next to them on the bench and Keri blinked away her own tears as she looked at him. She reached out, pushed his hair out of his eyes, then wrapped her arm around his shoulders, drawing him in close to her side. He'd grown up so much in the last few months. The little boy she knew was gone, replaced with a child much wiser than his years. She mourned his lost youth.

Looking up at the sky, the darkening horizon drew a long sigh from her lungs. Regardless of Sophie Ann's outburst, she couldn't sit here holding her until nightfall. She sat Sophie back down on the bench. A simple glance at Aaron, telling him silently to watch his little sister, was all it took for him to nod in acceptance.

"I'll be back," she said, smiling as she reached out to wipe Sophie's face again. "Please stay here. I don't want you wandering around town without me, okay?"

The children nodded their heads at her and Keri turned, heading back toward the buildings. She navigated town with practiced ease, avoided looking at anyone and hoped she blended in. She crossed the street near the stagecoach station, remembering to look and see if anyone was coming down the road this time. Making her way around the building, she and waited for nearly half an hour before the back door opened.

A portly woman with graying hair sat the bucket Keri had been waiting on by the back stoop before giving a shrill whistle and yelling, "Come and get it, dog, before it gets cold." The woman waited a few moments then turned, walked back inside, and closed the door behind her.

Keri waited another five minutes before sneaking over to the back of the building to look inside the bucket. She grimaced at the offering.

Day old stew, clumpy potatoes, and bits of bread swam in congealing grease. Keri's stomach turned, her heart breaking an instant later as tears filled her eyes. As miserable as life had been to them in the last little while, she knew this was the low point. Stealing scraps and slop from discarded buckets of waste meant for a dog to keep them fed.

She reached in with a trembling hand, scooped out a bit with two fingers and brought them to her mouth, tears scalding her throat as she tasted it. It was still warm, just as the woman said. She turned her head to one side, wiped her tears away with a shrug of her shoulder and grabbed the handle on the bucket, lifting it and turning. That's when she saw him. The dog the woman had called. He was as pitiful a sight as she was.

His brown coat was filthy with dried mud. He looked as emaciated as she felt and Keri sighed when he came to a stop a few feet away. He whined, lowered his head, his floppy ears dangling in his face and Keri felt something inside her break. Tears filled her eyes again and she blinked them away, put one hand under the bucket and dumped a good bit of the old stew onto the ground for the animal. She stared at him, hoped what she'd given him was enough to appease his hunger, and resolutely put him out of her mind. She had to. She had children to worry about. Worrying about the welfare of a dog would do her no good when she couldn't do anything about it anyway.

She sighed and turned, running around the side of the building before anyone saw her. Stopping at the corner of the building, she eyed those on the street. Music from the saloon filled the air and her eye was drawn to it the same as it was every time they ventured to town. She'd been tempted more than once to enter the building but her stomach always rolled at the thought and stopped her. She may not have a choice soon. They couldn't keep going like this and they certainly couldn't walk to California. She needed money and whoring herself out in the saloon may be the only option left.

Pushing the thought away for now, she scanned the street before venturing out of her hiding place. It took a bit of maneuvering to get back to the other side of town without being seen but she walked into the clearing behind the mercantile a few minutes later to find her children right where she'd left them.

Her heart nearly broke to see their gaunt faces but she smiled at them to hide her sorrow. Setting the bucket on the bench, she blinked away more tears. "It's stew," she said. "There's even a bit of meat in there, I think."

The kids looked into the bucket, their eyes wide and expectant. When they reached in, scooping the stew and potatoes out by the handfuls, Keri nearly suffocated, her throat tight and swelling as more tears threatened to fall. She sucked in large amounts of air, willing herself to be strong for them and sat down as they ate.

It was nearly nightfall when they'd finished. Aaron looked up at her, a frown marring his face. "Are you not going to eat, Ma?"

Keri smiled at him. "No love. You and your sister eat it. There will be more later for me."

When the residents of Willow Creek settled in for the night and the bucket was empty, Keri stood, held a finger to her lips to silence the children and crept to the back door of the mercantile. It opened with little resistance and she peeked over her shoulder, making sure Aaron and Sophie were still on the bench before she snuck inside.

She could hear the woman who ran the store in the upstairs loft talking to someone, and Keri paused when the floorboards under her feet creaked. She listened and held her breath before venturing farther into the room.

As before, she took only what she needed. Two loaves of bread, a jar of preserves, and a small bag of beans. She snuck back out, ran to the bench and gathered Aaron and Sophie, hurrying toward the outskirts of town and praying no one had seen her.

The walk back to the shack they'd been calling home was long, the night bitterly cold, but Keri smiled as she clutched her purloined loot. They would be able to eat for a week now thanks to her stolen goods. She looked toward the sky, the moon and stars blotted out by gathering clouds, and she hoped the weather held. If it snowed now, they were as good as dead.

CHAPTER TWO

The chicken coop was void of eggs again. Noah scratched at his beard while staring at the hens. He wasn't sure what was wrong with the critters but he hadn't seen an egg in over a week.

He shut the door to the coop and ventured to the barn. The cow had been milked but she was raising a fuss about something. He looked in on her, figured she just felt like bellowing this morning, and turned to tend his horse. He bridled him but left his saddle on the railing and led him out into the morning air. Clouds filled the sky and Noah looked up, staring at the darkening horizon and knew snow was coming. He could smell it on the breeze.

Taking up the brush, Noah groomed the horse until he shined, rubbed his neck and talked to the animal as if he were a real person. He'd found out pretty early that living alone took its toll if he never spoke, so his animals got a daily dose of stories and history as he'd seen it unfold, retold by an ex-confederate soldier who saw more death and destruction than any one man should have to endure.

He finished up another tale of bloodshed, remembering his

old friend Dwight Lytle, when he looked out across the valley. He saw smoke in the distance, lingering near the top of the trees that lined his property. Noah lowered the horse brush and stared at the thin ribbon of smoke. Was something on fire? His heart started racing at the thought.

Turning back to the barn, he raced in, tossed the brush away and grabbed his saddle, making quick work of getting it cinched on the horse. He ran to the cabin, grabbed his gun from the hook above the mantle—only an idiot traveled into the woods without one—and stored the weapon in the scabbard on the saddle before mounting.

The leather creaked under his weight and Noah adjusted his hat and pulled his collar up around his ears when the wind shifted. The first tiny flakes of snow drifted toward him, fluttering by his face as he took up the reins, giving them a small flick to get the horse moving.

The ride across the valley was slow. The snow fluttering in on a wisp of a breeze turned into a downpour within minutes, whiting out the countryside. Noah debated on going back to the cabin but that smoke was still there, black and thick amongst the trees.

He urged the horse forward and realized long moments later the smoke was coming from an old line shack that sat on the edge of his property. The building wasn't fit for anything other than firewood. It used to house cowboys watching over a herd in some long ago past, but Noah hadn't had a use for it. It leaned to one side, the roof sagging in the middle, and he was surprised it was still standing at all.

Dismounting, he tied the horse's reins to a nearby tree, pulled his rifle from the scabbard, and crept quietly toward the building. He could hear voices, a bit of laughter. Someone was in the shack. Squatters. Noah felt his blood race through his veins at the mere thought. His empty chicken coop came to mind and he knew why there were no eggs. Someone was stealing them. He'd bet his farm on it.

The horse chose that moment to nay and snort, stomping one hoof into the gathering snow. Noah looked back over his shoulder at the animal and scowled, willing him to be quiet.

The noise inside the shack stopped, someone making a shushing noise and Noah's blood pressure soared. He straightened, raised the rifle and aimed it at the door. "I know you're in there! Come on out."

He waited, watching the door, the silence deafening.

The snow slacked off, the flakes once again fluttering in front of him and the clink of small ice pellets began to fall. Noah waited, watching as his breath clouded the air in front of him and grew impatient. "Open up," he yelled, sighting the door with his rifle.

When the door hinges creaked, Noah eyed the opening, waiting. The darkness inside the small shack was disconcerting. He took a step forward, sleet and snow pelting his face. When he was close enough to touch the door, he lifted his leg, kicking it open while readying his rifle.

Startled gasps were followed by fright filled screams and the dirty faces of the street urchins he'd run into in town the day before filled his vision. They were huddled near the crumbling fireplace, the cherub-faced girl staring at him wide-eyed while she sucked on her thumb.

He stepped into the shack, lowering his gun as he stared at them, and narrowed his eyes. "What are you doing on my property?"

When they didn't answer, Noah took two more steps into the shack, his gaze landing on the boy. He met his stare head on and held it, but the slightest flicker to Noah's left side caught his attention moments before he realized someone was behind him. He turned to see the woman brandishing a frying pan, a startled look in her eyes as she lowered her arms, swinging the pan his way.

The metal caught him square in the forehead. He saw bright flashes of light as her face wavered, her large luminous eyes fear-stricken as the world seemed to shift. His knees buckled, his bones jarring as he hit the floor, both knees driving into the wooden floorboards. The woman lifted the frying pan again, holding the weapon above her head as the world tilted on its axis. Noah fell, his head connecting with the floor, her quiet, "I'm so sorry," ringing inside his head as he lost consciousness.

"Is he dead?"

Keri scowled at Aaron's question. "No, he isn't dead." At least she hoped he wasn't. She glanced back at the man's prone form. He hadn't made so much as a twitch since she'd hit him. She wasn't even sure he was breathing. It was hard to tell with the way he was lying.

Pacing nervously in front of him, Keri nearly chewed her bottom lip raw with worry while stealing glances at him. She recognized him. He was the man from town. The one she'd found Aaron and Sophie standing with on the sidewalk in front of the mercantile, the one who nearly ran her over in the street.

He'd scared her half to death when she first saw him. Nothing about the man had seemed friendly, his gray eyes cold and angry. Now, seeing him lie lifeless at her feet only intensified that earlier fear. What if she had killed him?

Aaron inched closer, his questions non-stop, and Keri pointed back toward the fireplace and waited until the boy did as she silently asked.

She stared at the man lying near her feet for long moments, then went to her knees in front of him. Sliding his rifle away, she reached out a hand, pushing his scraggly hair away from his face and laid one finger under his nose to see if he was still breathing. He was, thank the Lord.

Staring at his face, Keri's attention was drawn to a nasty scar running from his temple, down past his right eye and disappearing into his scraggly beard. The scar was puckered and white, which told her it was placed there years ago. She raised her hand, tentatively touching the furrowed skin. Whoever stitched it had done a poor job. The edges weren't even and it varied in width as it traveled down the length of his face.

He was a big man, his shoulders wide, and she knew the added bulk wasn't the thick coat he wore. His hands were big, the material of the black gloves he wore straining at the seams. His dark hair hung past his shoulders, the strands unkempt, his full beard long and bushy, and even though he smelled of soap, he looked as filthy as she was.

When he stirred, Keri scrambled to her feet and backed away. He blinked a few times, moaned, raised a hand and laid it against his forehead. Then he looked up at her.

His eyes were so pale gray they looked silver in the low light but it took only seconds for anger to darken his irises like storm clouds, his fury nearly tangible as the air in the room seemed to dissipate. When he moved, laying one hand on the floor in front of him and trying to sit up, she grabbed his rifle and lifted it, her hands shaking as she pointed the barrel in his direction.

It took him long minutes to climb to his feet and Keri's nerves were rattled by the time he stood to his full height in front of her. She swallowed a sudden lump forming in her throat and stared up at him, willing him to not harm them.

He locked eyes with her again, his cold gray stare piercing her where she stood and the gun barrel wavered. She gripped the weapon more securely and took another step back. "Don't move," she said, her voice cracking as she spoke. "I don't want to shoot you, but I will."

His gaze stayed with the gun and Keri was confident he

wouldn't try to rush her. She lowered her shoulders a fraction and motioned to the door. "You just get on out of here. I don't want no trouble."

He leaned his head to one side, his hair falling over the scarred side of his face as he narrowed his eyes at her. "This is my land, woman, so you're the one who'll be leaving."

Sophie made the smallest of noises and Keri glanced in her direction. It was a mistake. The man snatched the gun from her hands and had it turned, lifted, and pointed at her in a matter of seconds.

Noah studied the woman, taking in her bony arms, her short, limp hair, and the gauntness of her face. She was deathly pale, dark circles lay under her eyes like two large bruises and the clothes she wore weren't fit for cleaning rags. He turned his gaze to the children. His earlier assessment of them hadn't changed. They looked only slightly better than their mother did but not by much.

The inside of the shack was bare except for the fireplace. A bundle of twigs lay off to one side, and a small pot sat close to the coals, the aroma of beans filling the air. A half-eaten loaf of bread and a jar of what looked like preserves of some kind lay on the edge of an old blanket that was stretched out in front of the fire. There wasn't anything else. No furniture, no other clothing, nothing.

The woman made a small move and he turned his head to her. She froze and stared at him, her gaze flicking to the side of his face and he knew she was staring at that damnable scar. Heat surged through his body, embarrassment and anger filling him until he thought he'd burst from the need to scream at her. To tell her to stop staring at him like he was something foul. His pulse raced and every taunt he'd endured over the last decade assaulted him again with that one small glance. He met her gaze and lowered his head a fraction. "Get out."

Her eyes widened, her mouth opening as if to speak but she closed it with a snap. She glanced toward her children before meeting his hardened gaze again. "Please," she whispered. "We've nowhere else to go."

"And I care, why?"

She flinched, her eyes turning glassy. For a split second, the notion of letting her stay entered his mind but common sense prevailed a moment later. "Get your things and go," he said. "You've taken advantage of me enough as it is." He stared at all of them in turn before asking, "You been taking my eggs?"

The woman took a small step toward the kids and the boy sent an angry glare in Noah's direction. He lifted his chin, defiance shining in his eyes. "Them chickens barely lay any eggs," the kid said. "I've only taken four all week."

Just as Noah suspected. He knew his hens were still laying.

Turning to the door, Noah opened it and stood there staring at them. "There's other farms nearby. Go steal their eggs."

He watched them gather their few belongings, the little girl starting to sniffle, her eyes filling with tears, and Noah tried to ignore the voice in the back of his mind screaming what a miserable bastard he was. What sort of man would throw a defenseless woman and two youngins out into the cold?

One who didn't give two shits about anything anymore, that's what kind.

The threesome left the shack and headed deeper into the woods. Noah watched them until they were out of sight, his conscious nearly eating him alive as a silent battle went on inside his head.

He looked around the shack again, saw the pitiful fire still burning and crossed the room, disturbing the few coals still burning with the toe of his boot. When he was sure it wouldn't blaze—not that there was anything there to continue to burn—he left, pulling the door closed behind him, stored his rifle back in the scabbard and climbed into the saddle.

The ride back to his cabin was filled with a war of words inside his head. He was near deaf by the time the barn came into view. His back burned as if the woman's accusing glare was scorching his flesh and he clenched his jaw, trying to push her image from his mind.

Her gaunt face wouldn't leave.

Regardless of how hard he tried, those tired, soulless eyes of hers were still there, haunting him, begging him to let them stay.

"Damn it all to hell," he muttered, finally pulling on the horse's reins to get the animal to stop.

Snow was still falling, the fluttering flakes hitting his face and sticking to his beard. He lifted a hand, brushed most of it away and turned his head, looking back over his shoulder toward the woods.

Where had they gone? There was nothing out there, regardless of what he'd told them. Nothing but trees and the creek. No shelter from the wind or the snow. They'd be dead by morning if they had to sleep on the ground.

A barrage of hateful words filled his head, all of them directed at himself, and he realized in that moment, all the taunts he'd heard since the war ended were coming true. He really was a monster. He'd just turned a woman and two helpless little ones out into the cold.

Only a monster would be so heartless.

CHAPTER THREE

K eri heard the horse's heavy footfalls hitting the frozen ground seconds before she saw him. His misty figure slowly came into focus and she stopped, staring into the clearing, watching horse and rider with her heart in her throat. She ushered the children behind a large tree and waited, her blood rushing past her ears as she straightened her spine, trying not to look as terrified as she felt.

The man's anger was still evident, his eyes cold and menacing. He stopped, the horse dancing underneath him, and their gazes locked. He said nothing for long moments and Keri held her breath as she watched him. He was a terrifying sight. The black stallion he rode was powerful, his snorts crystallizing the air in front of him. She glanced back at the man astride the beast. The look on his face told her he'd rather be a hundred different places than sitting in front of her and she wondered what he wanted. Wondered if he'd come back for payment of those eggs Aaron had taken. At least he didn't know about the milk his cow had given up for them.

"What's your name?"

Keri was jarred from her silent musing by his question. He

had a distinct Southern accent she hadn't paid much attention to back in the cabin but the drawl was unmistakable. She wondered why he was in Montana but dismissed the thought when he shifted, one eyebrow lifting as he waited on her to answer his question. "Keri," she said, clearing her throat when her voice cracked. "Keri Hilam." He looked to her left and she saw Aaron out of the corner of her eye. He'd walked out from behind the tree. She frowned at him for not staying hidden, then said, "That's my boy, Aaron. He's ten."

"And the little one?"

"Sophie Ann is five." When she locked eyes with him again, it was all she could do to keep the tears from stealing her words. "Please." The word came out as a faint whisper. "That shack is the only thing keeping us alive at the moment. We'll surely die out here in the open."

He studied her for long moments, his gaze never faltering. Keri held her breath, willed him to see their precarious situation and hoped he showed them this one small mercy.

"Where's your man?"

Her heart thumped against her rib cage. "Dead." Keri swallowed to dislodge the knot forming in her throat. "He was thrown from a horse. We've been alone since spring."

"You've no other family to take you in?"

Sophie chose that moment to make her presence known. "Uncle Robert was mean to us."

Her soft spoken statement cut Keri like a knife, her gut wrenching as she looked over at her. "Hush, Sophie Ann."

The man stared at them for what seemed like an eternity before shifting in the saddle. Keri could tell he was reconsidering his earlier command for them to leave but she wasn't sure why. His gaze swept over her again from head to toe and fear coiled in her stomach. Would he be like every other man she'd encountered over the past few months? Expecting payment for his generosity by having a quick tumble with her between his bed sheets?

Her eyes burned, tears filling her vision until he became blurry and she bit her lip to keep it from trembling. Could no one help them without expecting something in return?

He sighed, his gaze flicking over the three of them before landing on her again. "You can stay as long as the snow falls. The moment it clears, leave." He turned the horse and rode away as fast as the beast would carry him in the snow.

Keri watched his retreating form in stunned silence until he disappeared, his image lost in the snowfall. He hadn't asked for anything. He offered her no lewd remarks or looks. Hadn't requested payment of any kind from her. The tears pooling in her eyes slipped past her eyelashes. She wiped them away and smiled down at Aaron and Sophie. "Let's go," she said. "For whatever reason, he's changed his mind."

They trudged back to the shack, laying their things inside and spent the next half hour picking up twigs and logs small enough to carry. The snow was still falling and Keri wasn't sure how long the storm would last. If it stayed like this, the fluttering snowflakes falling in soft wisps, they'd be all right.

Getting another fire going took longer than she would have liked and by the time a small blaze sparked, her hands were near frozen. She added more twigs, squeezed in a small log, and ushered the kids in closer.

They spent the rest of the evening nibbling on bread and the cold beans still sitting next to the fireplace and Keri listened to Aaron tell Sophie a story until her mind started to wander. The vision of the man on his black stallion filled her mind's eye. He was nothing like the angels she'd heard stories of but he was nothing less than angelic. His face was full of hard lines, the scar making him look cold and dangerous, but his mercy on them left no room for doubt in her mind. Actions always spoke louder than words and even though his were harsh and biting, Keri knew that under all that unkempt hair, a kind soul still lived.

By nightfall, snow and sleet pelted the cabin until the sound nearly drove Noah out of his mind. He paced the small space he called home and stopped every so often to stare out the darkened window into the blackness that lay beyond the glass.

He lifted his hands, laying them on either side of the small window, and stared in the direction that that old line shack stood. His thoughts hadn't strayed far from the woman and kids since he'd returned home and now that the storm had picked up into what could be nothing more than a blizzard, worry started to creep in.

Had the roof of the shack caved in yet? Would it? How long would those beans and that loaf of bread last them? Was the threadbare blanket he saw on the floor by the fire all they had to keep them warm? Did they find enough firewood?

"Damn it," he muttered as he lowered his head, his mind looping around question after question.

He turned away from the window and looked around his cabin. It was nothing special but it was warm, the walls sound. The small lean-to kitchen was functional, his larder filled with food enough to feed a small army of people all winter and the cedar chest at the foot of his bed held more blankets than he'd ever use.

All the comforts a man needed were at his fingertips. He'd not starve regardless of how long the storm lasted. He'd be warm, cozy even, and knowing it caused guilt to eat away at him until his throat was raw, loathing choking him where he stood.

The wind whistled against the walls again and he walked to the door, opening it. A blast of icy air chilled him to the bone, sleet and snow stinging his face. The night was so dark he could see nothing past the door frame.

He shut the door, bolted it from the inside, and walked back to the rocker that sat facing the fire. Hours ticked by, thoughts muddled inside his head until he couldn't stand the torment a moment longer before he readied himself for bed.

Laying his head down, he closed his eyes, exhausted, his conscience filled with worry he shouldn't have for those squatters in his line shack until everything went blessedly quiet as sleep claimed him.

It seemed as if he'd only shut the world off when he heard the rooster crow. He blinked against the light flooding the room and wondered how he'd slept so soundly with all that had plagued him the evening before.

He crawled from the bed, dressed and ventured outside. The snow was still falling but the rope he'd thought to tie between the barn and the cabin was still there and he followed it, pushing the doors to the barn open when he reached it and spent the next hour tending his animals. It wasn't until he'd finished that he bridled the horse, sat the saddle on his back and cinched it tight that he went back into the house, pulled those extra blankets from the chest at the foot of his bed and carried them back outside.

The trip across the valley toward the trees was long and hard, the horse doing his best to walk in the deepening snow. When the line shack came into view long minutes later, Noah was relieved to see the roof still in place but just as he'd suspected, it sagged in the middle, the snow lying on top too heavy for the old rafters to handle.

He dismounted, grabbed the blankets and walked into the shack without knocking. The woman, Keri, she'd said her name was, sat by the fire, only a single flame burning around a pile of twigs in the crumbling fireplace, her arms wrapped around her small frame. She looked up, startled.

The children were still sleeping. They were wrapped around each other, the threadbare blanket he'd seen the day before tucked underneath them until they were both cocooned in a small, warm roll.

The air inside the shack was frigid, his breath frosting the air in front of him and his earlier plan, to leave the blankets, was shot all to hell the moment he saw the woman shiver. They couldn't stay here. The blankets would do very little with the temperature still dropping, not to mention the condition of the roof. Another day of heavy snowfall and they'd be buried alive.

He bit back a curse and clenched his jaw, staring at her gaunt face before sighing. "Get your things," he said. "You can't stay here."

She stood, her eyes wide, and he was once again startled by how thin she was. How unhealthy the pallor of her skin appeared, her eyes sunken and hollow.

"But I thought..." She blinked up at him, her lashes fluttering against her cheeks before he saw her swallow. "You said we could stay until the snow stopped."

"Well that was before I knew a blizzard was rolling in!" She jumped at the tone and harshness of his voice, her little ones stirring in their blanket. He ignored her reaction, not caring if he scared her. He did most people and was used to the looks by now, used to the way others shied away from him.

But when Noah looked into her eyes, he noticed the absence of fear and disgust when she looked at him. She wasn't turning away in revulsion. She met his gaze head on, held it. How long had it been since a woman looked at him and didn't turn away or stare at that damn scar? He couldn't even remember. His chest tightened until he found it hard to breathe. He glanced up at the roof and motioned to it with a hand. "The roof is sagging. Another day and it'll cave in on you."

The breath left her lungs in an audible gush when she saw the deep swag in the middle of the roof.

Noah glanced at her sleeping kids. "Get them up. You can't stay here." When her frightened eyes met and locked with his, he regretted speaking without explaining first. "I'm taking you back to my cabin until the storm breaks." It took only seconds for the expression on her face to change. In a blink of an eye, she looked miserable. Did the prospect of staying with him disgust her so much? Noah felt the loathing he'd lived with so long return in a flash, the anger he harbored with life in general scalding his throat to the point he could barely swallow.

He narrowed his eyes. "Stay then, I couldn't care less what happens to you, but when you're buried alive don't expect me to dig you out." He tossed the blankets he'd brought to the floor and turned, hurried across the room and reached out to grab the door handle. He hadn't heard her follow him but she grabbed his hand to stop him from leaving. He jumped, startled she'd touched him, and took a step away from her.

"Please, don't go."

Noah looked over at her, the misery he'd seen on her face still present. She licked her lips, the small pink tip of her tongue darted out and his heart thumped in his chest at the sight. Her lips were full and pink, but dry and cracked. She wasn't the least bit appealing but he couldn't help his thoughts going places they shouldn't have all because she'd touched him. Looked at him without flinching.

"I have no money to pay you."

Her softly spoken words snapped him back to the present. She straightened her spine, met his gaze head on. Her corn-flower-blue eyes were large, luminous, and quite possibly the prettiest color he'd ever seen. "I didn't ask you for any money," he said, snapping out of his daze. That look filled her eyes again. Misery and.... shame. With nothing but the clothes on her back, the woman apparently still had her pride. He realized she wasn't refusing his charity. She just felt ill at ease doing it. He tilted his head, his hair falling over the scarred side of his face. "There are other ways to pay me back if you feel so inclined."

She closed her eyes, her shoulders lifting as she inhaled a large breath. She nodded, opening her eyes back up as resignation washed over her face. "Very well then."

As she woke the children, he busied himself putting out the fire. When the kids turned sleepy eyes his way, he looked at them both as they stood there bundled up in the blankets he'd brought. He met their gazes briefly, then looked to the woman. "Are you ready?" he asked. She nodded her head in reply. "All right, then. Let's go."

CHAPTER FOUR

To Keri's utter amazement, he'd placed her and the children on the horse and walked by their side, slogging through the nearly knee high snow while guiding the horse back to his cabin.

What sort of man required payment from a woman by having her whore herself out to him but still behaved like a perfect gentleman? She glanced down at him and shook her head. She didn't understand him.

She'd hoped to never be in a position to stoop so low again but the frigid night she'd spent by a single flame, listening to her children's teeth chattering, changed that. She couldn't bare it. Couldn't watch them starve or freeze to death and do nothing to prevent it. If she had to bare herself to this harsh, angry man and let him slake his desire, then so be it. She'd do so three times a day if she had to.

It was late afternoon before his place came into view and Keri held Sophie to her just a little bit tighter. His small farm looked similar to the old home she had shared with John. The memories of his death, and the aftermath of his passing assaulted her, the terror she'd felt before one desperate act on her part had gone so wrong nearly stealing her breath.

She blinked and pushed the thought out of her mind. It did no good to dwell on the past.

The man led the horse to the cabin and reached for Aaron then Sophie, lifting them before setting them on the ground. When he turned to her, Keri could tell he was as uncomfortable touching her as she was at having him do it. He grabbed her around the waist and lifted her as if she weighed less than air and set her feet on the ground, taking two steps back once he did.

He nodded to the cabin door. "Go on inside. I need to take care of the horse, then I'll be in."

Keri waited until he shut the barn door behind him before opening the door to his cabin. She ushered the children in before going in herself, pushing the door shut behind her.

It took a few moments for her eyes to adjust to the low light and she blinked rapidly until everything came into focus. The cabin consisted of a bed and a single rocking chair facing the fireplace. A large trunk sat at the foot of the bed, its latch open. Articles of clothing hung from pegs nailed into the wall by the bed. A lean-to kitchen was situated on the right of the door. She craned her neck to look inside. A stove and a small table with two chairs lined one wall, a sink on the other. Shelves lining the wall held plates, cups and more food than Keri had ever seen. Bags of dry good, jars of preserves and canned meats, baskets and bins filled to capacity left her in awe. This man had enough food to feed half the town.

The moment she thought of him, the door opened and she turned, grabbing Aaron and Sophie by the shoulders and pulled them next to her. The man hung his hat on a peg by the door then removed his coat, hanging it as well. When he turned to face them, he looked more uncomfortable than Keri felt.

He took up most of the space by the door. He stood at a height much taller than most. He looked strongly built and healthy. The beard covering his face was scraggly and much too long and it hid his features well. The white puckered scar on his face was probably why he wore it so unkempt and his hair didn't look as if it had been combed in some time. He looked...wild. Untamed.

Clearing his throat, he glanced around the room. "The cabin's not much but there's plenty to eat."

Sophie turned and looked up at her. "Can we eat now?"

Keri shushed her and looked back up at the man. He gave her a flickering glance, then crossed the room, added a few logs to the fire and had a good blaze going by the time he stood and faced her again.

For reasons she didn't understand, her heart started pounding. He was on the other side of the room but his presence seemed to suck all the air from the small space. She blinked, met his gaze, and ignored her pounding heart. "Are you sure about this arrangement?" He raised his hand to scratch at his beard and Keri noticed he hadn't taken off his gloves. She puzzled over the fact until he spoke.

"I wouldn't have wasted my morning bringing you back with me if I wasn't sure."

He sounded angry again. Keri glanced away from his disgruntled face. He really was an ill-tempered man. "You live alone?"

"Yes."

Turning back to face him, she met his gaze. "What shall we call you?"

He said nothing for long moments, the silence becoming unbearable before he finally said, "I'm Noah Lloyd."

Keri stared at him, wondering how he expected her to repay him in such a small space. She looked at Aaron and gave him a smile. "Take Sophie by the fire so she can get warm."

Aaron took Sophie's hand and led her away. Mr. Lloyd crossed the room again, closer to where she stood but still too far away for her to talk to him without the kids hearing.

She took a tentative step toward him, then another, his suspicious eyes narrowing the closer she got. When Keri was sure Aaron and Sophie Ann were out of hearing range, she wondered how to word what needed to be said.

A simple glance at his face and her confidence wavered. Could she really do this again? A small voice in the back of her mind whispered that she didn't have a choice.

Not able to meet his eyes, she chose to stare at his chest instead. "Not that I'm ungrateful for your generosity, but your cabin doesn't offer much in the way of privacy, Mr. Lloyd."

He glanced across the room, his brow scrunching as if thinking. "I can hang a blanket by the bed. It isn't much but it'll have to do."

Keri's stomach rolled. Did he expect her to spread her legs with her children in the same room with her? "When?" The word came out as a soft, breathy whisper.

"When what?"

She finally met his eyes. "When would you like payment for your hospitality?"

He stared at her for long minutes, confusion clouding his face. When it cleared, dread settled like a stone in her stomach.

"In the morning will be fine."

Keri sighed and glanced back at Aaron and Sophie. They were still by the fire, chatting softly. "If it's all the same to you, Mr. Lloyd, I'd just as soon get it over with." She glanced into the lean-to kitchen and nodded to it with her head. "In there. Aaron will keep Sophie occupied."

The confusion she'd seen on his face returned, only this time it didn't clear. He stared at her, his eyes narrowed. "I'm afraid I don't know what you're talking about."

Her face heated until she knew her skin reflected her embarrassment. She lifted her hands, clenched the collar of her shirt in her fingers, and glanced at his face. "For your payment," she said, her voice pitched low so Aaron and Sophie wouldn't hear. "I'd rather not prolong it. It will only make me more uncomfortable."

The confusion on his face grew. If he was waiting on her to say it point blank, he'd be waiting all night. His eyes suddenly cleared, then widened, before his cheeks darkened to a blistering red. He opened his mouth but closed it with a snap before turning and walking into the kitchen. Keri sighed, told Aaron and Sophie Ann to stay put, and followed him.

He stood facing the stove, his arms down by his side. He was clenching and unclenching his gloved fists. She watched him for long minutes before crossing the room. She hesitated when she reached him but sucked in a calming breath and stepped around him. His eyes were closed, small lines bracketing them and causing the scar to pucker more. She pondered his odd behavior. Had he changed his mind? Was he reconsidering the payment?

The strain on his face never lifted. She reached up and laid her palm to his chest. He flinched as if she'd shot him, his eyes snapping open to stare at her. "Have you changed your mind, Mr. Lloyd?"

His jaw clenched, his gaze boring into her as his face once again reddened. "What exactly are you offering me as payment, Mrs. Hilam?"

It was her turn to blush. "Well, myself…" The words came out as a strained croak. She cleared her throat and tried again. "Anything you'd like, Mr. Lloyd. There's not much I haven't already had to do, so nothing you ask for will shock me."

The moment the words were out of her mouth, all the blood in Noah's body drained into his lower extremities. His heart pounded, and even though the woman was bone thin and dirty, he pictured her naked, her limbs long and silky smooth as they wrapped around his hips. Her full pink lips on his skin, her body warm and wet and welcoming.

He sucked in a breath and willed his growing erection away as his neck and face heated, embarrassment burning until he couldn't breathe past it. Her hand still rested on his chest and he backed up to break the contact. "There's been some confusion, Mrs. Hilam. I don't want you in my bed."

Relief washed over her face, the strained lines bracketing her mouth vanishing quickly before another emotion all together flashed across her features. The scared, timid glint in her eyes changed in an instant, her blue eyes filling with hurt and embarrassment. She looked away, her head lowering a fraction. "I'm sorry. I assumed..." Her cheeks turned red, misery clouding her eyes again as she reached up to grab the high collar of her dress as if to hold the garment closed. "I'm afraid I misunderstood you. Others always wanted..." Her eyes closed briefly before she shook her head.

She didn't have to say what the others wanted from her and Noah was glad she didn't speak it aloud. He stared at her, visions of her climbing into someone's bed just so she could feed her children sickened him and his earlier thoughts of her naked and wanting him caused his stomach to churn, acid boiling inside his gut until he thought he'd be sick. Of course she didn't want him. Why would she?

His gaze swept her small frame again and he knew he shouldn't have brought her to the house. The townsfolk would talk when they found out. And they would find out. Nothing was a secret for long in Willow Creek. Once they knew, the rumors would fly unchecked. The homeless widow taking up with the town monster. He cringed just thinking about what they'd all say.

He pushed the thought out of his head, cleared his throat and pinched the bridge of his nose. "I only meant for you to do the cooking while you're here," he said, steering the conversation back to neutral ground. "It isn't necessary but if you wish to repay me, something other than beans and venison stew would be nice."

Her cheeks were still red but she lifted her gaze, met his own and nodded her head. "Is there anything in particular you'd like?"

The vision of her naked filled his mind again and he shook his head to dispel it. "No. Anything you'd like to cook is fine." She nodded her head and glanced around the small kitchen. He looked as well.

"Your provisions are enough to feed a small army, Mr. Lloyd."

"I don't like going to town," he said, taking in the shelves and bins of food he'd stockpiled. "I've enough to last all winter." He faced her again and inhaled a large breath. "There's stew there on the stove behind you. Bowls on the shelf over the sink. I'll go rig up that blanket around the bed while you feed those kids." He walked away but stopped when he reached the doorway. "There's hot water in the reservoir on the stove if you'd like to clean up." She nodded and he walked back into the main room. The kids talked quietly as they sat by the fire but looked up at him when he crossed the room. He ignored them, reached into the chest at the foot of the bed and dug out a few more blankets.

The woman called the kids, all three of them disappearing into the kitchen and Noah let out the pent up breath he'd been holding. What the hell was he doing? He avoided people as if they had the plague, didn't offer to speak to anyone he encountered, and tried his best to not be seen. So why did he invite this woman and her kids into his home? What had he been thinking?

The wind rattled the window and he glanced out at the darkening sky. He didn't know how long the storm would last but the moment the roads were passable, he'd take them into town and forget he'd ever seen them. They could be someone else's problem.

Soft laughter drifted into the room from the kitchen. He looked toward the doorway, imagining them around his small table and for some unexplainable reason, his heart gave a mighty thump at the noise. For the first time since moving to Willow Creek, his small cabin wasn't quiet. He barely heard the ticking of the clock on the mantel or the wood in the fireplace popping as it burnt. Childish giggles filled the air and he was loath to admit how nice it sounded.

A lifetime of regrets conjured images of a life he barely remembered living, his future changed in one tragic moment that still haunted him. He shook his head to clear the images and looked to the ceiling, wondering how he would secure the blankets, and ignored those gleeful sounds filling his home.

CHAPTER FIVE

I t was the first time she'd been full in months. Watching Aaron and Sophie eat, hearing them laugh and knowing they'd be warm when they drifted off to sleep caused the back of Keri's eyes to burn, her throat to clog and ache as tears threatened to fall. She pushed them away. She had no reason for useless emotions now. Not tonight. They were fed, warm, and for the first time since running from their previous nightmare, she felt safe.

Noah Lloyd was anything but friendly. His manner was gruff, his eyes hard and distrusting, but she knew they'd be okay here. After her embarrassing mistake in thinking he wanted her in his bed as payment, she could barely fathom the thought of looking him in the eye again. She wasn't sure who was more mortified by the proposition, him or her.

She pushed the thought away, glanced back down at Aaron and Sophie and smiled as they blinked sleepily at their bowls. Their bellies were full and both of them looked ready to fall asleep where they sat.

Grabbing a large bowl from the shelf above the sink, she filled it with warm water from the stove reservoir, found a washcloth and took her time cleaning the kids as thoroughly as she could without dunking them in a tub of water. She cleaned her own face, unbuttoned her shirtwaist and wiped off as much sweat and grime as she could and felt almost clean by the time she was finished.

Pouring out the water, she ushered Aaron and Sophie back into the main room. Blankets surrounded the bed. Noah Lloyd's shadow could be seen behind them but it was still enough privacy she didn't feel as if she was intruding too much. When he stepped around the blankets and saw them, he stopped, stared at her until she felt uncomfortable again, and cleared his throat, then crossed the room to the fireplace.

"The blankets should hold," he said, nodding toward the small bit of privacy in the room. "You and the children can take the bed."

"That isn't necessary," Keri said. "We're intruding enough as it is without taking your bed. Sleeping in front of the fire is quite fine."

His eyes narrowed as he shook his head. "It's not fine with me. Take the bed." His gruff command seemed to be his final word. He turned his back to them, sitting down in the rocker by the fire and started to remove his boots, effectively putting the argument to rest.

Keri stared at the back of his head for long moments, then guided Aaron and Sophie toward the bed, pulling the blankets aside, and stepping behind them. There were two long sleeve shirts and a long sleep shirt lying on the coverlet. For all his hateful ways, Noah Lloyd did have a bit of compassion in him. Keri smiled while looking at the garments. The thought of putting on something clean caused a shiver to race up her spine. She'd been wearing the same dress for months now.

Undressing Aaron and Sophie, she covered them with Mr. Lloyd's shirts, rolling up the sleeves so they fit somewhat better. She pulled down the blankets, listened as Aaron and Sophie giggled as they crawled onto the mattress and waited until they'd settled before turning her back to them and removing her dress.

The sleep shirt Noah laid out for her felt smooth against her skin when she slipped it on. It fell nearly to her feet. Lifting her arm, she inhaled the scent of soap on the sleeve of the shirt and smiled. Clean clothing seemed like such a luxury now after living in the same garments for so long.

She looked toward the blankets hung for privacy, her thoughts on the gruff man who had taken them in. A few cooked meals seemed like such a small thing for what he was doing for them. He'd invited them into his home, fed them, and given up his bed.

The wind still whistled past the small cabin and as Keri listened to the wall boards pop and crack around her, she knew he'd done more than filled their bellies and given them a warm place to sleep. He'd probably saved their life. Another night in that cold, drafty shack would have been the end of them. No, a few cooked meals would never be enough to repay him but if that's what he wanted in return, she'd feed him like he was one of her own.

The morning air was biting cold. Noah pulled up the collar of his coat, ducked his head and slogged through the snow to the barn, guided by the rope he'd tied to the door from the cabin.

Once inside, the animals stirred. The cow shifted in her stall, her neck stretching as she eyed him. He grabbed the bucket and stool, entered her pen and ran his hand over her head before setting the stool down to milk her. He was reaching under her when the barn door creaked open. Lifting his head, he tried to see over the railing, wondering if the wind had caught the door or if the woman had followed him out. She was still behind the curtain when he left the cabin and he couldn't think of one reason why she'd follow him.

Shaking his head when he heard nothing else, he went back to milking the cow, his thoughts on the woman. Images of her from the night before flashed inside his mind's eye. He saw her shadowy figure behind those blankets as she'd undressed, each curve and dip visible until he was sure he could sketch her without looking. Skinny as she was, her hips flared enticingly, the curve of her breasts high. It took everything in him to turn away, to settle in that old rocker knowing she was in his bed. He'd been so unsettled by the thought, he'd had half a mind of getting up and sleeping in the hay loft. If it hadn't been so cold, he would have.

He blinked the images away when the shuffle of feet caught his attention. He whipped his head to the left, startled to see the boy standing there watching him. His neck and face burned when he realized he'd been having such thoughts about the woman while her young son was but inches away. "What do you want?" he asked, his voice harsh.

The boy seemed unfazed by his tone. "Came to help."

Noah raised an eyebrow. "Help do what?"

The kid shrugged. "Whatever you need me to do." He walked fully into the stall and leaned back against the rail. "Uncle Robert used to make me and Sophie Ann milk the cow every morning." The kid swiped a hand across his nose. "He'd make us clean up after the horses too and gather up all the eggs."

"Yeah, well, I don't need your help." Noah's voice held every ounce of irritation he felt. He turned back to the cow and continued milking her, knowing the peace and quiet he found in the barn was lost as long as the kid hang around.

He hadn't had a moment's peace since finding them in the line shack, his thoughts a constant jumble of worries for that skinny woman and her kids. If he wouldn't have to walk the entire way, he'd load them up and take them into town before the sun set.

Hopefully the snow would stop falling soon. If it kept up much longer, he'd be stuck with them for the rest of the week.

It was times like this he wished he had a sled or another horse. He avoided people for a reason and seeing the kid out of the corner of his eye, he knew even this refuge was now gone. He should have never brought them back to the house.

Glancing back over at him, Noah heaved a breath. "Why are you still here?"

The boy actually smiled at him. "My ma said you was as grumpy as a bee-stung mule."

Noah narrowed his eyes. "She's right. I am. Now, go away." He didn't think the kid was going to listen but he eventually turned and left. When silence filled the barn again, he shook his head.

The woman thought he was grumpy, did she? He snorted a laugh. Grumpy was an understatement to how he felt most days. It was only bearable because he didn't have to see anyone. That changed the instant he let his conscience convince him that he needed to play the hero and rescue that waif of a woman and her gangly kids.

He scowled in disgust at his actions and finished milking the cow and stood, replacing the stool to the corner and setting the milk bucket aside. He fed the horse, made his way to the chicken coop and gathered up what eggs the hens had laid and returned to the barn, staring at nothing in particular, wondering what he was to do with himself now.

On any other day, he would have gone inside, fixed his breakfast and spent the morning with his drawings or reading until lunch. Those options were now gone with his unwanted house-guests taking up residence. He repositioned his hat. Grabbing the milk bucket and the eggs, he turned to the barn door. It opened before he reached it, the kid sticking his head back inside.

"My ma wanted me to tell you that your breakfast is ready."

The kid smiled and ducked back out of the barn, the door swinging as the wind caught it and smacked it against the frame a few times. Noah shook his head and crossed the rest of the barn, stepping outside and securing the door before venturing toward the house.

Wood smoke curled from the chimney and the smell of cooked meat filled the air as he reached the door. He hesitated a few moments, standing there in the cold as snow drifted along the collar of his coat. He could hear nothing from inside and stood there long enough his ears started burning from the cold.

He sighed. He was stalling. Purposely not wanting to go inside. Not wanting to face the woman again. He closed his eyes, turned his head left, then right, trying to get the kink out of his neck before opening his eyes. He couldn't avoid the house all day, every day. He had to face them eventually, converse with them on occasion. He might as well get it over with.

Reaching for the door, he opened it and walked inside.

Keri set Sophie and Aaron's plates down in front of them as they nestled in close to the fireplace. She handed them each a spoon as the door to the cabin opened. She stood and looked toward Noah as he came inside. He set the things in his hands down, removed his coat and hat, and bent to retrieve the bucket and basket by his feet and walked into the kitchen without a word. "You two eat quietly," she said, glancing at Aaron and Sophie before turning away.

She followed Noah into the kitchen and hesitated near the doorway. He was at the sink, his back to her. Entering the room fully, Keri approached the table, picked up an empty plate, and started filling it. Placing the plate at one of the empty chairs at the table, Keri glanced over her shoulder. Noah was staring at her. She averted her gaze and moved away from the table, picking up the remaining plate and serving herself.

Waking that morning dry and warm had left her a bit disoriented. She'd slept the entire night through, not waking once. She'd puzzled over the fact when she woke, listening to Noah move about the room before the sound of the door opening, and a cold blast of air, filtered in behind the blankets he'd hung for their privacy. She'd crawled from bed, dressed in the same grubby clothes she'd been wearing for nearly two months now and entered the kitchen, took stock of what sort of foodstuff he had, and planned a menu for breakfast.

She'd be embarrassed to admit she'd cooked with her own selfish wants foremost in her mind. She hadn't eaten decent food in so long, her mouth practically watered as she took stock of all the choices before her. Eggs with onions and bacon, biscuits and gravy and fresh butter from the larder had her mouth watering the entire time she cooked. Now, as she watched Noah take a seat and look at the fare she'd fixed, she wondered if she should have thought more of what he would have liked, not herself.

He started eating without a word and Keri finished filling her own plate. The small table in the kitchen only held two chairs, which was why she'd seated Aaron and Sophie in the other room, but now as she stared at that remaining chair, she wondered if Noah would want her company.

They'd not spoken to each other more than they needed to and from the looks of him, he didn't seem like the sort to want a dining companion. He glanced up as if he'd heard her thoughts. His eyes were still cold, unfriendly, and she lowered her gaze.

No, he definitely didn't want her company. She skirted around him and walked back into the main room to eat by the fire.

CHAPTER SIX

Noah dropped his fork, listening to it clank against his plate as he stared at the wall in front of him. He ground his back teeth together, anger swelling so thick inside him he nearly choked. He heard the soft whispers coming from the other room and it took everything in him not to go in there and…

And what? Force her to sit with him? Make her take the only remaining chair at the table and talk to him?

He sighed and tried to run a hand through his hair, his fingers snagging on the tangled strands. He realized how absurd his thoughts were. There wasn't a reason for the woman to want to join him. Why would she? He'd been nothing but surly since clapping eyes on the trio. He'd thrown scowls in their direction every time one of them caught his eye, thought endlessly of ways to make the trip into town despite the snow and had actually contemplated sleeping in the barn.

They'd disrupted his life, caused him concern for their well being when he otherwise wouldn't have given two shits less and now, having that slip of a woman pass him over for her snot-nosed kids caused something deep in his gut to ache and burn.

He raised his still gloved hand, scrubbed at the scar on his face and stared down at the half-eaten food on his plate. From the looks of it, she'd spent a good deal of time cooking. He couldn't remember the last time he had fresh biscuits. They were flaky and still warm, butter dripping off the tops of them and the gravy was thick, just the way he liked it. He sighed, shaking his head before picking his fork back up.

He finished his breakfast then stood to wash his plate. The sink was sitting full of dishes already. The notion of washing them for her swamped his thoughts but he dismissed it as quickly as it came. He wasn't catering to her. Why should he? She couldn't even grace him with her presence while she ate *his* food. Anger coursed through his veins again. He shoved his plate into the sink with the others, crossed the room and stepped through the kitchen doorway.

She looked up at him when he stepped fully into the room. The fire behind her bathed her skin in golden light. The dark circles he'd seen under her eyes the day before didn't look as dark today and her complexion was more pink than pasty white.

He blinked and turned toward the door, putting her out of his mind. Reaching for his coat, he slipped it back on, not really knowing what he was to do outside. The animals were all taken care of but sitting inside with her and those kids...

He couldn't do it. Couldn't pretend he was okay sharing his home with them. Given the choice, that woman would have turned her back and avoided looking at him the same as everyone else did. The only reason she didn't now was because she needed the comfort of his home, the warmth it provided and the food he'd been storing since late summer.

Jamming his hat onto his head, he grabbed the door handle but froze when she said, "Mr. Lloyd, please wait a moment."

Noah stared at the door, the sound of her skirts swishing as she crossed the room. She stopped right behind him. He could feel the weight of her presence and he clamped his jaw. She said nothing for long moments but finally cleared her throat.

"Would you happen to have a tub large enough for bathing?"

No sooner had the last word whispered past her lips did the vision of her standing in his home, naked, while water slid over her limbs filled his mind's eye. He closed his eyes, trying to rid himself of the images but they seemed to multiply as the seconds ticked on.

The curve of her breasts he'd seen the night before through the blankets filled his head. He wondered of their size, the fullness of them. Were her nipples soft pink or brown? He gritted his teeth and conjured images of the war, dispelling her as quickly as she came to him. "I have one in the barn." His voice cracked as he spoke and he cleared his throat. "I'll bring it in for you." He left, slamming the door behind him.

Trudging through the snow, he entered the barn, stood in the cold, chilly air and breathed deeply, trying, but failing, not to imagine Keri Hilam naked.

Shaking his head, he opened his eyes, glanced toward the tub and sighed. "You've been too long without a woman." Crossing the room, he grabbed the tub, hefted it onto his shoulder and started back toward the house determined not to think of her again.

It took some time but Keri managed to get a blanket hung in the kitchen doorway so she'd be able to bathe in private. Aaron was scrubbed clean and already by the fire in the oversized shirt he'd worn to bed, his filthy clothes soaking in the sink and Sophie Ann was splashing in the tub, her giggles filling the room.

Keri kneeled by the tub, washed Sophie's hair, scrubbed the dirt from behind her ears and the rest of her small body, and smiled at her now pink cheeks. "There," she said. "All done." She stood, held the same drying cloth she'd dried Aaron with and waited for Sophie to stand.

Dressing her in the night shirt, she sent her into the other room. She set Sophie Ann's dress into the soapy water and undressed herself, tossing her own clothes in, and sighed as she finally sank into the water.

It was pure bliss. The water was barely warm, not to mention dirty after bathing Aaron and Sophie, but Keri didn't mind. It was a bath, the first she'd had in months. She scrubbed and rinsed her hair until it was squeaky clean, washed her body, then lathered up and washed again, not stopping until she felt like a whole person, then leaned back, draping her arms over the side of the tub, stretched out her legs, and closed her eyes.

When Noah had brought the tub in, Keri had been surprised at the size of the thing. She'd imagined squatting in a small, round, half-barrel like the one she'd had back home, trying her best to bathe away the dirt on her body but what Noah had produced was nearly a full size bathtub big enough to lounge in. Big enough for a man the size of Noah, she reflected.

Thinking of him, she sighed again. She wasn't sure why, but she got the distinct impression he was surly and rude on purpose. It was no secret he rarely spoke and when he did, he was short and quick to say whatever it was he had to say. He rarely, if ever, made eye contact with her and more often than not, his head was tilted to one side, his hair lying flush against the scarred side of his face. She didn't think it was a conscious act, either. Probably something he'd done so long, he didn't even realize he still did it.

Her thoughts drifted to that scar, wondering how it had been made and why. She wasn't even entirely sure that was his only one. She'd yet to see him remove his gloves. He went so far as to eat with them on and to say it was a peculiar act was an understatement. Everything about him was peculiar, if you really looked hard enough. The amount of food he had stored was just this side of odd. He'd said he didn't like going into town as way of explanation and she had no reason not to believe him but it was still strange behavior.

Of course, she had her own unusual faults she supposed. Everyone did to some degree, but since the snow was still falling, it looked as if they'd be stuck with Noah Lloyd for some time yet. Not that she minded. Sure he seemed a bit cussed but she wasn't about to complain. She was warm, fed and oddly, felt protected in this small cabin with a man who seemed more likely to grunt an answer than speak one.

There was no hint of a woman anywhere in the cabin. Not one lacy curtain or doily. The air smelled of gun oil, horse hay and man. If Noah Lloyd had a woman friend, she didn't frequent his home often.

Keri fluffed her drying hair, the ringlet curls she'd grown to hate over the years bouncing back to life now that her hair wasn't coated in dirt and grime. Taking a glance down the line of her body, she ran a hand over her flat stomach. Her hip bones protruded a bit and her skin looked pale and unhealthy. She'd given up many meals so Aaron and Sophie could eat. She didn't regret doing so but her body had suffered from it. Where she was once soft and plump, she was now thin, her bones seen through her withering flesh. Her breasts were smaller, the fatty tissue that used to fill them out vanishing along with the rest of her. They barely filled her palm now.

Would Noah find someone as skinny as her attractive? Would any man, for that matter? With John gone, and the struggle to make it to San Francisco getting harder by the day, the thought of taking another husband looked more attractive now than ever. Did Noah Lloyd want a wife? One who was skin and bones and had less hair than he did? Doubtful. She'd be lucky if any man wanted her the way she looked.

Hearing the door to the cabin open, Keri stood, grabbed the small drying cloth and wrapped it around her body. She lifted a leg to step out of the tub and jumped, startled, when Noah bellowed, "What do you think you're doing?" loud enough to bounce off the rafters.

Sophie Ann screamed and Keri nearly fell as she jumped from the tub and ran toward the curtained doorway, bursting into the other room to see Noah reach down, grab Sophie by the front of her gown and lift her body off the ground, fury etched into every line on his face.

CHAPTER SEVEN

"**P**ut her down!" Keri ran across the room, wrapped one arm around Sophie's small waist and pulled her away from Noah. His face was all hard lines, rage contorting his features. She backed up, putting as much distance as she could between them, and didn't stop until her back hit the wall.

Shushing Sophie and trying to get her to stop crying, Keri glanced around the room and felt her heart hit her stomach. Dozens of pencils and papers littered the floor, a worn leather journal by the fireplace showing a few straggling pages and every sheet of paper she saw held drawings of some sort. Beautiful sketches of people and landscapes now ruined with Sophie's clumsy scribbling slashing across most every page. Her chest ached to see them, the air in her lungs leaving in one giant whoosh. "Oh, Sophie Ann, what have you done?"

Swallowing, and forcing her heart to stop pounding, Keri set Sophie on her feet. "Go get on the bed and don't move until I tell you to." She looked at Aaron who was huddled by the rocking chair and nodded to him. He took three steps away from the chair, grabbed Sophie's arm when she was near enough and ran with her to the blankets hanging around the bed, then ducked behind them.

Keri lifted her gaze to Noah. He was staring at the floor, his mouth a hard angry slash across his face before he bent to pick up one of the pages, then another. She bent her knees, grabbed the ones nearest her, scooping up the pencils as well, and didn't stop until the floor was once again bare.

She glanced down at the drawings she held. The one on top showed a woman, her dress as fancy as any Keri had ever seen. Her hair was long, draped across her shoulders in big curls and the smile on her face was flirtatious. The word, Isabelle, was scrawled under the likeness. Sophie's scribblings slashed across the page, cutting the woman's pretty face in half. Keri's chest ached looking at the ruined drawing.

Lifting her gaze, she locked eyes with Noah. He still looked angry. His eyes cold, his jaw clenching every few moments. She had no idea how to fix this.

Where had Sophie found the drawings? She wondered, looking around the room. There wasn't much in the cabin to begin with but the small desk by the window caught her attention. An oil lamp and a few books littered the top. The journal had to have been there. It was the only thing low enough for her to reach.

But why would she mark on the drawings? The back of her eyes burned as she looked back at Noah. "I'm so sorry, Mr. Lloyd," she said, her voice a soft whisper. "I didn't... I should have been quicker about my bath. I should have watched her better."

She blinked away tears and held out her arm, offering him the drawings and pencils. He snatched them away, then ran his gaze over her from head to toe, his jaw clenching again before he turned his back to her.

"Go dress yourself."

His harsh tone felt like ice over her flesh but a glance down at her body changed the cold shivers to molten lava as she cringed, humiliation burning so hot she thought she'd catch fire. She gasped, clutched the tiny drying cloth she wrapped around herself tighter and turned, running back to the kitchen and ducking behind the curtain.

Dropping the drying cloth, she grabbed the long nightshirt she'd worn to bed the night before, slipped it over her head and wondered if her face would ever stop burning. She glanced toward the sink where their clothes still sat in soapy water and shook her head. Not only had she stood in front of Noah with nothing more than a thin strip of cloth wrapped around her body, she would now have to walk back into the other room in nothing but his nightshirt. Her face burned hotter. "Oh, God, how humiliating."

Turning and seeing the blanket she'd hung over the doorway, she reached for it, tugging it loose, then draped it around her shoulders, wrapping it around her body until nothing could be seen but her head and her toes. When she stepped into the main room, the tension in the air was still thick, Sophie Ann's sniffles and the ticking of the clock the only sounds to be heard.

Crossing the room and stopping behind Noah, Keri inhaled a deep breath, then let it out slowly. "There's nothing I can say to make what Sophie Ann did all right, Mr. Lloyd, but for what it's worth, I truly am sorry."

He never turned to acknowledge her, just kept staring down at the loose pages in his hand. Keri fought back tears, blinking them away as she crossed the room and ducked behind the blanket with Aaron and Sophie Ann. They lunged for her the moment they saw her and as she sank into the bed, she let those tears she'd been fighting slide down her cheeks. Their safe haven from the winter storm was as good as gone now. Keri had no doubt Noah would want them out of his home and truth was, she had no desire to leave. Cantankerous as Noah Lloyd was, living under his roof was better than being alone.

Noah sank into the rocker, exhaling a long breath, years worth of memories staring up at him through the ruined pages of his journal. He thumbed through the drawings in silence. Nearly every page held some sort of scribbling on them.

He came to the drawing of Isabelle, his heart clenching as he took in the lines of her face. The impish smile she'd always given him. At one time, that smile had been enough to brighten his day. Now, it just reminded him of everything he'd lost.

The girl's clumsy pencil marks slashed across the page, right over Isabelle's face. Noah stared at it, anger once again filling him until he couldn't breathe past it. He could still hear the girl whimpering behind the blankets, the woman's soft voice lulling her with words he couldn't make out. He closed his eyes, seeing the entire incident replay in his mind's eye and knew he'd overreacted. He should have never yelled the way he had. Nor touched the girl. He wasn't even sure why he did. The drawings weren't valuable. They meant nothing to anyone but him but seeing them scattered across the floor as if they were rubbish....

He sighed, leaned his head back, and wished he could start the whole day over. The whole week. He wouldn't have chased down that smoke he'd seen through the trees. He wouldn't have encountered the woman and her kids huddling around a pitiful excuse for a fire. Wouldn't have felt compelled to take them in when the snow fell faster than even he expected. They weren't his responsibility. They meant nothing to him. He should have just left them alone.

And they would be dead out in the shack if you had.

Scrubbing a gloved hand across his face, he blew out a breath and thumbed through the drawings again, stopping when he ran across the one he'd drawn while sitting near the creek watching the water trickle down the stream. A few stick figures were drawn near the bottom of the page. His chest ached seeing them.

He remembered another drawing with those tiny stick figures buried in his memories. Judith, his sister, had done much the same. The pang of regret the memory produced stole his breath. As Judith had done all those years ago, he realized the Hilam girl had innocently been drawing. He couldn't chastise her for that. Besides, what else was the girl to do cooped up in the cabin all day?

Stuffing the drawings back into the journal, he stood and placed it on the fireplace mantel out of reach. He collected the pencils, placed them back in the box, and sat them on top of the journal.

The blankets around the bed moved and the woman stepped out from behind them. She was wrapped in a blanket, but the moment he saw her, in his mind, the blanket was replaced by that tiny drying cloth she'd been standing in earlier. His heart gave a thump, his blood rushing through his body to end up in his groin and the vision of her practically naked filled his mind's eye. That cloth she'd dried with had barely covered her breasts and fell to just below her bottom. Her legs seemed miles long, shapely, if not a little skinny, but good Lord, he hadn't seen that much soft woman flesh in years.

Her hair hung in soft ringlets, he noticed. It was blond and now that it was clean and falling around her face, he had to take back his earlier assessment of her. Keri Hilam may be a bony thing but there was an innocent sort of beauty to her. She looked soft, feminine, vulnerable.

She glanced around the room before meeting his gaze again, her cheeks turning pink. She opened her mouth as if to say something but closed it without a word. She looked uncomfortable and if truth be known, now that his body responded to her from nothing more than a glimpse of her, he was too.

He looked away and walked back to the door, grabbed his coat and hat, slipping them on before turning back to face her. "What time will supper be ready?"

She blinked at him, her mouth opening and closing a few times before she said, "Six."

Noah nodded, turned, and left the house. Once inside the barn, he sat on a bale of hay, stared at the animals, and wondered what the hell he'd do for the next three hours. Sitting inside the house would be too uncomfortable, especially seeing how Keri was dressed in his thin nightshirt. Not to mention, every time he thought of her he saw her standing in nothing but that small drying cloth. His body hardened the moment he thought of it, thoughts of touching, and tasting, all that soft creamy flesh she'd exposed to him consuming him. He closed his eyes, envisioned her in front of his fireplace, dropping that little cloth and beckoning him forward with the crook of one bent finger. And him crossing the room so fast he nearly tripped over his own feet.

He sighed and opened his eyes. "Put her out of your mind," he whispered, his words fading behind the gusts of wind whistling around the edge of the barn. The snow was still falling and to Noah's estimation, it couldn't melt fast enough. The sooner he got those three out of his house, the better off he'd be.

CHAPTER EIGHT

It took nearly a week for the snow to melt enough to travel. Noah hitched his horse to the wagon, made sure those kids were bundled in blankets, along with Keri, and started the long trek into town.

No one said a word as they jostled along the road and Noah was glad for it. The strain of the last week was finally starting to lift the closer to town they got. The silence he'd had to endure, and the long, cold days of hiding out in the barn, would be nothing but an unpleasant memory in a matter of hours. Once he deposited Keri Hilam and her kids into the marshal's care, things would go back to normal. He'd feed his animals, create more sketches from long ago memories, and wait for bedtime.

He frowned. Thinking of it now didn't seem as pleasant as he thought it would.

He glanced to his right, seeing Keri shiver in the blanket she'd pulled around herself, and for an insane moment, the thought of pulling her close to keep her warm filled his head. He dismissed the notion as quick as it came and scowled instead.

A look over his shoulder at the kids in the back of the wagon showed they too were shivering in the cold. It wasn't much of a surprise. As thin as they were, and as ragged as their clothes were, they should have frozen to death long before he found them. He guessed, all things considered, he'd done his good deed where they were concerned. He'd given them shelter and fed them until all three of them lost that sunken look to their faces. The dark circles under Keri's eyes were no longer visible and her cheeks had filled in a bit. She didn't look as gaunt as before. Neither did those scraggly kids. It was no wonder with the amount of food they'd put away since he'd found them. Not that he was complaining. Only a heartless bastard would begrudge a starving woman and her kids the food they needed to survive, especially when he'd stored enough to feed every resident of Willow Creek all winter long.

The town came into view in the distance and Keri shifted at his side. He glanced over at her, noticing her back was stiff, her head held high. The look on her face was unreadable but when she flashed a quick look his way, the despair in her eyes wasn't missed. What did she think was going to happen? That the marshal would lock them in the jail for being homeless?

He cleared his throat and shifted in his seat. "Marshal Avery is a good man. He'll do right by you."

She nodded her head but didn't say anything, smoothing the fabric of her skirt instead. Noah noticed her hands were shaking.

They didn't speak again until they reached town. When he pulled the wagon to a stop in front of the marshal's house, he set the brake with his foot, wrapped the reins around the brake lever, and jumped to the ground. He rounded the back side of the wagon and was making his way toward the front when Keri tried to step down, her foot catching in the torn hem of her skirt. She let out a startled gasp as she fell. Noah's heart crawled into his throat as he ran to grab her, barely getting his arms around her before she hit the ground, the impact of her body colliding with his driving him to his knees.

She sputtered, her eyes wide as she looked up at him. "T-Thank you."

Noah stared down at her, words failing him. Her hands were on his shoulders, her small frame pressed against him, and damn it all if his body didn't react as if she'd burned him, his skin scalding beneath his clothes. He stood and helped her to her feet and let go of her as quick as he dared to, making sure she had a good footing before backing away. He glanced at her face, noticed her curious gaze on him before he turned, grabbing each of those kids and setting them on the ground.

He didn't wait for any of them, turning to the house and opening the gate. The walkway was brushed clean of snow, the steps as well, and he took them two at a time, the door opening before he ever reached it.

The ruckus inside gave him pause. He didn't know much about Marshal Avery but he knew he didn't have a house full of kids. Two girls, last time he'd heard, but when Noah glanced inside the foyer, he counted no less than ten running down the hall, their voices loud and screechy.

"Hello."

Noah focused his attention on the woman at the door. The marshal's wife, if he remembered correctly. He removed his hat and nodded his head toward her. "Ma'am. Is the marshal home?"

She looked past him, her gaze settling on the three at his back before she once again gave him her attention. "Mr. Lloyd," she said, a pretty smile blooming on her face. "It's a pleasure to see you." She opened the door wider and stepped to one side. "Won't you come in?"

A squeal loud enough to cause a shiver to race up Noah's spine echoed off the walls of the house. The last thing he wanted was to be trapped inside that house with a passel of unruly kids. Having two underfoot for a week was enough. "I'd rather just speak to the marshal, if it's all the same to you, ma'am."

She nodded. "Morgan is over at the jail. He should be along

shortly if you want to wait or you can walk over there to speak to him."

"I'll go over to the jail." He turned to leave when Mrs. Avery called him back.

"Mr. Lloyd, you didn't introduce me to your... friends?"

Noah's eyes landed on Keri, then her kids, before he turned back to the door. "This is Keri Hilam and her kids, Aaron and Sophie Ann. I found them as the blizzard hit. I was hoping the marshal would know what to do with them."

"I see." Mrs. Avery smiled again, then stepped out onto the porch. "Mrs. Hilam? Would you and your children like to come inside for a bit? I've just put on a pot of tea."

Keri glanced at him, catching his eye before she motioned her kids forward. When they passed him on the porch, Keri paused by his side. He thought she was going to say something but she walked into the house without a word. Mrs. Avery gave him one final look before following Keri inside and shutting the door.

And just like that, Keri Hilam and her children were out of his life. Things could go back to normal now.

He descended the steps, walked to the gate and headed into town to find the marshal. A glance back at the house caused his steps to falter. Aaron and Sophie Ann were at the window staring at him. For some unexplainable reason, the sight of them caused his pulse to race. He didn't dare dwell on the why of it and turned his head, putting them out of his mind.

Keri reluctantly left Aaron and Sophie with the other children and followed Mrs. Avery, Abigail, she'd said as she introduced herself, into the kitchen. Another woman stood by the stove, a tea pot in one hand. When she turned and saw them, she smiled. "Well, who do we have here, Abigail?"

"This is Keri Hilam," Abigail said. "Keri, this is Laurel Avery, my sister-in-law. She's the school teacher here in Willow Creek."

"It's very nice to meet you." Keri took a look around the kitchen. It was the fanciest thing she'd ever seen. The fixtures sparkled, the stove gleaming white. The table was large enough to seat six people and was covered in a cloth of closely knitted lace. It was all very feminine looking. The tea service painted with small pink flowers that Laurel was setting out made it seem more so. Keri had only seen other tea sets like it in the catalogue she and John used to look through at the mercantile back home but those pictures were black and white drawings. She'd never seen one in color.

Abigail drew back a chair and smiled at her. "Would you like to join us?"

Keri hesitated. She'd never taken tea with proper ladies before. By the looks of these two women, they were probably every bit as refined and sophisticated as she was backwards and odd.

She glanced down at her dress. It was shabby, the skirt torn in a few places and her shirtwaist was dingy. She smoothed a hand over the fabric as humiliation raced through her veins.

Abigail still held her chair, an expectant look on her face. Keri gave her a nervous smile before taking the seat, watching as Laurel and Abigail sat, poured the tea and turned to her when they were settled.

"So," Abigail said, "You've been staying with Noah since the storm hit?"

Keri looked at both women in turn, noticing their curious gazes. What did they think she had to tell? "He found us in the shack we'd been staying in."

Laurel picked up her tea cup, took a small sip and set it back down. "You're alone?" she asked. "You and your children, I mean?"

"Yes." Keri wrapped her hands around the dainty cup, the warmth from the porcelain warming her to the bone. "We found the shack a few weeks back. It was abandoned and in bad shape but the fireplace was solid, the floor sturdy." She stared at her cooling tea. "I didn't know it belonged to anyone." She glanced back up and gave them a tiny smile. "Mr. Lloyd meant to throw us out but changed his mind and told me we could stay until the storm broke. He came back the next morning though, and took us home with him."

Abigail raised an eyebrow at her. "I'm surprised he even spoke to you," she said. "He's a man of few words. Why, what he said to me on the porch is the most I've ever heard him say and he's lived in Willow Creek nearly two years now."

"He's a bit reclusive," Laurel said. "Only comes to town once every few months and doesn't linger. He gets what supplies he needs, then leaves again, not pausing to speak to anyone."

Keri could see Noah doing that. He'd not spoken to her much in the past week and she'd been in the same room with him on many occasions. "He's quite reserved," she said. "Keeps to himself."

Both ladies nodded. Minutes ticked by in silence as they sipped their tea. A loud crash echoed through the house, Abigail shook her head before standing. "I hope whatever that was can be replaced."

Laurel took another sip of her tea and watched Abigail leave the room. "The blizzard caught us all off guard. I didn't even realize it was snowing until late in the day. The snow was too deep and falling too rapidly to send the children home so we've been camped out with Abigail and Morgan ever since. My husband is probably beside himself." She laughed. "Being stuck at home alone with our young son has probably driven him up the wall."

"You've not been home all week?"

Laurel laughed again. "No. We've all been stuck here. Three adults with ten screaming, fighting kids. It's enough to make me gray haired before my time. But, since Noah was able to get into town, I suspect others will too. I'm sure the parents are worried and anxious to see their kids again."

Abigail came back, a grim look on her face. "If we don't see some parents today, I'm going to make Morgan take every one of these wildlings home before dark. I'm not sure my nerves can handle another night of this." She settled back into her seat and refreshed her tea. "So, Keri, will you be staying in Willow Creek?"

CHAPTER NINE

Noah entered the jail and found Morgan at his desk scribbling something onto a stack of papers. The man looked up, smiled, and laid his pencil down as Noah shut the door.

"Noah. What a surprise." His smile faltered as he stood. "There isn't anything wrong, is there?"

Removing his hat, Noah cleared his throat. "Marshal," he said, nodding his head in greeting. "I found a woman and her kids in an abandoned line shack at the back of my property the day the blizzard hit. I've brought them to town." He twisted the hat in his hand, glancing around the room before meeting Morgan's gaze again. "I'm afraid I don't know what to do with them."

A hint of a smile tugged at the corner of Morgan's mouth but he hid it as quick as it came. He motioned to the vacant seat in front of his desk and waited until Noah had sat before taking his own seat. "So, what can you tell me about them?"

Noah opened his mouth but shut it a moment later. What could he tell him? Nothing much. "The woman's name is Keri Hilam. A widow, she said. Has two little ones with her. The boy is ten and the girl..." He shook his head. "I can't remember. She's younger." He shifted in his seat, propped his hat on his knee. "They were half starved when I found them. I'm not sure how long they've been on their own."

Morgan took in everything he said, kept asking questions Noah couldn't answer, and the longer he sat there, the more Noah wanted to leave. He was uncomfortable in town, always had been. Even though no one was in the room but Morgan, the need to flee was strong.

Now that he was here, trying to get the marshal to take responsibility for Keri and her kids, his thoughts drifted to her. He'd made no secret of his plan to drop her off on the marshal's doorstep once the storm passed and now that he'd done that, he couldn't help but wonder what would become of her. Why he cared, he couldn't say.

That woman and her kids had caused him a week of sleepless nights as he tried to get comfortable in that old rocker by the fire as they slumbered in his bed. He'd spent more time in the barn talking to his animals than any sane man should, and even though Keri Hilam cooked up a tasty array of vittles, having her in his house left him… twitchy. He wasn't used to being around people. Especially those of the female persuasion.

Since the day he left Charleston and headed west, he'd avoided most everyone and until a week ago, he was satisfied with his life. Happiness was something he didn't ever think to have again but things could be worse. His thoughts flashed back to the night his life changed and realized, yes, things could definitely be worse. He could be dead with the rest of the men he'd fought beside.

Morgan tapped a knuckle on his desk, drawing his attention back to the conversation and Noah blinked, watching as the marshal stood and grabbed his hat, placing it on his head before turning to the small pot belly stove in the corner. He banked the fire inside, shut the door and turned back to face him.

"Let's go see if your house guest can answer the questions you couldn't and we'll try to figure out what to do with her."

Noah stood and placed his own hat on his head. He didn't like how Morgan worded that last bit. He didn't want to care what happened to Keri Hilam and the longer he dwelled on the matter, the more involved he became.

They stepped out onto the sidewalk, the wind biting against his skin. He pulled his coat tighter, and waited as Morgan secured the door to the jail.

The walk back to the marshal's house was made in silence until they were stopped by a teenage boy. The youth smiled and tipped his hat. "Marshal," the kid said. "Thank you for letting me ride out the storm with ya but I'm gonna head back home."

Morgan laughed. "I can't believe you're going to leave me in a house full of women and children, Jesse. And here I thought you were on my side."

The boy grinned, the freckles on his face darkening to match his red hair. "I wish I could stay, but I have to get back to Grace. I'm sure Rafe has driven her half crazy by now."

The look in the boy's eyes changed the instant he mentioned Grace and Rafe. Noah remembered Grace. She was the woman Holden Avery had introduced him to in the mercantile the week before. Apparently, she found a husband after all.

Morgan and Jesse, the marshal had called him, talked for a few more minutes before the boy ran off toward the livery stable. Noah watched him go before they resumed their walk back to the marshal's house.

When they reached the gate, he paused. Morgan kept walking as he stood there and debated what to do. Common sense told him to get back into the wagon, ride away, and not look back.

So why was he still standing there?

Morgan stopped at the door and looked back at him. "You not coming in?"

The word, "no," was on the tip of his tongue but movement

near the window drew his attention and stalled the word. The cherub-faced Sophie Ann stood there smiling at him. She raised a hand, waved in his direction, and he looked behind him to see who she was waving at.

No one was there.

She was waving at him? Heat flooded his face, his pulse racing enough to make note of it. When Sophie Ann continued to stand there smiling and waving at him, the tightness in his chest lifted. It felt as if he was able to breathe for the first time in years. All because a pixie-faced girl was smiling at him?

He was getting too soft. Or Keri Hilam had poisoned his food. What else would explain his sudden desire to stay and see how things turned out? He sighed and muttered a soft, "damn it," before pushing the gate open and joining Morgan, who stood on the porch waiting for him.

The noise coming from inside the house was nearly unbearable. Noah glanced at Morgan and gave him a sympathetic look when they entered. He couldn't imagine living with that many kids, all of them trapped inside as a blizzard raged beyond the windows.

Standing in the foyer, Noah caught Aaron's eye, the boy smiling up at him. Noah nodded his head and followed the marshal through the house, stopping when they reached the kitchen. He found Keri there, sitting at the table looking uncomfortable. He saw her shoulders lift in a sigh as she spotted him, her gaze locking with his for a brief moment before she went back to staring at her hands.

Abigail stood, glanced in Keri's direction and smiled. "Mrs. Hilam is trying to find her brother, Morgan. She said he traveled to California but she doesn't know if he's still there. Do you know anyone who might be able to find him?"

"Maybe." Morgan sat at the table and looked at Keri. "Do you know where in California your brother was going?"

"San Francisco," she said. "He was going to attend a school there but I don't remember the name of it."

"What's his name?" Morgan asked.

"Peter Davis."

Keri told Morgan everything about her brother he wanted to know, the marshal jotting things down on a small pad of paper. Relief washed over Keri's face in small degrees, the lines of strain easing when Morgan said he'd contact someone to inquire about him.

When the marshal asked, "How did you end up alone in the middle of nowhere in a blizzard?" Keri's face paled more than usual. She glanced his way, then shifted in her seat. "My husband died two years ago."

"You didn't have any family to go to?"

She looked truly uncomfortable now. "No."

Two years ago? Noah remembered the encounter in the woods, of him asking where her man was. She'd told him he'd died but she'd said they'd been alone since spring. That was a hell of a long ways from two years ago. Had she lied to him? Or was she lying now? And if so, why?

He studied her face, watched her fidget as the marshal kept spouting off questions and realized she wasn't telling Morgan everything. The way Morgan lowered his head and peered at her said he knew it, too. He didn't press her though. "Where are you from?"

She hesitated, then said, "Great Falls."

Everyone in the room gaped at her. "You walked here from Great Falls?"

At Keri's nod, Noah shook his head. What was the fool woman thinking walking that damn far, alone? They could have been killed along the way with no one to protect them.

The West wasn't the safest place to be for a woman, especially one unaccompanied. Sleeping in the open when there were any number of predators roaming the land was stupid as well. Something quicker and stronger could have made a meal out of any of them before they had time to scream and she's damn lucky she hadn't run into the Indians that still roamed the area.

He focused on the conversation again when he noticed Morgan looking at him. "Did you say something?"

"Yeah, I said the hotel is booked. The storm trapped a stage-coach full of people in town and I'm not sure when they'll pull out again."

Noah's heart slammed against his ribcage. "There's nowhere for them, then?"

"The only place in town with an empty room is the saloon but it's no place for a woman with kids." Morgan stared at him for long moments, the look in his eyes questioning, before he sighed and looked away. "We can make room here, I suppose." He glanced at his wife. "We can move the girls into the spare room for a while."

Keri shot to her feet, her chair toppling over in her haste. Her face bloomed red as she turned and grabbed it, sitting it back up before turning to look at them. "That isn't necessary," she said, her voice pitched low. "I appreciate your offer but we've dawdled here too long as it is. Now that the storm is over, we really need to be on our way." She took a few steps toward the doorway, the lines on her face strained. "I thank you for your hospitality but please, don't go to any trouble. It isn't necessary."

She threw a look at him and Noah saw fear cloud her eyes. She hurried past him and through the house, her voice rising above the noise of the school children as she called for Aaron and Sophie Ann.

Abigail grabbed Morgan's arm. "You can't let her leave, Morgan. It's too cold for them to be sleeping under a tree some-where. They'll freeze to death."

Morgan stood and kissed his wife's worried cheek. "I'll not let her go. Stop frettin'." He crossed the room, gave Noah a pointed look and went after her. Noah followed, finding Keri bundling

Aaron and Sophie Ann in the blankets he'd given them before picking up her own and ushering both kids toward the door.

"Mrs. Hilam, wait." Morgan caught her before she could get the door open. "I can't let you leave."

Keri turned, her eyes large and questioning. "Why?" She glanced toward Noah, her gaze darting between him and the marshal. "We've done nothing wrong."

"I know you haven't," Morgan said. "But it's not safe for you out there alone."

Her throat moved as she swallowed. "We can't stay. I have to find my brother." Her voice was barely above a whisper and Noah noticed her eyes turn glassy, tears shining brightly before she blinked them away.

Sophie Ann stepped around Keri and looked up, her blond hair shining in the light. "I don't want to go yet," she said. "There's gonna be a Christmas party." She turned and looked into the other room where the rest of the children were gathered. "Betsy said there's candy and oranges and sometimes presents."

Keri ran her hand over Sophie Ann's head. "It's weeks yet until Christmas, love. I promise we won't miss it."

The school teacher startled Noah when she stepped up beside him. She smiled and looked down at Sophie. "We would love to have you at our party, Sophie Ann. You and your brother."

Aaron's face lit up and Noah's gaze darted to Keri's. She looked miserable in that moment. Stuck between wanting to leave and granting the quiet desires of her children.

The noisy chatter of the school kids in the other room wasn't missed even though they were no longer screaming. Aaron and Sophie Ann looked between their mother and those kids with longing in their eyes. They should be in school, Noah thought.

Keri was talking quietly to them now, her words lost as she whispered. Noah watched them, heaving a breath before glancing at the door. He should leave. Push right past Keri and those kids, jump into his wagon, and head back home. He could wash his hands of them, let them be the marshal's problem, just like he said he was going to do the day he found them.

So why wasn't he leaving? And why did he not want to, yet?

Keri knew the moment Sophie looked up at her with tears in her eyes that leaving Willow Creek wouldn't be as easy as it had been in the past. Every small town they'd left behind had been nothing but one meaningless stop along the way. Willow Creek wasn't one of those towns. Here, they had a reason to stay. The chance at making friends, of finding a place they fit in, had them ready to plant their boot heels into the dirt. She'd felt the same way a time or two over the last week, too.

Above all else, Aaron and Sophie were tired. She could see it in their tiny faces, in the way they carried themselves. What had seemed like such a simple plan six months ago was falling apart around them.

Leaving in the middle of the night all those months ago had been impulsive and dangerous, but the alternative wasn't acceptable. She couldn't stay with John's brother another day. He'd already taken so much from her. From them. To know where his sick mind was headed still caused a shudder of disgust to fill her until she was ready to scream from it. Her setting out alone may seem idiotic to most but it saved Sophie Ann from a monster. She could take whatever cruelty he heaped upon her, and did on a daily basis, but Sophie couldn't. She wouldn't have understood. But telling them why they couldn't stay was too horrible to fathom. They'd never look at her the same if they knew, not to mention, if Marshal Avery found out, he'd throw her so far under the jail no one would even remember she existed.

Keri pushed the thought away and smiled, trying to mask her feelings, and smoothed back Sophie's curls to busy her hands. "Listen to me, love," she said, keeping her voice pitched low.

"When we find Uncle Peter, we'll have the biggest Christmas party you've ever seen. We'll get a tree with all the trimmings and gifts and all the oranges you can eat. I promise."

"But we won't find him in time," Aaron said. "Christmas will be here soon."

"We've a few weeks yet until then, Aaron."

"I know but we won't make it to California by then. Why can't we just stay until after Christmas? We can leave after it's all over."

Keri looked at his stricken face. "We've nowhere to stay, Aaron. We can't live in that shack all winter with no food. Besides, Mr. Lloyd doesn't want us there, he's made that perfectly clear."

"Well, we can stay here, then," he argued. "I heard the marshal say we could."

Keri stooped down to be eye level with them and turned her back to the adults in the room. Her eyes burned with unshed tears, the quiet pleas of her children breaking her heart. "I don't want us to be a burden to anyone, Aaron." She pulled him and Sophie close so her whispered words could be heard. "There's no place for us in Willow Creek. We have to move on. The only reason we've stayed this long is because of the snow storm."

"We can stay with Mr. Lloyd."

When Aaron looked up at Noah, Keri's chest ached. She'd seen that look on the boy's face before. It was there when his uncle strolled into their house to rescue them from the burdens left when John died. It was admiration in its most innocent form. It had been wasted on Robert, though, and giving it to Noah, a man none of them knew well enough, seemed a bit misplaced as well, especially seeing how Noah Lloyd was the most unfriendly, grumpy man, she'd ever met. "He doesn't want us there either, Aaron. That's why he brought us to town. We have to move on."

Aaron's face went red, his lips bloodless and he clenched his teeth together, his eyes filling with tears. "Uncle Peter won't want us either! Nobody does, so what difference does it make if we stay here or keep going. We should have never left." He started crying, the tears in his eyes falling so quickly, Keri had trouble brushing them away. He sniffled, and hiccuped, and tried to talk through his sobs. "You said things would be better but they're not. They're worse! You and Sophie Ann can go to California. I'm staying here."

Before she could react, Aaron threw off the blanket she'd wrapped around him and ran out the front door. She gasped and stood, rushing for the doorway as Aaron ran the length of the sidewalk and out into the snow covered road. "Aaron!" A choked sob crawled into her throat as she watched him run away. "Aaron, come back!"

CHAPTER TEN

She was halfway down the walkway, running frantically toward the gate when Noah caught her. He grabbed her arm, ignored her desperate cries, and turned her back toward the house. "Go back inside," he yelled. "You've no coat on and it's too cold to be out here without one. I'll go get him."

He didn't wait to see if she'd done as he said and took off at a run after Aaron. The kid was making a quick getaway despite the snow that still lingered on the sidewalks in town and Noah slipped twice, regaining his footing without falling, and ducked between the buildings as Aaron had.

The clearing behind the mercantile was vacant and Aaron's footprints were clearly visible. Noah followed them through a thicket of trees, snow falling from the limbs above to collect at the back of his neck when he walked under them. He growled in frustration, pushed the limbs away and came out on the other side. Aaron's footprints had disappeared.

Looking back into the thicket, Noah searched the brush, ducking to look under low lying bushes and finally saw him. He was huddled under a cluster of undergrowth, the ground underneath him void of snow. The sparse grass had been beaten down, dirt showing in most of the area, and Noah squatted and tilted his head to look in. "You plan on riding out the winter in this rabbit hole?"

The kid drew his knees in and crossed his arms over them before burying his head. "It stays dry," he said, his voice muffled.

"And how would you know that?"

"We stayed here before we found your old shack."

Noah stared in at the small clearing and shook his head. They'd stayed here? Under a thicket of trees, sleeping on frozen ground, with no way to warm themselves? His conscience pricked the moment he remembered seeing them huddled around the pitiful fire in the line shack. A shack he'd initially run them out of.

He closed his eyes, fighting back disgust at himself, and scrubbed a hand over his face before pushing the thought away and looking back up. "Your mother was pretty upset when you ran off. You can't abandon her like that. With your father gone, you're the man in the family now. It's your place to see to her and your sister."

Aaron looked up, incredulous. "I'm only ten. I'm not old enough to be the man in the family."

Noah shrugged his shoulder. "Your age doesn't matter. I was fourteen when my father died. I stepped into his role and saw to a plantation larger than this whole town and provided stability for my mother and sister when they didn't know what else to do. We aren't given what we want in life. We have to make do with what we're handed, even if we don't want it."

The boy stared at him for long minutes before shaking his head. "I can't take care of them," he said, tears once again filling his eyes.

"But you already have been."

Aaron shook his head. "No, I've not."

"Sure you have." Noah shifted, his knees aching from squatting in the same position too long. The boy was no longer crying outright but his eyes were still filled with tears. "The first time I saw you, you were chasing after Sophie Ann. Your mother trusted you to watch over your little sister, didn't she?"

"But that was just so she could find us something to eat. She wasn't gone too long."

"That's not the point. She still expected you to protect Sophie Ann. What will she do if you leave them now?"

Aaron huffed out a breath. "Same as she always did. Keep walking to California and steal what food she can find. Me being there won't make a bit of difference."

Noah knew that for a lie but didn't say so. He might not know much about Keri Hilam but he'd bet every possession he had she wouldn't leave without her children, regardless of what Aaron thought. "You're wrong about that," he said. "You being with her will make all the difference." He tilted his head, making sure he caught Aaron's eye. "If you don't want to go on, then you need to convince her to stay. You can't go on stealing every bit of food you get, nor can you sleep on frozen ground forever and you'll never make it to California on foot. You might as well put down roots here." To his horror, Aaron's eyes filled with tears again, his cheeks growing red before he let out a wail that made Noah cringe.

"It don't matter," Aaron cried. "We'll still have to sleep under the trees. The marshal was just being nice when he said we could stay with him. Only reason he said it was because you don't want us in your house no more." He looked up, misery so profound shining in his eyes, Noah felt a twinge of pain in his chest just looking at him.

Aaron swiped a hand under his nose, then wiped his eyes dry. "Uncle Robert didn't want us either. He just wanted my pa's land." He sighed and laid his head back on his knees. "No one wants us."

Noah's neck and face heated as shame and embarrassment at Aaron's words slammed into him hard enough to cause his chest to ache. *No one wants us*, the words echoed in his head. He knew all too well how that felt. It seemed like a lifetime ago but the pain was still there if he thought on it too much.

Looking away, he stared at the back of the mercantile, thoughts running rampant in his head. He'd spent the last week counting the minutes until he could get his unwanted house guests out from under his roof but he'd seen the look Morgan gave him when discussing what to do with them. The man *had* only offered a room to them because he didn't want to. Aaron may be young but he'd had to grow up in a hurry. He was more perceptive than Noah had given him credit for.

He repositioned his hat and stood, working the kinks out of his back and legs. Getting Aaron out from under those bushes was the least of his problems, he realized. The bigger issue was Keri herself. He wasn't sure why she'd tried to leave so quickly when Morgan suggested she could stay with him and his family. Was she in such a hurry to find her brother that she'd brave the cold with no protection to do it? It was idiotic. No one could withstand a Montana winter out in the elements. Only a fool would think they could.

But she'd already done it to some small degree. She was probably delusional enough to think she still could.

The blizzard that blew in wouldn't be the last of them. Noah had spent enough time in these parts to know the cold weather was brutal when it set in good. The mild winter they'd had recently wasn't normal and if Keri had been in these parts for any amount of time, she may think it was. They'd freeze to death if they tried living as they had been.

But what choice did they have? Where would they go?

No one wants us. The words whispered inside his head again. "Damn it." Irritation gnawed at him. *This* was the reason he avoided people and had been doing so for the better part of twelve years. He didn't want to be bothered with anything, or anyone, for any reason. Not even friendship. Those sorts of attachments only led to misery sometime down the road. Best to just not get involved, period.

But as much as he wanted to leave, to wash his hands of this whole mess, something kept his feet planted. He'd had more than enough opportunities to leave. Hell, he could go right now. Just walk away, leave the kid under the bushes and go home. He'd done his part. He'd dropped Keri and her kids off at the marshal's house like he said he was going to. They were supposed to be Morgan's responsibility now.

Yet, here he stood, freezing his ass off while talking to a kid with snot running down over his lip.

Annoyance fierce enough to scald his flesh washed over him and he looked back down at the brush Aaron was hiding under. His temper flared an instant later. "Get out from under there, Aaron. You've wasted enough of my time as it is." To his amazement, Aaron crawled out and stood, his head bowed. "Get back to the marshal's house. You've worried your mother enough for one day."

He followed the boy back, his thoughts a jumbled mess. Keri ran down the walkway when she spotted them, tears leaving wet trails down her cheeks. She grabbed Aaron when she reached him, fell to her knees there in the snow, and wrapped him in her arms and sobbed. Noah stopped at the gate, watching them. Would Keri stay with the Avery's or would she try to leave at the first opportunity she had? They'd left the comfort of their home for reasons Keri had yet to tell him about so what was to stop her from doing so again?

She looked up at him, her eyes large and filled with tears, gratitude shining so bright the sight twisted inside Noah's chest. Idiotic thoughts filled his head a moment later. Thoughts of letting her stay with him until her brother could be found. He tried to chase the notion away by reminding himself he'd slept in a chair for a solid week, but the idea nagged at his conscience until he seriously thought about it.

It's a bad idea. The words whispered inside his head until a reason it wasn't chased the doubt away. A reason he didn't want to think about, especially when Keri stood, her hands resting on Aaron's bony shoulders as she held his gaze and smiled. It was the tiniest curve at the corners of her mouth but the effect it had on him caused his entire body to jolt. The strain on her face melted away as she looked at him, her eyes, still glassy with unshed tears, locked with his own, and everything around him seemed to narrow down into a pinprick of light until nothing remained inside of it but her. This waif of a woman with eyes so soulful he felt as if he was drowning in them.

He blinked and looked away, trying to get his overactive imagination under control. The curve of her lips could barely even be called a smile, yet the effect was felt as if she bestowed him with one so blindingly brilliant he'd been dazzled by it. And maybe he had. Maybe the fact she could look at him without disgust or pity filling her eyes was enough. The fact she offered him that tiny smile to begin with. Whatever it was, Noah knew he'd been wrong about one thing. Keri Hilam wasn't the fool. It was him. A fool to even think of keeping her when every fiber of his being begged him to walk away, to forget she even existed. But the moment he looked back up and saw her captivating eyes still fixed on him, his heart gave one mighty thump in his chest hard enough to let him know he was still alive.

And for the first time since the war ended, he was actually glad he was.

"Come back inside, Keri. You look frozen through."

Abigail touched her arm and was tugging her away before she could find words enough to thank Noah for going after Aaron. For rescuing and taking care of them when the storm hit. For everything.

She glanced over her shoulder at him as they entered the house. He was still by the fence, staring up at her as Abigail shut the door behind them, and she knew she'd not get a chance to thank him. He'd been too eager to be rid of them and was probably climbing into his wagon this very moment.

The warmth of the house enveloped her as she entered the foyer. She spotted Sophie Ann. She was staring out the front window, her face pressed against the glass.

"Come back into the kitchen, Keri. We need to get you two warmed up."

She followed Abigail and sat back down in the chair she'd vacated earlier, her arms still around Aaron.

"How about some more tea?" Laurel asked her. "It'll warm you up in no time."

"All right," Keri said. "Thank you."

Laurel refilled her tea cup and even poured one for Aaron. They sat in silence for long minutes, drinking from their mugs until the chill was chased away from her bones.

Laurel and Abigail left the room, their hushed whispers filling the air and Keri closed her eyes, trying to escape her reality for a brief moment. She had no idea what to do now. As much as she hated the thought of imposing on the marshal, and risking him finding out what she'd done, she didn't have much of a choice. Regardless of how it looked to others, she wasn't stupid. She knew she couldn't walk to California in the dead of winter. If she were honest with herself, she'd acknowledge the fact that they wouldn't be able to do it had it been summer. She'd taken her kids from the only home they'd ever known and turned them into homeless beggars.

She sighed, finished her tea, and glanced into the hall where the women were talking. Movement past Abigail's shoulder caught her attention and leaning back enabled her to see around the woman. Marshal Avery stood just inside the front door and to her surprise, Noah was with him, the two men deep in their own conversation. When the marshal broke away and joined the women, Keri looked away. They were discussing her, trying to figure out what to do with them. She didn't need to be told to know so and embarrassment burned her cheeks. They pitied her. Talking in soft whispers so she couldn't hear and humiliation burned hot in her chest. She swallowed and nudged Aaron away so she could stand.

Noah startled her when she turned. She hadn't heard him enter the room. He glanced at Aaron, told him to "go find your sister," and waited until he had before he looked back over at her. His shoulders lifted as he inhaled a breath, his gaze locked with hers. "You and the kids will be coming back home with me." Keri blinked up at him. "I've things to pick up at the mercantile. Be ready to go when I return."

She opened her mouth to discuss the matter but he turned before she could get a word out, walked back down the hall and out the front door. Morgan followed him after a few moments. The two women broke apart, Laurel grabbing her coat and slipping it on before leaving the house while Abigail hurried up the stairs.

What was going on? Where was everyone going? And why had Noah decided to take them back home with him when she knew it was the last thing he wanted to do?

CHAPTER ELEVEN

L aurel returned a short time later, her arms draped in clothes. She smiled at Keri as she hustled into the room to the right of the front door. An office from the looks of it. A light flared in the room as a lamp was lit and Abigail's footsteps tapped on the stairs a moment later. Her arms were also filled with clothes.

The uncomfortable feeling she'd had when they all left intensified as the two women busied themselves in the office and Keri craned her neck to see what they were doing. When Laurel called her name, she jumped, startled by the noise.

She entered the room, her eyes scanning the clothing the women had. Small dresses and stockings. Hair ribbons and nightgowns. Trousers and shirts that looked as if they'd seem better days but still better than the rags Aaron was wearing.

These strangers had gathered clothing for her kids?

Tears filled Keri's eyes again. She'd cried so much today, her head felt stopped up, her throat aching with the emotion.

Laurel smiled her way as she folded the trousers and shirts. "These aren't the best," she said, "but it's all we have on such short notice. They're hand-me-downs mostly, from the box over at the school, but they come in handy on occasion." Her smile brightened. "Like now. They'll do for Aaron until something better can be found for him."

Keri couldn't say a word in reply. Abigail was folding dresses, adding them to the pile of trousers and shirts. When everything was sorted, Abigail found a bit of twine in one of the desk drawers and tied everything together.

"There," she said, smiling. "That should help out a bit."

"I can't..." Keri cleared her throat twice before getting the words out. "I can't take these."

"Sure you can," Laurel said. "They were just sitting in a box. It isn't as if we took them from someone who needed them."

Keri looked at Abigail. "The dresses?" she asked, quietly. "Will your daughters not need them?"

Abigail smiled. "Not for a while yet. They belonged to my niece, Alex, but they're still a bit too big for my girls. They'll probably be too big for Sophie Ann as well, but I have this." She held up a small black box and laid it on top of the clothes. "It's a sewing kit," she said. "You can tack up the hem or take the sides in a bit if they're too big for Sophie."

The marshal and Noah returned a few moments later and for some unexplainable reason, the moment Noah turned to look at her, the anxiety she felt eased a bit. "Ready?" he asked, his head once again tilting a fraction to one side.

She stared at him, wondering why he was willing to take them back. She crossed the room and joined him in the foyer. "Why are you doing this?" she asked, her voice pitched low so the Averys wouldn't hear. "I know you don't want us in your house and it's okay. We'll be okay."

"Are you going to stay here with the marshal until your brother can be found?"

Her heart ached, misery causing the back of her throat to tighten while tears filled her eyes again. "I don't want us to be a burden to anyone."

"So, you're going to, what?" Noah said, his eyes darkening. "Sneak away again? Make it to Missoula before the next storm hits? Then what?" He glowered at her, his eyebrows pulled down as he frowned. "You don't look like a stupid woman to me, Keri. Don't prove me wrong."

She looked away, saw the faces of her children and knew Noah *was* wrong. She was stupid. Stupid for dragging her babies halfway across the territory when she could have found a husband anywhere along the way. She may not have been happy but they would have been warm, fed and cared for.

And not a burden to these people.

Noah grabbed the blanket she'd used to wrap herself in on the way to town and held it out to her. "It's just until the marshal can find your brother."

She sighed and stared at him, still unsure why he was taking them back in. "You didn't answer my question, Noah. Why are you doing this? I thought you wanted us gone."

"I did." He shifted his weight from one foot to the other but never took his eyes off her. "And truth be known, taking you back home with me is the last thing I want to do but I can't let you leave, Keri. You can't drag these kids across the country in the dead of winter and if I have to be inconvenienced for a time to prevent you from doing that, then so be it."

"So instead of us being a burden to the marshal, we'll be a burden to you?" He never answered but the look on his face changed. Something in his eyes told her he didn't really see them as a burden, regardless of his surly manner. Did he want them to come back so they wouldn't leave Willow Creek or because he really wanted them to stay?

The answers never came and the longer she stared at Noah, the more she realized she didn't really have a choice. Not now. She either went with Noah or stayed here with the Averys. They couldn't survive the winter in the open.

She bit her bottom lip and stared at Noah's bearded face.

"What will people say?" she asked. "About us staying with you, I mean?"

He shrugged. "I don't care what they say. They'll talk regardless of what I do."

"That may be, but..."

The marshal took a step forward, his arms crossed over his chest. "As far as the townsfolk are concerned, Noah rode into Missoula and got himself a wife. He rarely comes to town so no one will question it. Stop worrying, Mrs. Hilam. Everything will be fine."

Keri thought of another dozen excuses why this was a bad idea but in the end, it made little difference. They needed somewhere to stay through the winter and imposing on the marshal made her feel uneasy. He was a family man with children. He didn't need more people to worry about. At least with Noah, she was comfortable around him—when he wasn't acting like a disgruntled bear—and he lived alone. She wouldn't be putting anyone out. Well, no one other than Noah. Maybe she could talk him into taking his bed back. At least she wouldn't feel so bad then.

Decision made, she glanced into the other room where Aaron and Sophie Ann sat watching the school children play a game that didn't involve screaming. She called Aaron's name until he noticed her and stood, grabbing Sophie Ann's hand and walking her across the room to where she stood. The blankets they'd been using to ward off the cold were gathered and wrapped around them again as the front door was opened. Going back home with Noah was a complete contradiction to what she'd meant to do but as she followed him out of the house, she didn't dismiss the sense of relief she felt.

She followed Noah quietly, Morgan in step behind her, his arms filled with the clothes the women had packed. Reaching the wagon, Keri stared at the small cot sitting in the back. She glanced at Noah and wondered where it had come from, but decided to ask later.

When the kids were settled, Marshal Avery saying his good-byes and walking away, Noah turned to help her into the wagon. She looked down at his outstretched hand, the black leather gloves she'd never seen him take off still in place, and she didn't hesitate placing her hand in his to let him help her into the wagon. For whatever reason, he had invited them back into his home. She was too stunned to ask for the real reason why, and sat silently all the way back to his cabin.

Noah parked the wagon near the door and helped her down, picked up Sophie Ann and placed her feet on the ground, and reached for the cot and mattress, hauling them in and setting them along the farthest wall opposite the bed. The bundles of clothes were brought inside, the blankets they'd been wrapped in folded and put back inside the chest at the foot of the bed, and it wasn't until Noah went to unhitch the horse from the wagon that she turned to look at Aaron. "What happened when Noah chased you down?"

Aaron sighed and leaned against the bed. "We talked, mostly."

"About what?"

"All kinds of stuff." He shrugged and gave her a wide-eyed look. "He said I had to be the man in our family now since Pa was dead and that you and Sophie Ann wouldn't be able to get along without me."

Keri smiled, her heart aching as she looked at him. "He's right. I'd probably wither up and die if you weren't here." That earned her a smile from him. "Do you plan on staying, then?"

"I don't think I got no choice," he said. "After Noah was done talking, he told me to come out of my hiding spot and get back to the marshal's house. He didn't sound like he was asking me either."

Keri raised an eyebrow. "He yelled at you?"

Aaron shook his head. "No. He didn't have to. I knew by the

sound of him he'd probably snatch me up by one ear if I didn't do as he said, so I just did it."

She'd heard Noah's deep, demanding voice enough to know the power behind it and Aaron was at least smart enough to know not to test the man. Of course, after he reacted so badly to Sophie Ann getting into his drawings, she was sure both kids would tread lightly around him.

When the door opened, she turned, watching Noah come inside, a large package wrapped in brown paper under one arm. He removed his coat and hat, then looked in her direction. Keri could tell he wanted to say something. He apparently had as much trouble speaking up as she did at the moment. She glanced at the package then raised her eyes to his. "Is there anything in particular you'd like for supper?"

He shook his head. "No. Anything you'd like to fix is fine." He took a step, then stopped and held out the package. "This is for you. It's all the mercantile had."

That beard of his hid so much of his face, it was a wonder Keri could even tell he was blushing, but there was no mistaking the red tint glowing on his cheeks. She crossed the room and reached for the package. "Thank you." He nodded once, turned and left her standing there. She watched him reach for the leather journal Sophie had nearly destroyed and the box of pencils before taking a seat in the rocker. Laying the package on the bed, she debated on opening it. What had he bought? And why?

"Can we eat soon?"

Keri looked down at Sophie Ann when she spoke and smiled. "Yes, love. We'll eat soon. Can you sit out here with Aaron and not get into any trouble?" Sophie Ann grinned and nodded her head. Leaving them to entertain themselves quietly, Keri headed for the kitchen.

. . .

* * * *

Noah could see her out of the corner of his eye. She was inching closer, her blond curls bouncing over her shoulders. He looked over at her. She stopped walking the moment she realized he'd seen her. She held his gaze until he turned his head.

The pages she'd ripped out of his journal were beyond repair. He stuffed them in the back of the book and scanned through the pages, pulling out the ones she'd scribbled on. The book itself was in good shape although more than a few pages fell free from the binding.

Sophie Ann had nearly reached his chair when he grabbed his pencil and laid it against a blank page. The first few strokes across the paper looked stark against the background. His touch was light, the pencil strokes long and he had a vague outline by the time Sophie Ann reached him. She leaned against the arm of the chair, peering down at what he was doing. She never said a word, just watched quietly as he drew.

The ticking of the clock sounded loud in the stillness but for once, it didn't cause the melancholy that usually invaded him every evening. The thought should have alarmed him but for some reason, it didn't. As much as he disliked being around people, these scruffy kids, and their soft spoken mother, didn't bother him much.

He didn't waste time perfecting the sketch and held back a pleased smile when Sophie Ann gasped as the picture started to take shape. He glanced at her, noticing her wide eyes before she smiled.

"That looks like me," she whispered.

Noah didn't reply. There wasn't a need to. He worked on the sketch as the scent of food filled the air, the soft pattering sounds of Keri in the kitchen causing something in his chest to tighten. He still didn't know why he'd brought them home with him. It wasn't his intention when he'd bundled them up and took them to town, or when he fetched Aaron and returned him to the marshal's place. But when Abigail had taken Keri back to the house and she looked over her shoulder at him, he'd already made his decision. He'd take them home with him and keep them until Morgan could locate Keri's brother. And if Peter Davis couldn't be found...

Well, he'd cross that bridge when he came to it.

When the drawing was finished, he scribbled *Sophie Ann* and a date on the page and turned the book so she could see it. She grinned, grabbed the journal with both hands and stared at it so long he wasn't sure she was going to give it back.

"Can you do a horse?" she asked, her big eyes imploring as she looked up at him.

"After supper I can." He pocketed the pencil, Keri coming into view as she stepped back into the room.

"Aaron, you and Sophie Ann get washed up. Supper is almost ready."

Sophie Ann whirled, the journal still in her hands, and ran across the room, holding the book up to show her mother. Keri's face lit from within, her surprise evident. When she glanced at him, heat burned along his neck until she looked back down at Sophie Ann when the girl said, "He's going to draw me a horse after supper."

"Is he?" Keri said. "Well, you best get cleaned up so we can eat, then."

The girl ran back across the room and handed him the journal before darting off again. She hadn't made it halfway across the room before she turned back to face him. A frown tugged at her lips. "I'm sorry I messed up the other pictures."

Her voice was pitched so low, Noah barely heard it. He glanced at Keri before turning his attention to Sophie Ann. "Apology accepted." Her frown vanished in an instant. Closing the book, he set it aside as both kids disappeared into the kitchen, the sound of water splashing as they washed was heard before both of them came barreling back into the room and plunking down near the fire. When Keri followed them with two plates, he knew he'd have to get two more chairs. The floor wasn't a place anyone should have to eat from.

Following Keri into the kitchen, he noticed his plate was already filled and sitting in front of his chair. He sat, picked up his fork and kept the expression on his face neutral when Keri grabbed her plate and left him sitting in the kitchen alone. He couldn't say why the sound of her retreating footsteps felt so dismissive. He hadn't done anything to make them feel welcome. He barely spoke to them, if truth be known.

As he listened to them laugh and talk in the other room, he ate in silence, the question of why he'd brought them back whispering inside his head again. He couldn't think of one reason that stood out from the others but he had to admit, hearing something other than that damn clock ticking made the evening seem a little less bleak.

CHAPTER TWELVE

Noah had no sooner sat by the cow when he heard the barn door open. He turned his head, not surprised to see Aaron looking at him. The boy was wearing the clothes the Avery women had given him. They were a bit big, the pant legs rolled several times to keep from dragging the ground, but he didn't look nearly as homely as he had the first time he saw him.

Aaron walked into the stall and nodded his head toward the cow. "Want me to milk her?"

It was the same thing he'd asked the first time he'd followed him into the barn. The expectant look on Aaron's face was what made Noah stand up. The smile the kid shot him took him by surprise. "I've never seen anyone so eager to milk a cow."

Aaron sat on the stool and got straight to work. Noah raised an eyebrow at him. He hadn't been lying that first day when he said he could help out.

Noah stepped out of the stall, folding his arms over the rail, and looked back in. Aaron's arms worked, one then the other, his gaze focused and intense. He looked much too serious for such a menial job.

"This cow seems less ornery than the one we had. Ethel," the kid said, glancing up at him, "that was our cow's name, she used to try and step on me when I milked her. Sophie Ann would talk to her just so she wouldn't pay no attention to me." Aaron tilted his head to see him, an inquisitive look on his face. "This cow got a name?"

"No."

Aaron shook his head. "Sophie Ann will name her. She names every critter she comes across. She named every one of our piglets and chickens and there was a whole mess of 'em."

Noah readjusted his hat. "Sounds like you had a pretty good size farm."

"I guess we did. We had a few goats and pigs, two horses, the chickens and Ethel." Aaron paused, then frowned. "Well, we had a lot of animals until Uncle Robert got there. He sold the ones he didn't butcher."

At the mention of the man's name, questions by the dozens popped into Noah's head. None of them were any of his business, but he knew he'd drive himself insane if he didn't know why they'd left home, alone, to try and walk through four territories to find a relative they didn't even know was still alive. "Sophie Ann mentioned your uncle Robert was mean. Is that why you left?"

"Partly, I think." Aaron shifted on the stool. "Ma never said outright why we was leaving but with the way Uncle Robert yelled at me and Sophie Ann, I figure that's why she wanted to leave. He didn't like us to talk too much and he'd yell at Ma when she tried to calm him down." He stilled, a frown covering his face. "He used to hit her sometimes."

"Who?" Noah asked. "Sophie Ann?"

"No, my ma." Aaron looked up, fire dancing in his eyes, the frown now gone. "The first time I saw Uncle Robert hit her, I got so scared I ran half way to the Johnson place before I remembered I'd left Sophie Ann behind. When I got back home, Sophie and my ma were crying." He shook his head, his jaw clamping tight. "Ma's mouth was bleeding and one whole side of her face was red. I ain't never wanted to kill nobody until I saw that." He met Noah's gaze. "Do you think they'd lock a little kid up for killing a man?"

Would they? Hell if he knew. "Hard to say," he told him. "I guess it would depend on what a kid killed a man for."

"I had lots of reasons to kill Uncle Robert by the time we left." He pulled the bucket out from under the cow, setting it aside before standing. "When he found out my pa died, he just walked in our house like it was his to take and started bossing us around." Aaron's face turned blistering red, his eyes downcast. "He treated my ma like she was his wife too, even though she wasn't."

Noah stared at him, knowing by that scarlet blush on his face exactly what it was he wasn't saying. Dear ole' Uncle Robert had invited himself into Keri's bed. His heart thumped inside his chest. Had Robert forced himself on her? Or had she accepted him?

Aaron picked up the milk bucket and walked to the stall door with it, sloshing milk over the sides. Noah reached for it, setting it aside before he spilled all of it. He pulled the stall door shut and secured it, then stepped over to his horse.

He tended the rest of the animals, Aaron's voice following him around the dimly lit barn as he told him more about their life on a distant farm. John Hilam had been older than their mother. Streaks of gray had been in his hair according to the boy, which led Noah to believe he was much older than Keri. He finished with the horse, secured the stall door and listened to Aaron talk until he was sure the sun would go down before the kid lost steam. Apparently when he got going, he didn't know when to shut up. Everything he said seemed to bleed together until he heard Aaron mention the war. Everything in him froze and his body tensed.

"Was you in the war?" Aaron asked.

Noah couldn't find his voice and nodded his head instead.

Aaron sighed. "So was my pa. He used to tell me about it sometimes but my ma would always give him funny looks when his stories got too bloody." He looked up. "Is that where you got that scar on your face?" he asked. "From the war?"

Memories assaulted him so fast, his chest tightened. His vision dimmed until he saw nothing but black... then vibrant red. He could smell the smoke, the stench of burning flesh and hair, and felt the panic that usually came with the memories over-whelming him an instant before Aaron grabbed his hand, the gentle touch shocking him so badly, his body jolted.

"You all right?" Aaron asked. "You look a bit funny."

Noah swallowed the panic, taking deep breaths as his head cleared. He nodded once and turned on his heel, grabbed the chicken feed and bolted out into the cold air as fast as his feet would carry him.

Keri saw the package Noah had given her the night before the moment she stood and reached for her dingy dress. She'd placed the paper wrapped parcel on the chest at the foot of the bed and had forgotten all about it.

She reached for it and untied the string holding it together and sucked in a soft breath when she saw what was inside. Three calico dresses in soft, pale colors lay beneath that brown paper, along with several pairs of socks, stockings, a new chemise and underwear. Heat blazed against her face as she stared at the undergarments. Had Noah picked them out? Surely not.

She picked up the chemise, ran a finger over the pink silk ribbon that held the front together, then grabbed the underwear. There was lace around the bottom of the legs, the material so white it reminded her of freshly fallen snow. The lace looked expensive and she'd never owned anything so fine in all her life.

She'd seen fancy undergarments like these before but couldn't figure out why one would need such embellishments. Underwear only served one purpose and having fancy lace edging and pink drawstrings seemed like a bit of a waste.

Unless they weren't just for practicality. Were fancy drawers like these made to entice men instead?

Heat blazed across her face at the thought and she couldn't stop imagining Noah picking out her undergarments with the intentions of seeing her in them. Of him touching them. The heat in her face increased. How would she ever manage to look at him and not be reminded that he'd bought her underwear. Fancy, lace trimmed underwear with dainty pink ribbons and bows.

Her nervous laughter filled the cabin and she smothered it before she woke Sophie Ann. Removing her nightdress, she put the bloomers on, slid the chemise over her head and tied the ribbon, then stared at each of the dresses. They weren't fancy. Simple work dresses, really, but the fabrics were as pretty as any she'd ever seen.

The brown dress dotted with small pink flowers drew her eye first, followed by the pink flowers on a white background, then the blue and red. She grabbed the brown dress, slipped it on, then turned to the mirror on the wall and tried to see what she looked like. The mirror was too small to see much but it was enough. She smiled, then made a face when she saw her hair. The curls that hadn't been a problem when her hair had been long were now a riot of tight ringlets about her head. She tucked what she could behind her ears, pulled on the curls in hopes they would settle a bit and blew out a breath when she realized it was useless.

She grabbed the other two dresses and hung them on one of the numerous pegs along the wall and turned back to grab the socks. Another small wrapped package was lying underneath them. She unwrapped it, her eyes widening as she saw the soap. The bar was pink, the writing on the white label wrapped around it in a language she couldn't read. The scent of flowers filled the air in front of her. She lifted the soap to her face and inhaled the aroma deeply, imagining what it would feel like to bathe in that soap, for the scent to linger on her skin all day.

Laying everything aside, she stepped out from behind the blankets, smoothing a hand down the front of her new dress and headed to the kitchen. Aaron wasn't in the cabin and her pulse leaped. Had he left after she'd gone to sleep? Rushing to the door, she stepped outside, searching the yard and saw the barn door swing open, then closed. She ran toward the building but stopped when she reached the door. She could hear Aaron talking. "Thank God," she whispered, her hand going to her chest. She listened for several minutes before heading back to the house and started on breakfast.

The heat inside that small kitchen would have been unbearable in summer. The stove took up most of the room, the cabinet not nearly long enough, but she managed to get everything going at once. Sophie Ann startled her when she tugged on her skirt and Keri smiled when she saw her tiny face. "Did you sleep well, love?"

Sophie Ann yawned, her jaw popping. "Yeah."

Keri noticed she was still carrying the drawing Noah had given her after supper the night before. A horse with a rider who looked suspiciously like Sophie. "You're going to ruin that picture if you keep carrying it around."

"I'll be careful," she said, staring down at it. "Noah said he'd make me another one today." She looked up and smiled. "I wonder if he can draw kittens."

Keri had a hard time imagining Noah with something so delicate as kittens. He seemed too harsh for such a frail thing. But, appearances could be deceiving. She'd thought Robert to be a gentleman once too and look how that turned out. She shuddered and glanced back down at Sophie. "Run out and tell Aaron and Mr. Lloyd that breakfast is ready."

When she came back inside, panting for breath, her cheeks

pink from the cold, Keri fixed two plates and settled Sophie near the fire, setting Aaron's plate beside her for when he came in. He bolted through the door a moment later and ran to the kitchen. Keri followed him and raised an eyebrow when she saw him washing up without having to be told.

Aaron and Sophie Ann were already eating by the time Noah came inside. Keri heard him enter the kitchen, the scrape of his chair across the floor screeching, and her stomach did a little flip. Nervous butterflies dipped and swam and her neck and face burned the moment she thought of the underwear she was wearing. Lacy underwear he'd bought for her. She hoped her cheeks weren't as red as they felt. She quickly set Noah's plate in front of him, and turned to fill her own.

She lingered with her back to him so long, she knew he had to be wondering what she was doing. She could hear his fork scraping against his plate and she closed her eyes, told herself to stop being such a girl, and faced him, her gaze focused on her plate as she started toward the table. She paused when he glanced up at her, his eyes giving a fast sweep of her form from head to toe before he looked back down.

The empty chair caught her attention and for the second time since he'd found them in that line shack, she wondered if he'd want her company. The new clothes he'd bought her could mean any number of things and she wasn't about to examine any of them now but, the fact he'd gone to the trouble gave her courage enough to ask. "Would you mind if I sat at the table with you?"

He looked up as if startled and she wished she'd never spoke. If he said no, she'd never be able to get rid of her damning blush. To her surprise, he said, "I don't mind."

Keri flashed him a quick smile and sat down.

CHAPTER THIRTEEN

There it was again, Noah thought, a smile just for him. His insides were shaking like some schoolboy with his first crush by the time she'd settled. He was disgusted at the mere thought of such girlie notions as butterflies fluttering in his stomach all because she smiled at him. He was a grown man, being nervous around a woman was ridiculous.

Of course, he hadn't spent more than a few moments talking to a woman in so damn long, it was little wonder Keri made him feel like he was about to jump out of his skin. It also didn't help that she kept flashing those shy smiles his way. It made him think things he shouldn't. Things that weren't possible. Not now, at least. Not with the way he looked.

He'd been ignoring the small shaving mirror hanging on the wall for years. The loathing he felt when he saw himself sucked what little soul he had left out. He noticed nothing when looking at his reflection other than that scar and he knew that was all anyone else saw, too. It was why people turned their heads when they saw him. Why children stared. That damn scar was why he didn't bother shaving. His beard hid most of that jagged line etched across his face and his hair seemed to cover the rest. He probably looked a sight, though. He hadn't been able to get a comb through his hair in ages.

Keri cleared her throat, her soft voice drawing his gaze to her. "Thank you for the drawing," she said. "The one you drew for Sophie Ann. She's carried it around with her all morning." She looked down at her plate, a small frown covering her face. "And I'm sorry she ruined the others." She met his gaze again. "I truly am."

Noah looked away. "It's done now. I can redraw them if I wish." Long minutes passed, both of them eating in silence until Keri asked him how long he'd been drawing. "Since I was a boy."

"They're quite beautiful. I've seen sketches like yours before but I've never known anyone who could actually draw them."

The compliment felt so foreign he wasn't sure how to respond to it. The way she looked at him left him lightheaded as well. Her gaze was intent, as if she cared about what he said. He lifted his mug, downed half the coffee she'd poured into it and shifted in his seat. When she started eating again, he peeked up at her.

Her blond curls looked a bit wild this morning, the light coming from the small window in the room shining off the strands. He could only imagine what her hair had looked like tumbling down her back, a glossy veil of spun gold falling to her hips. His fingers twitched to touch it. To see if it was as soft as it looked.

He glanced at his gloved hands and held back a sigh. He'd never be able to feel it anyway. He hadn't removed the gloves since they'd arrived and he didn't plan on it. He'd taken them off in the barn when he was alone, flexing his fingers, stretching them and feeling the texture of things before slipping the leather back on, but he'd never let them see.

Putting the thought out of his mind, he finished eating and refilled his coffee mug. He watched Keri as she took small bites of her eggs, his gaze sliding over the dress Mrs. Jenkins had picked out for her. It fit perfectly, the fabric just snug enough to draw his eye to her breasts. They weren't overly large but he was sure they'd fill his palm. The old dress she'd been wearing when he found them had been big and baggy and hid her figure. This dress hugged the curve of her hips, showed him how small her waist was. She was still too thin but far from unappealing.

When the Avery women mentioned having extra clothing for Aaron and Sophie, he knew Keri would need a few things too. That dress she'd been wearing was so threadbare, he was surprised it hadn't fallen apart after she washed it, so he'd headed to the mercantile when the women went off to gather things for the kids. He'd been clueless as to what a woman needed though, and the shopkeeper had taken on the painful task of picking things out for him upon Morgan's request for her to do so. The marshal's little white lie of him marrying a widow in Missoula had earned him a curious look from Mrs. Jenkins before she reluctantly nodded to Morgan and started gathering everything for Keri he'd asked for.

Thanking her for her trouble had been useless. Mrs. Jenkins either didn't hear him or ignored him outright. He'd bet money on her ignoring him but didn't dwell on it. He'd made a business out of ignoring others, it was only fair they repaid him in kind.

When Mrs. Jenkins' set everything on the counter and started totaling it all up, he spotted scented soap in a basket on the counter. The label said it came from France. He had no idea if it really did but the scent had caught his attention. It was just the sort of thing a woman would want. Why he cared he couldn't say, but he'd bought it anyway, slipping the pink bar onto the pile of clothes. It had been an impulsive move. He still wasn't sure why he'd done it.

Keri laid her fork down and glanced up at him, her cheeks turning pink. He realized he'd been staring at her and averted his gaze, taking another drink from his mug. When she did the same, he cleared his throat. "What happened to your hair?"

She reached up, pushing the strands behind her ear. "I sold it."

When her eyes met his, he knew how much she'd hated doing it. It was there on her face, etched in bleak sadness. "We ran out of food," she said. "At the time, I hated the thought of stealing and I had nothing else of value. When I saw a sign in the window of a millinery that said they bought hair, I walked in and asked what they'd give me for mine." She smiled. "Apparently unruly ringlets are in high demand. The money was enough to buy quite a bit of provisions but it didn't last forever."

"You started stealing what you needed then." It wasn't a question and she knew it wasn't.

"I had to feed my children." Her voice was pitched so low Noah barely heard her. The despair on her face was obvious, though. Judging by the condition they were in when he found them, she hadn't been a very adapt thief. The three of them looked like skin and bones that first day. Not so much now. Their hollow cheeks had filled out. The dark circles under their eyes had lightened and the pallor of their skin was beginning to look healthy again.

She stood and started to clear away the dishes and he sat there watching her, drinking in the sight of her as if he'd never seen another woman. Never one in his kitchen, that's for sure. When she caught his eye, she stopped. "What?"

"Why did you leave home?"

The color leached from her face so quickly, Noah feared she'd pass out. Her eyes looked a bit too wide as she turned her back to him, her hands now shaking as she reached for the remaining dirty dishes. He stood, waited for her to answer, but knew she wasn't going to say anything when she shook her head.

He didn't press the matter. It wasn't any of his business anyway. He thanked her for breakfast and walked into the other room. The kids looked up at him from where they sat on the floor before they stood, grabbed their empty plates, and carried them away. "I need more chairs," he mumbled. He glanced around the small cabin, his eye landing on the blankets hanging around the bed and the small cot under the window. "I need a bigger house."

The thought conjured images in his mind of additions, bedrooms for privacy, a proper kitchen with work space, a new stove and a table big enough to seat a large family. He had more money than he'd ever spend in his lifetime so building on to the cabin wouldn't take much. He could place the order for wood at the mercantile and have it delivered right to his door.

Sophie Ann and Aaron ran back into the room laughing about something but stopped abruptly when they looked at him. All thoughts of building on to the cabin vanished in an instant. This wasn't his family and they weren't staying. Once Morgan found Keri's brother, they'd leave, his life could get back to normal and those extra bedrooms and big kitchen would be wasted space.

He turned away and sat in his rocker, staring into the fire. He'd given up his chance for a normal life the day he'd returned home from the war and saw disgust and pity on Isabelle's face when she looked at him. For all her beauty, she'd been as shallow as those other snotty debutantes that flounced around Charleston.

Isabelle had wanted wealth, something he had in abundance, but it wasn't enough. Not for her. Not after she'd seen him stripped bare and got a good look at what he'd become.

The scar on his face had still been raw and red, the stitches the sorry excuse for a doctor put in, uneven and crooked. As horrible as the scar was, the rest of him had looked worse. The horrified expression on her face left him praying infection would set in. Dying would have been preferable to seeing the pity on everyone's face but days had turned into weeks, then months, and the scars started to heal regardless of him wishing for his own death.

The memories nearly took his breath. He blinked, tried to chase them away by focusing on the noise in the room. Sophie Ann and Aaron talking, the sound of water splashing in the kitchen as Keri washed the dishes. That damn, irritating, ticking clock up on the mantel.

He opened his eyes when the rocker moved. Sophie was leaning against the arm of the chair, her small face turned up to look at him. "When you going to draw me another picture?"

"Depends on what you want me to draw."

"Kittens," she shrieked, her tinkling laughter filling the room.

It was the last thing he wanted to draw but her excited face drew him up from the chair to reach for the journal he'd placed on the mantel out of her reach. When he sat back down and flipped to a clean page, then grabbed his pencil, Sophie nearly lay on top of him she was stretched over the arm of the chair so far. And for some reason, he didn't mind that she was there.

T hree days after the visit to Marshal Avery's home, Keri was startled to hear a knock on the door. She answered it, her eyes widening when she saw Laurel Avery, the school teacher standing there. The woman smiled, her pretty, unusual amber eyes shining as she said, "Good day, Mrs. Hilam. Can I come in?"

Keri nodded and stepped back, peeking out the door to see a man she'd never seen before by the barn talking to Noah. Aaron and Sophie were there as well, a small boy and an older girl talking to them. She shut the door and looked at her guest, wondering what she was doing there. "Is anything wrong?" she asked.

"Oh, mercy no," she said, shrugging out of her coat and draping it over her arm. "I just wanted to talk with you about something."

Keri's stomach flipped. Talk about what? She swung her arm toward the kitchen. "We can sit at the table, Mrs. Avery."

"Oh please, call me Laurel."

"Only if you call me Keri." Laurel smiled and Keri followed

her into the kitchen, wringing her hands as the woman sat down, laying her coat across her lap. She smiled nervously and tucked a strand of hair behind her ear. "I don't think Noah has any tea but I could make coffee if you'd like."

Laurel raised a hand, making a shooing motion as she shook her head. "Don't go to any trouble," she said. "Come and sit down."

When Keri had taken a seat, Laurel smiled and looked around the kitchen. "This little cabin is quite homey, isn't it?"

Keri nodded. "Yes. Perfect for someone who lives alone."

Laurel raised an eyebrow at her. "But not for another adult and a couple of kids?"

A short laugh spilled past her lips. "No. There's no privacy, nor enough beds." She shook her head. "I feel bad every night me and the kids crawl into bed knowing Mr. Lloyd is on that small cot, but he wouldn't have it any other way."

Laurel leaned forward and lowered her voice a bit. "What sort of man is Noah Lloyd?" she asked, curiously. "He's such a mystery to everyone. He's been here a couple of years and no one knows anything about him. His accent tells me he's from down South somewhere but other than that..." She sat back up and shrugged. "He rarely speaks and when he does, it's in as few words as possible."

Keri smiled and nodded her head. "That sounds like him." Her mind drifted to him. "He's pretty quiet here as well. Doesn't talk much. Well, he hadn't before this morning. I think we had out first real conversation over breakfast. It's the most I've ever heard him say."

"Does he get along with the children?"

The day Sophie Ann got into his drawings came to mind. The way he'd yelled and lifted her from the floor, racing into her mind. "For the most part," she said. "They had been staying out of his way when we first got here but Aaron helps him in the barn most mornings now and Sophie Ann's taken a liking to the pictures he draws for her. He sketches pictures that look so life-like. They're really quite beautiful." At Laurel's inquisitive look, Keri blushed.

Laurel changed the subject, which Keri was glad for, but at the mention of school, she sighed.

"I'm sure they get bored here all day," Laurel was saying. "At least they'd have something to do for a few hours they were in town with me. Besides, it's my last year teaching. I'd love to get to know them before my replacement shows up in the spring."

Dread skated along Keri's spine. "I'm sure they'd enjoy it but I see little point in it. The marshal said he'd send a wire to the sheriff in Missoula and try to get someone to track Peter down. Once he's found, we'll be leaving. If they get into a routine here, it'll be harder for them to let go."

"And if your brother isn't found?"

Keri didn't like to think he wouldn't be. She had to believe he was out there somewhere. He'd send for them the moment he knew they were trying to reach him, especially after being so vocal about her not marrying John to begin with. With their parents gone, she hadn't wanted to burden Peter with taking care of her, but he'd disliked the Hilam family. He thought John was decent enough, but he'd begged her not to marry him. His family wasn't good enough for her in his eyes and John was nearly fifteen years older than her. She could do better, he'd said, but she'd married John anyway. If he knew she needed him now, he'd not refuse them. "I can't think about that."

"You need to," Laurel said. "There's a very big possibility they won't find him. California is large, Keri. I don't know how you thought you were going to find him in the first place."

Keri's eyes burned with tears. She blinked them away and stared down at her hands as an old misery resurfaced. She'd thought the same thing almost daily as they trekked across Montana but it was either try to find her brother or let Robert destroy them completely. Swallowing the lump in her throat she said, "I have no other choice."

"Sure you do." Laurel reached out, taking hold of her hand. "You can stay right here in Willow Creek."

"No." Keri shook her head. "I've already burdened more people than I would have ever dreamed. I'll not continue doing it." She looked up and met Laurel's eyes. "Taking advantage of Noah is hard enough. I can't do it indefinitely."

A peculiar look crossed Laurel's face before the woman smiled. "Well, instead of pretending, you could actually marry the man."

CHAPTER FOURTEEN

K eri's eyes widened. "Marry Noah?"

Laurel grinned. "Why not? You'd be a responsibility then, not a burden."

"I can't see that happening."

"Why?"

She laughed. "Well, I'm not even sure he wants us here. I've still not figured out why he took us back in."

"Maybe he does want you here."

Keri thought on it, then shook her head. "No. I think he just felt obligated. There wasn't anywhere else for us to go so he brought us back."

"Maybe. It's something to think about, but for now the issue is Aaron and Sophie. They really should be in school. At least for a little while. They need interaction with others their own age. Besides, it's almost Christmas. I have so much planned this year and I'd hate for them to miss out." Laurel stood and draped her coat across her arm again. "Please say you'll think about it."

Keri sighed, then stood. "I'll think about it."

Laurel smiled brightly. "Great. School starts at eight sharp every morning. I'll be looking for them."

She left as quickly as she came. Keri stood in the kitchen for long minutes, the ticking of the clock in the other room loud in the stillness. She knew Aaron and Sophie Ann would love attending school. Aaron had gone for a short time before John had passed but Robert refused to take him once he took over the farm. Sophie Ann had been too young, so it would be a new adventure for her.

Could she really deny them this one small thing after everything they'd been through? What harm would really come of them spending the holiday happy and enjoying themselves?

But they'd not want to leave if she let them go. They'd fall in love with Willow Creek, with the people who made it special, and when Peter sent for them, she'd break their hearts by forcing them to leave.

The door swung open and Sophie Ann and Aaron came running inside, the blankets they used to keep warm outside flung to the floor once the door was shut. The moment she saw them, she knew someone had mentioned going to school. Had Laurel taken the decision out of her hands after all? Anger built inside her until she thought she'd pop. It vanished in a heartbeat, though. One look at their delighted faces and her heart ached. She hadn't seen them look so happy in years. How could she deny them this one small thing?

They ran into the kitchen, jumping with excitement and Aaron was the first to reach her. "The school teacher's daughter said they'd come visiting so they could ask if we wanted to come to school. Please say we can."

"Please!" Sophie Ann piped in, her cheeks red from the cool wind outside.

Seeing their happy faces and hearing their excited laughter, Keri didn't know how she could deny them. Noah appeared in the kitchen doorway. He looked at the kids, then her, but didn't comment.

Aaron turned and looked over his shoulder at Noah. "Tell her you'd take us. That's what you said outside, isn't it?"

Noah met her gaze again and nodded. "I don't mind taking them every morning but it's up to you."

She glanced back down, both of them smiling up at her, and her heart melted. They'd had so little to be happy about in their short lives, what would this one small thing really do? Catching Noah's eye again, she gave him a questioning look. At his nod, she gathered Aaron and Sophie Ann to keep them from bouncing around the room and squeezed them. "Fine," she said, kissing them on top of the head. "You can go to school."

They jumped out of her arms, hoops and hollers ringing inside the small cabin, their happy laughter filling her to the brim with love. She grinned as she watched them grab the blankets and run back outside. When the cabin was quiet again, Noah was still there. Still watching her. "Are you sure you don't mind?"

"I'm sure." He straightened and readjusted his hat. "There's not enough around here to keep me busy anyway. A trip into town every morning will at least give me something to do. Besides, they'll realize how tedious school is pretty quick. They'll be begging you to stay home before the week is over."

For the first time since meeting him, Keri thought she saw him smile. He turned to leave so fast it was hard to tell with that bushy beard all but obscuring his mouth, but it was there in his eyes, the way the skin wrinkled around them, and in the slight shift of his jaw. If Noah Lloyd was smiling now instead of scowling at them, then maybe Laurel was right. Maybe Noah did want them around. But why?

Monday morning, the kids were up before the sun. Keri had covered her head with the blankets when they bounced on the bed, trying to wake her. She laughed at their antics until she remembered Noah was just on the other side of the blankets. "You're going to wake Mr. Lloyd with all that racket."

"He's already up." Aaron jumped to the floor, dressed for school. "And we need breakfast before we leave so you got to get up, too."

Keri grinned and sighed dramatically. "Fine. I'll get up."

The morning passed in a blur and it wasn't until she was in the front seat of the wagon, the kids in back bundled in blankets to keep them warm, that a case of nerves hit her. What if they got scared without her? Or one of them got hurt or sick? And what would she do all day with them gone?

Questions by the dozen plagued her until they reached town. When the school came into view, the fear rolled over her until she couldn't breathe.

"They'll be fine."

She turned to look at Noah, his quiet words doing nothing to calm her fears. He pulled the wagon to a stop and set the brake. "I'll come around and help you down."

Keri's face heated when she remembered the last time she'd tried to get out of the wagon alone. Falling had been embarrassing but winding up in Noah's arms had left her a bit rattled, especially after the way he'd looked down at her, his arms tightening around her for a brief moment before he helped her to her feet and released her so fast, she stumbled. The whole incident was confusing.

She put it out of her mind when Noah reached her side of the wagon and offered her a hand, helping her down without incident. He lifted the kids out of the back and turned to face her. "I have a few things to get from the mercantile."

"Okay," she said, waiting until he'd crossed the street before looking up at the school. The gate squeaked when she opened it and ushered Aaron and Sophie Ann inside, all three of them hurrying up the walkway. The air was frigid this morning, and without the warmth of the blankets they bundled themselves in whenever they had to be outside, it was almost unbearable.

Once inside the building, Laurel turned, her smile lighting the room when she spotted them. "Oh, I'm so glad you came." She made her way toward them, greeted Aaron and Sophie Ann, and reassured Keri they'd be fine.

Keri stayed long enough to see that they were settled, both of them taking a seat with the other students, joyous smiles on their faces. The small schoolhouse was warm and the smell of wood smoke and chalk filled the air. Aaron and Sophie Ann hadn't turned to look at her once. She smiled and left before she talked herself out of leaving them behind.

Noah wasn't back from the mercantile and she had no idea how long he'd be. She walked to the wagon, wondered if she should wait for him or seek him out. Following along behind him might give him the wrong impression but truth be told, her hands were near frozen.

She hurried across the street, then down the sidewalk and entered Jenkins Mercantile, the bell on the door tinkling as she pushed it back shut. The heat from a pot belly stove in the middle of the store warmed her in an instant.

Her curious gaze lit on the interior of the store as if she was seeing it for the first time. She was, in a way. It was the first time she'd been inside the building during store hours. Every other time she'd ventured inside, she'd been there to steal what she could. Embarrassment heated her cheeks but she tamped it down. There was little she could do about it now. She had no way of repaying the store for what she'd taken so she did what she always did when faced with a problem there was no solution to. She put it out of her mind.

Crossing the store, she stopped by the stove, holding her hands out to warm them and looked for Noah. She didn't see him. A curtain behind the counter swung to one side, a thin woman with spectacles perched on her nose coming through.

Mrs. Jenkins, she assumed, the woman's head turning in both directions before she spotted her. Keri smiled. "Good morning."

"Mornin'," she said. "Anything I can do for you?"

"No, thank you. I'm waiting for someone. Um, Noah Lloyd. Has he been in yet?"

The look on the woman's face clearly told Keri she didn't like Noah. She puzzled over the fact until the shopkeeper said, "He's over at the hotel but he'll be right back."

"All right. Thank you."

Mrs. Jenkins stared at her until Keri was uncomfortable. She smiled at the woman again, a nervous reaction she needed to get a hold of, and cleared her throat. "Think we'll get more snow?"

The woman raised one eyebrow. "Yes. Lots of it, too." She walked to the end of the counter and leaned one slim hip against the wood. "You the woman he married?"

Keri started at the question, the little white lie Morgan Avery said they'd tell finally making an appearance. "Yes," she said, the word coming out in a soft whisper. She cleared her throat and tried again. "Yes. Going on a month now."

The woman kept staring as if she couldn't believe what she was hearing. She remembered the look on Mrs. Jenkins's face when she'd asked for Noah and thinking the woman didn't like him much. Was that why she looked so peculiar now? Because she didn't think anyone would willingly marry Noah?

Keri finally turned her head, looking around the room again as she waited for Noah to return. She didn't have to wait long, thankfully. The bell above the door chimed when he came inside and he paused briefly when he saw her, then crossed the room to the counter. He spoke quietly to the store keeper, then reached into his coat pocket.

He was paying her for something, she realized. Mrs. Jenkins took the money and pushed a large, brown paper covered package toward him. Noah lifted it and turned, making his way back toward her. "Ready to go?"

Keri nodded and walked out of the store when he opened the door. The sun was bright, the snow nearly gone now, but the air was still cold. Keri wasted no time returning to the wagon. She slowed her steps and glanced at the school. The desire to go back inside was strong but she borrowed trouble doing it. She knew Aaron and Sophie would be fine but having them right by her side for so long made it hard to give them up, even for a few hours.

Stopping by the wagon, she saw two chairs now sitting in the back. Were they for the kitchen table? She hid a smile and turned when the sound of paper rattling caught her attention. Noah was opening the package he'd carried from the store. He lifted the top item from inside the brown paper and turned, unfolding it, and Keri was sure her heart stopped beating when she saw what it was.

The green coat he held was the finest she'd ever seen. She raised her eyes to his, silently asking if it was for her, and her throat ached painfully when he closed the distance between them and held it open.

Noah Lloyd had gone above and beyond what anyone else had ever done for them. He'd given them a place to stay that was warm and dry, fed them until their bellies were full, bought her dresses to replace the torn, dingy one she'd been wearing and arranged for Aaron and Sophie Ann to have decent things as well. Now, he'd bought her a coat. One look at his face, at the understanding in his eyes, and tears filled her own. She swallowed past the tight knot forming in her throat and willed the tears away, focusing her attention on the coat instead of Noah.

Light colored fur lined the inside of the dark green wool. She could see it around the cuff of the sleeves and along the high collar and hemline, too. When Noah nodded at her, prompting her to slip her arms inside, she did so while her heart pounded against her rib cage. Warmth enveloped her instantly, the fur rich and soft. She turned and met his gaze. "You didn't have..."

"I know," he said, cutting her off before she could finish. "You needed coats." His gaze ran the length of her. "Button that up." He turned back to the wagon, reached again for the paper, and the tears she'd been trying so desperately to hold back slid past her lashes when he pulled a smaller version of her coat, blue instead of green, and a sheepskin coat much like the one he was wearing, out of the package. It was small enough for Aaron, the blue wool perfect for Sophie Ann. He draped the coats across his arm, picked the remaining items up and turned, handing her a fur lined bonnet and a fur hand muff that matched her coat. She saw gloves and hats for the kids as he walked past her to the school.

The moment he was out of earshot, Keri let out a string of sobs that caused her entire body to hurt. She scrubbed her face, wiping away her tears as fast as they fell, and tried to get her emotions in check before he came back out. She'd let those tears come when she was alone. The last thing she wanted to do was to embarrass him by falling apart. Acts of kindness didn't seem like something Noah Lloyd did on a daily basis and why he was doing them for her puzzled her more than anything in her life ever had.

When he came back outside, she turned, faced the wagon, and wiped her face dry one last time. She wondered if she could get back into the wagon without his help but he was at her side before she could try. He lifted her up, folded the paper the coats were in and laid it, and the string that held the package together in the back, then rounded the side of the wagon and climbed up.

He never said a word, never even looked her way, and Keri was glad for it. She didn't know what to say anyway. How did you express your gratitude for something so outrageously decadent? The coat was expensive. Any fool could see that. The wool was thick, the fur soft against her skin. Where had he gotten the money to pay for it?

"That bonnet does you little good if you don't wear it."

Keri turned her head to look at him. He held her gaze for a few moments before looking back at the road. His hair was still as wild and out of control as always, the beard too long, too thick, but despite his gruff and standoffish manner when they met, he now gave them a home. He'd stopped scowling at them, too.

So who was this man that provided for them without question and asked for nothing in return but a hot, cooked meal?

Putting the bonnet on, Keri tied the silk ribbon under her chin and slipped her hands into the fur muff. She'd never owned anything so beautiful in all her life. She felt the tears burning her eyes again and blinked them away.

For whatever reason, Noah Lloyd was giving her everything she and the kids needed. She wasn't going to question his motives. He may not even have any, but she knew she'd never be able to repay his kindness.

CHAPTER FIFTEEN

Damn. Noah readjusted his hat and resisted the urge to sigh. He didn't know she would cry. Hell, the thought never even crossed his mind. He'd given Isabelle gifts by the dozens. She'd never cried. She'd squealed loud enough to pierce his ear drums and ran about town showing every friend she had, and some she didn't, what he'd given her, but not once had she cried. Those expensive baubles he bought her were worth tears, in his opinion, but she'd never shed one. Keri's gift, nothing more than a coat, had produced an onslaught of them and he wasn't sure what to make of it.

She sniffled again. He glanced at her out of the corner of his eye. Her face was red and puffy, her cheeks tear streaked, but she looked pretty as a picture in that fancy coat and bonnet. He was glad he'd let Mrs. Jenkins talk him into it, now. He'd known the woman had been trying to make a bigger sale, and she did, but he'd admit, grudgingly of course, that she'd been right. He just wished it hadn't taken the coats so long to come in. Keri and those kids had been over a week without anything to keep them warm except those old blankets.

The trip back home was made in silence. Not that he thought

it wouldn't have been. It wasn't as if they had much to talk about anyway and he was okay with that. He was used to silence. After years of listening to women prattle on about anything and everything, it was nice to be near one who didn't find it necessary to blather on.

He pulled the wagon into the yard, set the brake and jumped to the ground, rounded the wagon and helped Keri down. Their gazes clashed briefly, enough for him to see her give him another of those tiny smiles, and he watched her walk away, the back and forth sway of her hips not going unnoticed.

Shaking his head, he put her out of his mind, led the horse to the barn and unhitched him from the wagon, then put the animal back in his stall. Lifting the chairs from the back of the wagon, he carried them outside and looked them over again, making sure Mr. Brighton, the hotel and restaurant owner, hadn't sold him broken chairs. Satisfied there were no cracks in the wood, he carried them into the house.

The blankets around the bed moved when he shut the front door, Keri stepping out from behind them. She glanced at him, then at the chairs. "The mercantile sells furniture?"

"They do from a catalog, but these came from the restaurant." He carried the chairs into the kitchen and pulled the table away from the wall, setting the chairs around it. It would be cramped with four people eating there but at least no one would have to sit on the floor now.

"Think we'll all fit?"

She'd read his mind. He shrugged his shoulders. "I guess we'll find out this evening."

He left her in the kitchen, headed back to the barn, and sat on the bale of hay next to the wall and stared at the animals. He felt a bit cowardly hiding out in the barn instead of staying inside but at least here he didn't feel compelled to try and think of things to say.

They had nothing in common, he and Keri. They knew

nothing about each other that would steer a conversation, so what was the point of sitting inside where it was warm? Besides, being inside the drafty barn kept his mind off the fact that since the kids were in school, he and Keri were very much alone and would be every day. A fact he'd been trying to ignore since leaving town.

The uncomfortable silence made lunch unbearable. Keri picked at her food and wondered why Noah was suddenly so standoffish. He'd seemed fine this morning but the moment they got back home, he ran off to the barn and took his time coming back inside.

She glanced up at him. His whole face was obscured by all that wild hair, and she wondered what he looked like underneath it all. Not that it mattered. The way someone looked said very little about what sort of person they were. She'd seen beautiful women with souls so ugly it tainted every aspect of them. Her own husband, John, hadn't been a handsome man but he was good to her. He'd worked hard, provided for them without complaint, and gave them everything they needed. He never hit her or raised his voice. She couldn't say the same for his brother, Robert. He'd been the worst sort of monster and it still amazed her he and John were even related.

The ticking of the clock in the other room seemed loud for some reason and the silence was enough to drive her to distraction. After hearing Aaron and Sophie Ann's voice every day, all day, she wasn't sure she'd ever get used to the silence.

She took a sip of her water and glanced up at Noah. "Where are you from?" she asked. Even the sound of her own voice was better than nothing. "Your accent tells me somewhere down South."

Noah looked startled at her question and was quiet so long

she wasn't sure he'd answer. When he finally said, "Charleston," she smiled. "Oh, I hear it's beautiful there."

"It was."

He said nothing more and Keri held back a smile. If she knew nothing else about Noah Lloyd, it was that he was a man of very few words. His short answers to everything proved that. "Did you live near the ocean?"

"Yes."

She took another sip of her water. "I saw a drawing of the ocean once. I hoped when we found Peter I'd get a chance to see it in person." Noah continued to eat without commenting. "What made you settle in the middle of nowhere, Montana?"

He stiffened, his fork raised halfway to his mouth. His eyes were downcast but Keri could see the tension the question caused. His entire body looked stiff. She realized the reason he left Charleston for Montana was none of her business, and she imagined he wanted to tell her just that.

It was obvious by his lack of answers that he wasn't in the mood to talk to her. He rarely did. Just because Aaron and Sophie Ann weren't there didn't mean he'd spend his day entertaining her. And by the look of him, sitting there having lunch with her wasn't something he wanted to be doing either.

"I'm sorry," she said, quietly. "Your life is none of my business. I shouldn't have pried. Forget I said anything."

She continued to pick at her food, keeping her remaining questions to herself as her thoughts strayed to Aaron and Sophie Ann again. She wondered if they were all right, if they'd made new friends, and if they missed her as much as she missed them. Sighing, she stood and set her still full plate by the sink. She'd finish it later if she got hungry before supper.

When she turned, she ran into Noah, crashing into his muscled chest. She let out a startled gasp, both of them taking a step away from the other. "I'm sorry," she said. "I didn't realize you'd stood up." He was holding his empty plate. She took it from him, then turned her back to him again.

She listened for his retreating footsteps but they never came. With her back still to him, she wondered what he was doing just standing there and blinked in surprise when he said, "I was injured in the war. There wasn't anything left for me when I got back to Charleston so I left."

His quiet statement held no emotion, his voice flat, but when she glanced over her shoulder at him, his eyes held every ounce of pain he felt. She knew without asking that the war was how he got that scar. John had more than his share of them, too. Nothing as noticeable as Noah's but there just the same.

She glanced at those black leather gloves he never took off. She'd bet money that scar on his face wasn't his only injury. What exactly had happened to him? She met his eyes again. His physical scars must have been horrific for him to hide under years worth of facial hair and keep gloves on twenty-four hours a day. She wasn't about to ask him, though. He didn't strike her as the sharing type of person. He was reserved and kept to himself and the silence was something she was going to have to get used to even if it made for very long days.

He left without another word and she had hours yet before it would be time to get Aaron and Sophie. Cleaning the kitchen would be the highlight of her day, it seemed.

The privacy she gained by not having the kids underfoot all day, and Noah avoiding the house, did give her the opportunity to indulge herself a bit. She gathered a bucket of warm water and stepped behind the blankets hanging around the bed, stripped out of her clothes, and spent the next ten minutes lathering her body in the sweet smelling soap Noah had given her. When she was dressed again, she headed to the kitchen and washed her hair, the scent of the soap filling the air around her. She closed her eyes and breathed it in as she took a drying cloth to her short locks, scrubbing at her head to dry the water from her hair.

The curls were in a wild riot by the time she'd finished and finger-combing the strands did little for them. She sat on the hearth, letting the heat from the fire remove any remaining dampness from her hair and jumped when a loud knock rapped on the door. She stared at it, wondering why Noah was knocking.

Crossing the room, she opened the door. A man she'd never seen stood staring back at her. Her heart gave one powerful thump against her ribcage at seeing him.

His clothes were as ragged as the ones she'd been wearing when Noah found her and the stench coming off him told her he'd been as unfortunate as she had in the past few months. "Can I help you?"

"Afternoon, ma'am." He removed his bowler hat and smiled, his dingy teeth causing a wash of revulsion through her system. "I'm wondering if I might bother you for a drink o' water?" He glanced over her shoulder into the cabin. "I been walking since the sun come up and for once, its warmed me up more than I would have thought on such a cold day."

Keri's pulse was leaping. She wasn't even sure why. The man looked innocent enough but he made her uneasy. She glanced toward the barn. The door was closed tight, but the desire to call out to Noah was so strong she nearly choked on the need to do so.

The man shifted on his feet. He looked to be in his thirties, his skin dark and leathery from too much sunlight. His gaze was darting around the interior of the cabin and the uneasy feeling she had only grew. Lifting her chin in what she hoped was a confident stance, she gripped the edge of the door. "Wait here," she said. "I'll bring you a glass."

She shut the door and hurried to the kitchen, filling a glass, and taking a quick look out the small window above the sink. The barn door was still closed. She went to turn but a wavering shadow on the side of the building drew her attention. She narrowed her eyes, then widened them when she saw a man round the corner of the barn and creep along the front. He held a revolver in his right hand and she gasped, the cup she held slipping from her fingers, the sound of breaking glass loud in the stillness.

Keri spun on her heel and swallowed a shocked gasp when she saw the man she'd left on the stoop. He was standing in the kitchen doorway grinning at her.

CHAPTER SIXTEEN

"It's a cold one out today." The man who'd invited himself into the cabin turned and looked away from the doorway. He removed his coat, tossing it to the floor along with his hat and glanced around the room again, stuck his thumbs behind his suspender straps and nodded his head. "Mighty fine home you got here. Nice and cozy." He looked back at her, his gaze skating down her body before climbing back up and landing on her breasts. "Your man build it himself?"

Keri didn't answer. Couldn't have if she'd tried. Her heart was hammering inside her chest, her nerves rattled enough to cause her entire body to shake.

She had no idea what these men wanted but the gleam in this one's eyes, and the way his gaze kept lingering on her breasts, caused bile to churn in her stomach. She'd seen that same look a time or two on Robert's face, the memory of him taking her against her will still vivid in her mind. She'd not fought him after that first time. Not when he'd threatened her with things so vile, she'd not been able to eat for days afterwards.

The man motioned to the main room with his head. "Come on out here," he said. "I don't want you at my back."

Keri did as he asked only because she needed to be closer to the door. The moment she stepped into the main room, he came toward her. She sidestepped him, her gaze darting to the door as she moved farther away from it. Could she make it outside without him stopping her?

"What's your name, pretty lady?"

Keri swallowed the lump forming in her throat and tried to take even breaths. Her heart was racing, her thoughts on Noah. "You best get on out of here."

He grinned, his broken, brown teeth only adding to her disgust. "Got no intentions on leaving, darlin'. Once my friend takes care of your man out there in the barn, we're all going to have us a nice relaxin' evening." He crossed to the fireplace, picked up a few of the items Noah had sitting on the mantel, then turned back to face her. His eyes were roaming again, the look in them easily readable. "What say you and me get better acquainted while we wait on Hershel to come in."

His voice echoed in Keri's head, a barrage of images playing inside her mind's eye, and she took several hasty steps back when he advanced on her. She couldn't breathe as she watched him, her heart beating out a fast tattoo against her ribcage as she looked toward the door again. Fear stole her voice, her throat aching with the need to yell for Noah before remembering the man she'd seen creeping toward the barn door. Hershel, this one had called him. Would Noah see him in time or would the man kill him? Fear he might caused the back of her eyes to burn.

The blankets hanging around the bed brushed against her back and Keri stopped, grabbed the material in her hands and sucked in a few harsh breaths. "Stay where you are," she said. "Just take what you want and be gone."

"Oh, I planned on doing that, sweet thing." Reaching for his belt, he unfastened it. "But what I want at the moment is you." He grinned again, then chuckled. "Now don't go looking at me like that. I promise, by the time I'm through with you, you won't even remember your man's name." His gaze roamed her body again.

Keri flung the blankets aside, darting behind the privacy curtain Noah had hung and searched desperately for something to use as a weapon. The sound of ripping material echoed in the room as the man yanked at the blankets, pulling them from the nails securing them from the ceiling. Keri scrambled onto the bed, crawling across to the other side, and screamed when he latched onto her leg, his fingers digging into her flesh.

Kicking as he pulled her back across the bed, the world seemed to dim, the light in the room fading, the sound of her screams hollow to her own ears. Fear exploded in her chest and stole her breath. She raised both arms, flinging her fists at him as he grabbed at her skirts, jerking her body to the edge of the bed.

The loud report of a gun going off outside nearly stopped her heart. The man sneaking into the barn, the gun she'd seen in his hand filling her mind's eye. A choked sob strangled her as she thought of Noah, of the man, Hershel, killing him. Of him then coming inside to help this foul creature assault her, and she kicked and fought harder, tears blinding her as she tried to get him off her and a knee to his groin finally doubled him over.

She jumped from the bed, her feet barely touching the floor before he grabbed her and swung her around. She fell against the small table by the bed, the oil lamp tipping to one side. Grabbing it, Keri twisted, screamed and slammed it against the man's head.

It shattered into a hundred tiny pieces. The man's yell was followed by an outraged bellow that nearly stopped her heart. He raised his hands, swiped at his eyes, then threw a murderous look at her seconds before he flung her back to the mattress.

His face was red, rage clouding his eyes as he gritted his teeth, his hand lifting before he brought it down, slapping her face hard enough to stun her. She clawed at him and managed to turn her head when he raised a fist to her. The impact dazed her, her head snapping back moments before he hit her again, and again, and again, the pain intense enough to numb every other sensation in her body. She slumped against the bed, his voice a dull echo in the room as everything around her started to go dark.

He flipped her to her stomach, grabbed both her arms and pulled them behind her back, then lifted her skirts. Keri blinked, trying to get her dazed brain to function. Her legs were dangling over the side of the bed, his hands were tugging at her bloomers, and the only thought going through her head was, would he kill her when he was through? Would his friend? And what would happen to her babies if they did?

The pain in her arms increased, his hold on her forcing her shoulder blades to nearly touch. Spots flashed before her eyes as the material of her bloomers ripped, cool air hitting her bottom moments before he stepped between her legs, his fingers probing and digging into her flesh. She let out a strangled sob, kicked her legs to try and dislodge him and winced when a loud crash, followed by a yell so feral filled the room that her heart skipped a beat before the weight of him was suddenly pulled from her back.

Noah flung him to the other side of the room, rage burning so hot his blood felt near to boiling. The man bounced off the wall, then slumped to the floor, his eyes wide as he turned his head to look at him before trying to stand. Crossing to the fireplace, he yanked the shotgun he kept hanging above the mantel down and raised to his shoulder, the gun cocked and aimed at the man's head before he gained his feet.

"Don't shoot!" The man scrambled back, crawling across the floor toward the door, fear causing his complexion to turn pasty white.

The gun barrel wavered. Noah realized his hands were shaking.

He'd killed so many men during his time in the war, the

deaths caused nightmares to plague his dreams. He regretted the loss of every life he took and prayed for their souls nightly, but looking at the man cowering at his feet...

Noah had never wanted a life so badly as he did in that moment.

Keri let out a small sob. He could see her out of the corner of his eye. She was on the floor, her skirts twisted around her thighs. A trickle of blood ran from her lip and just seeing her wide, frightened eyes caused bloodlust so fierce to cloud his vision, his finger tightened on the gun's trigger.

The man in the barn had taken him so completely unaware, his heart had yet to stop pounding. He'd heard the barn door open and thought it was Keri, his anger at her invading his personal space scalding his throat until he turned and saw a man he'd never seen before. The moment he spotted the gun in his hand, Keri's face shimmered in his mind's eye seconds before he heard her scream. Fear for what would happen to her filled his head as the man advanced on him, raised the pistol, and fired the gun.

He'd ducked, the bullet hitting the wall behind him. He stayed low and ran at him, his shoulders connecting with his middle and they both went down. When Keri screamed again, the fear for her safety intensified. Noah tossed the gun away, grabbed the man's arm and brought it down over his upraised knee, the sound of breaking bone loud in the stillness. The man's bellow of pain was cut short when Noah punched him in the face, then did it again, a satisfied warmth rushing through his limbs when the man's eyes rolled to the back of his head and he slumped to the ground. He'd drug him outside, dropped him by the barn door, and ran for the house.

The blinding rage that filled him when he walked in to see Keri sprawled on his bed with some unknown man's filthy hands on her took all rational thought from his mind. The need to kill him was still there. The only thing that stopped him from pulling the trigger was the sound of Keri crying. It tore a piece of his heart out to hear it.

He'd been so cold and dead inside for so long, he wasn't even aware he was capable of feeling anything anymore but one quick look at her left him breathless. She was staring at him, her eyes wide and luminous, her head shaking from side to side. A soft whispered, "don't," slipping past her lips was enough to stay his hand.

Noah turned back to the man still on the floor. "Get up." He stood, reaching for his discarded coat and hat as he scrambled to his feet. "Your friend is lying out by the barn. Drag him off my property and if I see either of you again, I'll not hesitate to kill you. Am I clear?"

The man nodded and had the gall to look back over at Keri. Noah took three steps toward him and had the gun barrel pressed into the side of his head so fast, the man gasped.

"We'll go," he said, the words coming out breathy and high pitched. "We'll not be back. I swear it."

Easing his finger from the trigger, Noah motioned to the door with his head and followed the man out when he left. He stood by the side of the house, watched as he ran to the barn and grabbed his friend by the shoulders of his coat and started dragging him away. He didn't lower the gun barrel until both of them were out of sight.

He went back inside and slid the bolt on the door. Keri was still sitting on the floor. She'd stopped crying but her complexion was so pale he feared she was hurt worse than he thought.

Propping the gun against the wall, he approached her, bent to one knee and curved a finger under her chin, raising her head so he could see her. The left side of her face was bruising. The bastard must have hit her hard for discoloration to already be forming. Her lip was bleeding as well. He glanced down the line of her body. She'd yet to pull her skirts down. Red marks slashed across her thighs from hands holding her too tightly. The sight of all those little bruises made him want to run outside and chase those bastards down and shoot them point blank whether Keri wanted him to or not.

Her whole body was shaking, tears swimming in her eyes. A few of them spilled over her lashes to run the length of her cheeks. Noah wiped them away with his right hand and smoothed her hair back with the other. "It's all right," he said. "They're gone." She nodded, fear still clouding her cornflower-blue eyes. She tried to get up but he put a hand on her shoulder. "Just stay right here for a minute."

She nodded her head again and closed her eyes, taking a few deep breaths. "He asked for water and came in when my back was turned."

Noah watched her hands start to shake, her eyelids sweeping up. Tears still pooled in her eyes and the sight tightened his chest. "I didn't much think you invited him in." She stared up at him, his gaze roaming her face before he gently swiped the blood from her lip.

"I thought the other one killed you," she said.

Her words were so soft, he barely heard them, but the look in her eyes came across loud and clear. She'd been afraid. For him. His pulse raced at the thought. "He tried," he said. "but I ducked the moment I saw the gun. Once I heard you scream, I didn't give him a chance to fire another shot."

Within seconds, a torrent of tears filled her eyes, then spilled over her lashes, a soft, strangled sob tearing from her throat. The sound caused his anger to return, to burn hot and fierce enough to scald his lungs as he tried to breathe past it. She lowered her head, grabbed onto the sleeves of his coat, her fingers gripping the material until her knuckles turned white, and cried as if her heart was breaking. Before he even had time to contemplate what he was doing, he grabbed her, sat down next to her and pulled her into his lap, tucking her tightly against his chest.

She clung to him and buried her face against the side of his neck, her tears warm and wet against his skin. Her whole body trembled as she slid her hands inside his coat and wrapped her arms around his waist. Noah ran a hand over her head, whispering soft words to her, telling her he wouldn't let anything happen to her and continued to hold on to her long after her tears had dried.

They sat in silence, the ticking of the clock and the occasional pop of firewood filling the room. Noah wasn't sure when he'd closed his eyes, or buried his face in the wild curls of her hair, but as he sat there, breathing in the scent of her, he couldn't deny how good she felt. How nice it was to hold her. It had been twelve years since he'd let anyone this close to him and he'd missed it. Missed the feel of someone touching him, even the innocent contact of Keri's hand on his back, her face warming the skin on his neck.

She shifted, sniffled once, and moved her head, tucking it under his chin before sighing. Her arms loosened around his waist just a fraction and the sweet scent of the flowery soap he'd given her filled his senses.

He raised his head, tucked a finger under her chin and raised her face so he could see her. Another trickle of blood had run down her chin. He wiped it away, noticing her lip was already swelling. Lightly swiping her lip with his thumb, he had an overwhelming urge to kiss her. To soothe all those aches he knew she had, to chase that haunted look from her eyes.

To protect her and keep her safe. Always.

Noah smoothed her hair back and tucked the short strands behind her ear. "Are you all right?"

"I am now." She heaved a huge sigh. "I've been holding that in for months now." Her eyes lowered, her hand raising to brush across his shoulder. "I didn't mean to cry all over you."

"It'll dry." He stared at her for long moments, his chest tightening again when she looked back up at him. He was loath to move. Would have been content to sit there the rest of the day just holding her but knew it wasn't possible.

He helped her to her feet instead, then sat her on the bed. A glance at the clock had him straightening and crossing the room to grab her coat and hat. "Put these on," he said, laying them on the bed. "I'll go hitch up the wagon. It'll be time to pick up Aaron and Sophie Ann soon."

CHAPTER SEVENTEEN

They headed into town without a word spoken between them. Noah kept his gaze on the trees lining the road, watchful of the two men he'd run off. That is, when he wasn't stealing glances of Keri. That bruise on her face was darkening by the minute and her hands were still shaking.

When he pulled the wagon to a stop next to the school, he rounded the horse and helped Keri to the ground. Class wouldn't be dismissed for another hour and at her questioning look, he took her by the arm and crossed the street, guiding her to the new building the townsfolk had just finished erecting.

The words, Dr. Evan Reid, were printed in fine script across a painted piece of wood that hung on the wall. Noah had seen the new doctor on his last trip into town. He saw him sitting behind a desk when he looked in through the glass on the door. He knocked, opening the door when he motioned them in.

"What are we doing here?" Keri asked, her whispered words barely audible. Noah glanced at her face, at the bruise on her cheek and her busted, swollen lip, and turned his attention to the doctor.

Evan Reid was tall with brown hair and a kindly smile. He

seemed a bit young to be a doctor, Noah thought, but he supposed the man knew what he was doing if the framed certificates lining the wall were any way to judge. He smiled at them, held out his hand, and Noah shook it, pleased at the tight grip. "Noah Lloyd," he said, nodding his head when Dr. Reid introduced himself as well. "And this is Keri." He hesitated, glanced at Keri out of the corner of his eye, and said, "my wife."

The man looked over at Keri, his head tilted a fraction as he looked at her face. "Run into a bit of trouble?"

"Something like that." Noah let go of her arm, placing his hand on her back instead. "I think she's okay but I'd like you to look her over anyway just to be sure."

Dr. Reid nodded, catching his eye once before motioning Keri to a table along the right hand side of the room. "Come have a seat, Mrs. Lloyd, and let me take a good look at you."

Keri looked back over at him and held his gaze so long, his pulse started racing for no reason whatsoever. Noah pushed the "why" of it out of his mind to examine later. "I'll be back to fetch you in a few minutes," he said before turning to the door. "I need to speak with the marshal."

He left her in Dr. Reid's care and headed across town, ducking into the marshal's office. It took a few moments for his eyes to adjust to the low light in the building and he blinked repeatedly as Morgan stood from his chair and greeted him.

"Noah? Something wrong?"

The explanation took less time than Noah thought it should have. Morgan listened to his recounting of what happened, then sat back in his seat. "You didn't recognize either of them?"

"No," Noah said. "I think they were drifters."

Morgan nodded. "Is Mrs. Hilam all right?"

"I think so. She's bruised up and scared but I don't think she's seriously hurt. I took her over to Dr. Reid's just to be sure though."

Morgan asked him a few more questions, jotted things down

on a piece of paper and told him he'd keep his eye out for the two men. Noah walked back to the doctor's office, noticing as he crossed the street that school had been dismissed, the gaggle of screaming kids running from the building and spreading over the sidewalk and the small playground sitting next to the school.

Stepping back into Dr. Reid's office, Keri looked up at him, a faint smile touching her lips. He looked toward the doctor. "She's all right?"

"Yes." He stood and rounded the desk. "The bruises will probably get a bit more nasty looking but they'll fade eventually. I've given her something for pain." Dr. Reid looked over at her. "A bit of rest will do wonders for her."

Noah nodded, paid the man, then held out his hand to Keri. "Come on. Let's get you home."

They crossed the street and headed back to the school, Keri's head darting in every direction as she looked for Aaron and Sophie Ann. Noah spotted them by the side of the building, both of them on their knees petting the sorriest excuse for a dog he'd ever seen.

The critter was all legs and ears. His coat was dingy brown and he wasn't sure if it was dirt or just the color of him. The animal's ribs were poking against his skin. He was half starved from the looks of him. Sophie Ann and Aaron were both petting him, scratching his head, and laughing. Noah knew trouble when he saw it. Those kids had the look about them that said they'd fallen in love with that mangy mutt. He sighed while watching them.

Aaron was the first to look up. He shot to his feet and grinned. "We found a dog!" He reached down and laid a hand to the animal's head. "Can we keep him?"

Noah opened his mouth to say no, but the words stuck in his throat. The dog looked his way, his bony tail wagging back and forth as Sophie Ann cooed and talked to him. The dog let out a loud, "woof," his whole body twitching as his tail swung from side to side and his tongue lolled from his mouth.

The dog let out a series of barks, the sound deep and loud, and Noah wondered if that dog would have let him know someone was on his property. He didn't look like much of a watch dog, but if the critter let him know if someone was messing around the house, he'd be worth the trouble of keeping him.

He looked to Aaron and Sophie Ann, saw the moment they noticed the bruises on Keri's face. They both stilled, their eyes wide as they stared at her. She stiffened by his side and he stepped in front of her and motioned toward the dog. "What's his name?"

"He ain't got one yet," Sophie Ann said.

Noah nodded and crossed his arms over his chest. "Dog has to have a name." He looked the mutt over again. "Can't call him dog all the time."

Aaron's face lit up. "Does that mean we can keep him?"

It was probably a mistake but it wouldn't be the first he'd ever made. "Just until he decides he doesn't want to be kept."

The kids let out an excited squeal and laughed, telling the dog he was coming home with them, the dog's, "woofs" just as loud as Aaron and Sophie Ann's yells. Noah turned and looked down at Keri, her questioning eyes, for once, not filled with tears. He shrugged. "It'll keep them distracted."

She tried to smile but it was a weak attempt. Loading them all into the wagon, the dog included, he headed back home. Aaron and Sophie Ann said nothing about the bruises on Keri's face but they kept giving him weary looks. He reluctantly told them what happened, a watered down version of course, and once Keri assured them she was fine, they quieted.

The entire day played back inside his head as the buckboard bounced over the weathered rode. He saw every detail of his day, guilt assaulting him when he realized his hiding out in the barn like a coward was the reason Keri had been hurt. If he'd just stayed inside, he would have been there when that bastard had knocked on the door.

He turned his head to look at her, the bruises on her face darker now, and silently vowed to keep her safe. As long as she was in his house, her and those kids were his responsibility. A responsibility he surprisingly realized, he didn't mind having.

Keri couldn't stop shaking. The fear she'd felt when the stranger came inside the house and grabbed her was gone now that Noah was beside her but her insides were still jumping. The wagon jostled along the road, the kids laughing as they sat in back with the dog. She glanced over her shoulder and recognized the mutt. It was the same one she'd seen behind the stagecoach station, the one the bucket of food had been set out for. The food she'd taken from him.

When the house came into view, a thin ribbon of smoke rising through the air from the chimney, the sense of relief she felt was staggering. Noah's small cabin wasn't a place she could really call home but just seeing it brought feelings of safety.

She'd been so relieved when Noah had come inside and pulled the drifter off her. For a brief moment, she thought he'd shoot him, the look on his face said he was thinking hard about it. She didn't want the man's death weighing on Noah's soul because of her, though, and had been glad when he ordered the man out, threatening him if he ever came back.

Shock had already settled into her bones by the time he came back in. She'd been numb until he came to her, the concern clouding his eyes breaking through the calm she'd desperately been holding on to. The moment he wiped her tears away and she saw genuine concern on his face for her, she'd lost it. Fallen apart as he pulled her into his arms. Two years worth of worry and fear poured out and she couldn't seem to stop crying once she got started.

He'd held her, whispered words she'd had trouble making out and squeezed her so tight, she'd not wanted him to let go. She'd felt safe for the first time since sneaking off in the middle of the night to escape a monster.

Noah said her name and touched her. Keri started and saw his gloved hand covering her own, and looked up. They were home. "Let's get you inside," he said, grabbing her around the waist and lifting her from the wagon.

The dog was yipping, jumping around and sniffing everything he came to while Sophie Ann and Aaron chased along behind him. Noah guided her into the house, helped her take off her coat and with a hand on her back, ushered her to the bed.

"Lie down for a bit. I'll see to the kids."

"You don't have to."

"I know I don't." He left, going back outside and Keri let out a long breath and looked around the room. The blankets were still dangling from the ceiling, glass from the shattered lamp shining on the hardwood floors like small diamonds. The place needed a good tidying up. She glanced at the bed, weary to the bone all of a sudden, and sat down.

She slipped her boots off, and lay back, trying to forget the entire day. She dozed off and didn't wake again until the smell of food pulled her from a dreamless sleep. Whispered voices filled the air and she rolled over, blinking against the light from the fireplace. The dog was there, sleeping on the rug in front of the fire. Either the light was just dim enough, or they'd given the mutt a bath, because he didn't look quite so homely now.

Aaron walked into the room from the kitchen and smiled when he saw her. "She's awake," he said, turning to look back into the kitchen.

Sophie Ann ran into the room, her smile bright enough to

chase the gloom. "I got to help cook!" she squealed. "Noah said I was the best bread baker he ever seen."

Both Aaron and Sophie Ann walked to the bed and looked down at her. "You want to come eat with us?" Aaron asked.

Keri nodded. "Yes. I'm starved."

They grinned and waited until she sat up before running back into the kitchen. Keri glanced at the floor, mindful of the broken glass. The floor was swept clean, the blankets, she noticed, once again hanging from their nails.

She smiled, stood, and made her way to the kitchen, her eyes landing on Noah the moment she stepped into the room. He was by the stove dishing food into plates. When he turned and saw her, he locked eyes with her for a brief moment then set the plate in his hand on the table.

When they settled, all four of them around that small table, Keri looked at each of them. The kids looked happy, their smiles bright, and she wondered if they'd asked Noah again about what happened to her. The whole left side of her face felt swollen and she dreaded even seeing it. She could only imagine what she looked like. The fact the kids hadn't commented on it now told her Noah had to have told them something more. Whatever it was, was enough to calm any fears they may have had because supper was a lighthearted affair filled with smiles and laughter. And for once, Noah didn't keep his head bowed and his eyes downcast. Every time she looked up, he was staring at her.

CHAPTER EIGHTEEN

I t was so quiet, Keri thought she could hear her own heart beating. The wind blew past the windows, causing a faint whistle, and the logs burning in the fireplace popped every now and then, but other than that, it was deathly still.

Ever since that drifter showed up and forced himself inside the house, Noah spent the majority of his day in the cabin. He rarely stayed in the barn more than half an hour now and Keri knew it was because of what had happened three weeks before.

Everything seemed to change once the shock of the attack wore off, Noah's behavior being the most noticeable. The kids were quieter and that old dog they'd brought home perked his long ears up at the slightest sound. Keri suspected Noah thought that dog would serve for more than just a distraction to Aaron and Sophie Ann. The dog, Duke, the name the kids picked out for him, let them know if something outside wasn't quite right.

The swelling and bruises she'd been wearing had faded and everyone settled into a routine. One that still left Keri a bit bewildered. She went with Noah every morning to take the kids to school and spent the rest of the day doing odd bits of things around the cabin, all while keeping a curious eye on him. Noah spent the majority of his day sketching in his journal, reading, or sitting by the fire, staring at the orange and red flames as they danced around the wood. Their gazes locked often and he didn't look away as he once did. She wasn't sure what had changed, but Noah seemed more at ease around them. She'd even caught him smiling on a few occasions.

She glanced up at him from her seat next to the fire. As always, he wore a pensive look on his face. She would have paid money to know what was on his mind most days. After asking why he'd moved to Montana and got very few answers, she didn't ask about his life. It didn't stop her curiosity, though. And really, how could one not be curious?

Noah was stoic at best. He'd shown very little emotion other than when he first found them in the line shack and the day she was attacked. He talked with the kids more, drawing pictures for Sophie Ann when she asked for them, and Aaron helped him in the barn every morning and evening, but other than catching him stealing glances at her, he said nothing more to her than he had to.

And it was driving her insane.

Inhaling a frustrated breath, she bit the string loose from the dress she was hemming and laid the garment aside. "Do you have anything that needs mending?"

Noah looked over at her, glanced at the needle and string still in her hand and said, "No."

When he looked back at the fire, Keri shook her head and stood, picking up Sophie Ann's dress. She hung it on one of the nails driven into the wall by the bed and crossed the room, tucking her needle and thread back into the small sewing box Abigail had given her, then looked at the clock. Two more hours until school was dismissed. Two more hours of silence.

"How often did Robert hit you?"

The question came out of nowhere. Noah was still staring into the flames, his hands clasped together in front of him, but the slight tilt of his head let her know he was waiting for an answer.

She retook her seat, settling into one of the chairs from the kitchen, and just sat there staring at him.

"Aaron told me he saw Robert strike you." He turned to look at her, the expression on his face unreadable. "If a man is low-down enough to hit a woman in anger once, chances are he'll do it again."

Keri lowered her head, clenched the material of her dress in her hands and sighed. "I learned real quick what set Robert off and we went out of our way to accommodate him. To give him what he wanted so he wouldn't get angry." She glanced at him and looked away again. "He never went so far as to beat me, but he slapped me when the mood struck him."

"He moved in and took possession of your farm?" She nodded her head. "And then you?"

That last bit was spoken softly but the implications were loud. She glanced toward the fire, images she'd rather forget playing back through her mind. "I fought him the first time." Her stomach churned, those old feelings of helplessness returning. "The second time he came to my bed, he just stood there staring at me, the look on his face blank." She looked up. "He told me I'd never fight him again. That I'd do anything he asked of me and I'd live to regret it if I didn't. I was used to being slapped around by then so his threats didn't bother me much, but then he called Sophie Ann into the room. He picked her up and asked her if she wanted him to help her get ready for bed. Then he asked me where her nightgown was. Something in his eyes ... It didn't take me very long to figure out what he was actually threatening me with."

Noah looked as horrified as she'd felt, his eyes locked on hers so long she felt as if he were reading her mind. "Did he ever..."

He left the question unfinished. "No. I gave him anything he wanted, just like he said I would, but as the months wore on, I noticed him watching her. The look in his eyes when he did scared me so bad, I started saving every penny I found and stored as much food as I could. Once the weather turned warm..." She licked her lips and averted her gaze, memories of that night assaulting her faster than she could stop them. She'd put the entire night out of her mind and tried not to think on it but now every second of that night played in slow motion inside her head. Her stomach ached, her head spinning for brief moments before she pushed the thoughts away. "I waited for him to go to sleep," she said, nearly choking on the words, "then I gathered the kids and we ran."

Neither said anything for a while, both of them staring into the fire, the ticking of the clock on the mantel loud in the stillness. Keri didn't know why Noah was so interested in her life but after weeks of silence, she wasn't going to complain, even if the subject matter left her feeling uncomfortable. She had questions of her own and started to ask him one when he said, "What was your husband like?"

"John was ... practical." His image filled her mind's eye. "He worked too hard and smiled too little. He was also stubborn, which is why he climbed onto that horse when everyone told him not to. He should have never tried to break a horse as wild as that one."

Noah turned his head to her, his gaze intent and curious. "Aaron said he was older than you."

Keri nodded. "He was, by fifteen years."

"Were you happy?" The question threw her a bit.

"I guess it depends on your definition of happy."

"Meaning?"

What exactly did being happy mean? Keri wasn't sure she knew anymore.

Noah spent his days repeating the same actions like clockwork. He fed the animals, took Aaron and Sophie Ann to school, always insisting she go along with them, then sat by the fire until time to head back into town to get the kids. He was quiet for the most part, but nothing about him said he was a man happy with the lot life had given him. But he didn't look miserable either. "Well," she said, "would you consider yourself happy?"

He took so long to answer, she wasn't sure he was going to. "I don't remember what happiness feels like."

The tone of his voice pierced her heart, the look in his eyes causing the ache in her chest to intensify. "I was satisfied," she said, answering his question. "I wasn't unhappy but..."

He leaned forward a bit, his head titling a fraction more when she stopped talking. "But what?"

Meeting his gaze, she held it. "There were days when life was so mundane, I would have given anything for a violent storm or some minor catastrophe just so something would be different. John said, 'hold lunch for me. I may be late getting back in,' every day before he headed out of the house and every night as we settled in to sleep, he'd huff out a huge breath and say, 'we made it through another one.'" She frowned, then shook her head. "I don't think John was very happy either."

"Was your marriage loveless?"

"Yes." Keri didn't hesitate to answer. There had been no love between her and John. Their marriage wasn't born of soft feelings and romantic notions. It was born of necessity. "My brother wanted to attend school but wouldn't make the commitment to do so because of me. We lost our parents the winter Peter turned eighteen and I didn't want to be the reason Peter gave up his dreams, so when I heard John was looking for a wife, I made it known I would marry him if he asked." She shrugged her shoulders. "It solved a lot of problems marrying him. He got a wife and I was no longer my brother's responsibility. Peter sold the farm and moved to California a month after John and I were married."

Noah continued to stare at her and his questions only fueled her own. Why his sudden interest? she wondered. She blurted, "Were you ever in love?" before she even had time to ask herself why she wanted to know.

He let out a long breath and to her surprise, answered. "I thought I was once." The old rocker he was sitting in groaned under his weight when he shifted, stretching his legs out in front of him. "I realized when I got home from the war that an emotion like love did very little for you when faced with something we'd rather not have to deal with." He turned his head and stared back into the fire. "The girl I thought to spend my life with couldn't look at me without turning away in disgust. Whatever I felt for her died when she broke our engagement." He laughed, but the sound was bitter and dull. "Apparently wealth and prominent standing in the community weren't enough when faced with the prospect of being married to a man no one had a desire to look at."

"I'm sorry."

"Don't be." He locked eyes with her again. "Isabelle couldn't look me in the face without the horror of my injuries shining in her eyes. I'd rather be alone than spend a day with someone who pretended to love me while secretly cringing every time I touched her."

He held her gaze, unblinking for long minutes as if searching for some answer in her face. He must have found it. His shoulders dropped slightly, the tension in his body seeming to disappear as she looked at him. He shifted again, glanced away for a moment then stood and said, "It'll be time to get the kids soon. I'll go hitch the wagon." Keri stared after him wondering why he'd asked her those particular questions. And why he'd answered hers when he'd been so defensive last time she'd asked.

But the newfound knowledge he'd given her hinted at his former life. Wealth and standing in the community, he'd said. Had Noah been wealthy before coming here? She looked around the cabin. Nothing here screamed the trappings of someone used to the finer things in life. She dismissed the possibility. She must have misunderstood what he'd meant.

She remembered the name, Isabelle, though. She'd seen it

under one of the drawings in his journal. She glanced up at the mantel, to the leather bound book Noah sketched in every evening. The desire to look through it, to find the ruined picture of Isabelle was strong, but going through his things was wrong, even if her desire to see the girl who obviously broke his heart urged her to stand and take a peek.

The pain in his voice when he'd mentioned his return from the war told her how much Isabelle's actions affected him. It also told her that Isabelle was the reason Noah had left Charleston. Why he kept to himself and had no one he could call a friend. Why he hid behind all that hair.

Standing, she banked the fire, grabbed her coat and hat, slipping them on before picking up the fur hand muff. A smile lit her face every time she saw it. She'd seen similar hand muffs carried by the more wealthy ladies back home but never thought to own one herself, but here she was, a single mother running from a life she no longer wanted while playing house with a man who couldn't decide from one day to the next if he wanted them around or not.

Today, he seemed to want her there.

Staring at the soft furred hand muff, Keri raised a puzzled brow. A pair of gloves like the ones Noah had bought for Aaron and Sophie Ann would have been more practical for her but he'd bought her something she knew was expensive. A luxury to most. His comments about wealth whispered inside her mind again. If he were wealthy, why would he live in such an out of the way place in a cabin barely big enough for him?

The questions would never be answered, so she put them out of her mind and opened the door. It was snowing again, a light dusting covering everything. She made her way across the yard, inhaling the fresh clean air as the cold wind chilled her face. As pretty as the snow was coating the surrounding trees, she hoped they weren't in for another blizzard.

She stopped when she reached the barn, watching Noah as he

hitched the horse to the wagon. The falling snow caught in his hair and beard and she imagined Isabelle, and her reaction to seeing him when he returned home with that scar, was why he kept his hair so long and unkempt. Truth be told, she barely noticed the scar anymore. No one would, given enough time. So why did he stay hidden from the world? Surely he didn't think people would judge him for something like a scar?

As standoffish as he was at times, Noah Lloyd had every reason to walk with his head held high. He was kind even when he tried not to be. He took her and Aaron and Sophie Ann in even though Keri knew it galled him to do so. He gave them a home, provided for them, and protected her from strangers bent on doing her harm.

And he'd done it all without asking for a thing in return.

She'd given plenty of herself in the past few months to see them through a rough spot. Done things she was ashamed of but never regretted. She'd thought once that Noah had wanted the same thing. She'd been embarrassed when she realized she'd been wrong. And humiliated she'd offered herself to him when bedding her had been the furthest thing from his mind.

But she wasn't so sure he didn't think of it now. Over the last several weeks, she'd caught him gazing at her numerous times. The look in his eyes as he watched her was filled with heat and the desire she saw flickering there caused his eyes to shift from gray to silver. She could almost believe he was imagining her naked in those stolen glances. And if truth be known, her pulse raced every time she caught him looking at her like that.

But those lingering looks was all he ever gave her.

As quiet as Noah was at times, his eyes told a story of their own. The pain was still there, the loneliness he'd lived with for so many years, but every once in a while, she'd glimpse a bit of hope shining in his eyes. It was such a small thing to have—hope—and it would change his life if he just believed he was worth the trouble.

If he thought he was capable of being loved.

She blinked and realized she was staring at him. Noah noticed too. He stood by the side of the wagon, his gaze locked on her, and for a reason she didn't quite understand, her breath hitched when he held his hand out to her.

He'd been helping her in and out of that wagon ever since she'd fallen out of it in town, always steadying her as she climbed up, but today when she reached his side, he settled his hands on her waist, his touch light, and Keri could only stare up at him. That heated look she'd seen so many times over the past several weeks once again burned in his gray eyes as his gaze roamed her face, then settled on her lips.

Her pulse jumped when his fingers tightened against her waist. His pupils dilated, his chest expanding as his breaths quickened and if she didn't know any better, she would swear he was going to kiss her.

CHAPTER NINETEEN

Noah slapped the reins down, getting the horse to moving and tried to convince himself the sight of Keri didn't force all the blood in his body to head south, but every passing second in her presence told him otherwise. He couldn't get her out of his head. He couldn't look at her without remembering what she'd felt like in his arms. How her warm breath had felt against his neck.

How badly he wanted to kiss her when he'd caught her staring at him as if she'd wanted him.

His good sense prevailed when he reminded himself that just because he wanted her did not mean she felt the same way. So he'd given one last lingering look at her pink lips and put her in the wagon. Then spent the next ten minutes trying to decide if the look on her face was disappointment or relief.

The questions about her life with Robert and her husband had come from nowhere. He wasn't even sure why he asked them, especially since he'd been so rude to her when she'd asked him why he'd moved to Montana. He'd not wanted to tell her how miserable he'd been after Isabelle's rejection but today, he'd wanted to see her reaction. Wanted to see how she'd respond when faced with the same thing. To see if she found him as repulsive as Isabelle did. For some reason, he didn't think so.

A gust of wind blew snow and sleet at them, pelting their faces until Keri let out a small shriek, then laughed before trying to tuck her head inside the neck of her coat. Noah reached behind the seat, grabbed one of the blankets he kept back there for the kids to bundle up in and lifted it, trying to open it by giving it a hard shake. Keri took it, snapped it into the wind, then twirled it around her shoulders. Instead of laying it against her to ward off the cold, she held her arms up and turned her body toward him, blocking the wind-blown snow and cocooning them in a semi-warm, snow-free haven. She was so close, her knees rested against his thigh and he could smell the perfumed soap on her skin.

"Is this another blizzard blowing in?"

He glanced over at her. She was staring up at him, her blue eyes as captivating as she was. He cleared his throat and looked back at the road. "Hard to say." He looked up into the sky. The clouds were thick and gray but the snow fell in small flakes. "I guess we'll find out soon enough."

Reaching town took longer than it should have. The snow was falling harder by then and they ran into the school to collect the kids, smiling a greeting at Laurel when she saw them. Aaron and Sophie were huddled in a corner with a few other students, drawing something. Noah stood off to one side as he waited.

"I hope this snow isn't the start of another blizzard," Laurel said as she smiled up at them. "Everyone will be disappointed if we have to cancel the Christmas party. You'll be bringing the kids, won't you?"

Noah looked at Keri. He'd heard Aaron and Sophie Ann talking about the party, of the food and music, the dancing and games, and wondered if Keri would want to go. He imagined she did, and some small buried part of him wanted to take them. Wanted to see them smile and enjoy themselves. The part that preferred to stay hidden balked at the idea, but seeing Keri's eyes shine with excitement at the possibility made the decision for him. He'd bring them even if he had to sit in the wagon until time to go home. "They'll be here."

Laurel's face lit up as she smiled. "Wonderful! The children will be so excited. They weren't sure you'd be able to make it."

Aaron and Sophie finished whatever it was they were doing and raced across the room, talking on top of each other as they bundled up in their coats and gloves.

"Remember, a week from Friday at the stagecoach station," Laurel told them as they exited the school.

They hurried back to the wagon, covered the kids with one of the blankets and made it back to the house just as the snow stopped falling.

Aaron helped him unhitch the wagon and feed the animals while talking nonstop about the upcoming party. When they walked into the house, supper was waiting like it was every evening. Keri smiled at him when he entered the kitchen and heat spread through his limbs at the sight. The fact he enjoyed her smiles should have had him hunting a place for her and those kids to settle in to. Most days, the thought never entered his mind but when it did, a simple smile and her blue eyes seeking him out were all it took to convince himself that her and those kids were exactly where they needed to be.

Where he wanted them to be.

He'd lived alone for the last twelve years, cooking for himself and spending his evenings in quiet solitude. How was it a mere slip of a woman and her kids could turn his whole world around in a matter of weeks? He had no explanation for it. He avoided most everyone he came into contact with and the thought of speaking to a woman nearly choked the life out of him. He'd seen many a pretty faces. Many that, a lifetime ago, he would have pursued without thought. But not anymore.

Well, not until Keri.

Her, he spoke to, and the simple act of her doing things for him caused feelings to stir he thought long dead. Feelings he knew would have him acting like a fool in the very near future.

He sat in his chair, listening to the chatter of Aaron and Sophie Ann and watched Keri move around the room, filling plates and smiling at whatever the kids were talking about. She caught his eye, staring at him for long moments before her cheeks turned a pretty shade of pink. The fact she blushed from nothing more than a look from him left him dazed, especially when he recalled what he looked like. For the first time in years, he wished he was the man he used to be.

Setting his plate down in front of him, Keri glanced at him as she settled into her seat, those pink tinted cheeks turning darker by the second.

The joy he felt seeing her blush stirred that part of him he'd buried the day he left Charleston. He'd given up his dreams of a wife and children when Isabelle shunned him and he traveled halfway across the country to escape the pain of her rejection, resigning himself to always being alone. But Keri made him want those things again. He just wasn't sure how to go about getting them.

CHAPTER TWENTY

The town Christmas party was an event not to be missed, or that's what Keri had been told every day for the last week. Aaron and Sophie Ann made sure she knew how much they wanted to go. Fear she'd change her mind at the last moment clouded their eyes with worry regardless of how much she reassured them. They wouldn't be happy until they were in that stagecoach station surrounded by food, music, and good old fashioned fun.

Getting them to school knowing they'd have to wait all day before the party made her glad she wouldn't have to sit with them while the hours ticked away. That job had been left to Laurel and Keri didn't envy her at all. She couldn't begin to imagine how rowdy those school kids would be while waiting. Laurel had laughed and said, "I'm used to rambunctious kids."

When they returned from town, Keri was surprised when Noah brought the large bathing tub into the house and sat it in the kitchen by the stove. He filled it with hot water from the stove's reservoir then hung a blanket over the doorway for privacy and asked her if she'd like a bath. She stumped her toe on the bed frame in her haste to gather her soap, clean clothes and a drying cloth, and cursed a blue streak under her breath while limping back to the kitchen. If Noah heard her he didn't say anything.

The bath eased every drop of tension she felt, the floral scented soap making her feel pretty despite her skinny frame and chopped off hair. She washed it, working a lather through the curls, and did it all over again before climbing out and dressing in the pink and white work dress she owned.

The moment she sat down by the fire to dry her hair, Noah grabbed a stack of clothing off the side of the desk and walked into the kitchen, pulling the curtain closed behind him and the sound of splashing water stunned Keri so much, she could do nothing but stare at that blanket covering the doorway. When he finally stepped back around the curtain long minutes later in clean clothes, his hair wet and lying across his shoulders, she barely recognized him. She stared until she realized he was talking to her. "I'm sorry, what did you say?"

He shifted on his feet, his chest lifting as he inhaled a deep breath. "I asked if you would mind cutting my hair."

His voice was pitched so low, Keri barely heard him. But hear him she did. He wanted her to cut his hair. She was standing without even realizing she'd moved, a twinge of anticipation causing her pulse to leap. "I don't mind," she finally said, realizing he was still waiting for an answer.

Noah nodded, then turned and grabbed a chair out of the kitchen and sat it near the fire. He collected a comb and a pair of scissors and handed them both to her before sitting down.

Keri spent the next ten minutes combing the tangles out of his hair. The strands were long, the ends falling way past his shoulder blades and once it was gnarl free, she ran her fingers through it, amazed he was allowing her to groom him.

"Any preference to length?"

He didn't answer right away but eventually said, "Whatever you think."

Keri cut the length to lie against his shoulders. He'd been hiding behind that hair for so long, she imagined cutting it too short would have him hiding out in the cabin until it grew back. At least with a little length he'd *feel* like he could still hide. Not that he needed to.

She thinned it by half, ran her fingers through it as it slowly dried, and could only stare as she stepped around him. As unruly as his hair had been, the dark strands now fell smoothly around his face. For some reason, he didn't look quite as intimidating without that wild mane of knots and gnarls sticking about his head. He looked as tame as his hair did.

His beard was still three years too long, though. She smiled and locked eyes with him. "What about this?" she said, raising a hand and tugging at the facial hair. "A good trim wouldn't be a bad idea."

A flash of panic sprang into his eyes and she saw a vein on his temple thump against his skin as his pulse raced. She could almost see the reasons to leave that beard flash across his brain, the same reasons he'd probably clung to when growing it so long to begin with.

He met her gaze and held it until the air around them seemed to go still.

Keri felt his panic as she looked into his eyes. Saw his fear at being so exposed. "You've no reason to hide, Noah." She smiled at him and saw a flicker of hope blaze in his eyes. "Besides, what good is a fancy new haircut if you let this bushy thing distract people from even noticing?"

He drummed a finger against his leg, those blasted gloves still encasing his hands. She'd have to work on getting those off too now that he seemed to be coming out of whatever shell he'd been hiding in. Whatever he was hiding under that leather couldn't be so bad as to never remove them.

His nod was so slight, she barely caught it. "Is that a yes?"

"Yes."

The word was whispered but Keri took it as a good sign. She grabbed the drying cloth he'd used on his hair and laid it across the front of his chest, draping the ends over his shoulders. "Hold the front of this."

With the cloth underneath him to catch the hair she snipped away, Keri bent slightly and started cutting. Noah shut his eyes with the first clip. Getting as close to his face as she could, she cut at that scraggly beard until she could make out the shape of his jaw and the curve of his chin. Until she could see how perfectly his lips were formed.

Keri combed and clipped his beard until it was shorn close to his face. She made the last cut and didn't realize she was holding her breath until her lungs started to burn. She looked down at his face, at the smooth lines he'd hidden for so long and felt her heart flutter as she stared at him. Noah Lloyd had been hiding a handsome man underneath all that hair.

She took the ends of the cloth from him, folding it so none of the hair would slip out and set it, and the scissors and comb aside then turned back to face him. The scar he'd tried to hide ended just under his chin. The crooked, white line cut a slash down the length of his face. She could only imagine what it had looked like right after it had been done. How it looked when Isabelle saw it.

The puckered skin was white now, its zig-zag pattern over his cheek noticeable, but not as hideous as he makes it out to be. His Isabelle must have ripped his heart in two. Life was passing him by while he let the actions of some silly girl who should have loved him enough to comfort him, not turn away in disgust, force him into seclusion.

She raised a hand, tracing the path of it from his eye down. He grabbed her hand, stilled her movements, and whispered, "Don't."

More than twelve years had passed since he was hurt and the emotional pain was still there. Keri could see it in the lines of his face. Rubbing her thumb across his cheek, she said, "It's just a scar, Noah. A minor imperfection. It doesn't define who you are."

Her soft spoken words tore a hole in his heart. How could she act as if it made no difference? Isabelle had cried when she saw him, shook her head as if to deny what she was seeing. Begged him to have someone fix it. But there was nothing to fix. His face was ruined, his body riddled with scars that made the one on his face seem like such an insignificant thing.

But Keri wasn't flinching or looking away, instead, she was touching him, her fingers warm and soft against his face. A mere caress.

As nice as it felt to have her touch him, he'd never felt so exposed in his life. Fully clothed he felt naked, as if the entire town of Willow Creek was sitting there in his cabin laughing at the town monster who thought he was good enough for someone to love. He kept his eyes closed, not able to bear the pity he knew he'd see if he looked up at her.

Her thumb slid across his cheek again, the small touch leaving a trail of fire behind it. She moved closer, stepping between his legs until the heat from her body warmed him, the scent of that floral scented soap that lingered on her skin filling his senses.

A fluttering touch against his lip forced his eyes open. Keri traced the outer edges with the tip of one finger. The look on her face was his undoing. The disgust he'd seen cross Isabelle's features wasn't present as Keri looked at him.

The fear of rejection he'd lived with since Isabelle turned her back on him shattered as he looked up at Keri, desire shining so brightly in her beautiful eyes his body jolted, his pulse leaping and dancing under his skin.

She ran soft fingers over his face, smoothed both of her hands over his bristled jaw and looked up, her heart shining in her eyes. "You've no reason to ever hide, Noah." She cupped his face in her hands, her thumbs grazing his cheeks.

Then she kissed him.

His entire body clenched tight at the first touch of her soft lips. The air was sucked from his lungs and he sat there unmoving as she sealed her mouth over his, her tongue darting out to tease his bottom lip. He hardened in an instant, ached to have her with a craving so fierce it burned over every inch of his flesh.

He grabbed her, pulled her flush against him, and slid his tongue inside her mouth, tasting her sweetness as her arms wove around his neck.

Good God, how had he lived so long without the simple pleasure of a kiss? She felt so good, tasted as sweet as the finest wine, and caused his body to pulse with need. Threading his fingers into her hair, he angled her head the way he wanted and used his other arm to pull her flush against him.

She moaned deep in her throat, the sound vibrating through his body as her fingers dug into his scalp, her hold bordering on pain, and it still wasn't close enough. He wanted to feel her against his skin, to drown in the scent of her. To end the agonizing yearning to sink into a soft, willing woman.

His hands spanned her waist, sliding up her ribs to the underside of her breasts. He wanted to touch her, to cup them in his hands, to feel them against his palms.

He needed to stop before he wasn't able to.

Grabbing her arms, he broke the kiss, pushed her away from him and stood, knocking the chair over in his haste.

They were both breathing heavily, Keri's lips swollen and plump, her gaze darting over his face. "What's wrong?"

Hell's fire. She was flushed pink, her eyes wide and luminous and every harsh breath she took raised her chest, drawing his gaze to those breasts he wanted to see and touch. He groaned, his erection throbbing at the sight of her nipples pebbled and poking against the material. The pain in his groin cleared his head enough to turn and head for the door. He had to get away from her.

"Noah, wait! Don't leave."

He stopped with his hand on the door, his head bowed while every nerve in his body fired tingling zaps through his limbs. "I haven't kissed a woman in twelve years, Keri. Much more of that and I won't be able to stop myself from taking you."

"Then don't try."

His breath caught at her words. Was she suggesting...

He closed his eyes, imagined what her pale flesh would look like exposed as she sprawled across his bed. Every muscle tightened, tension coiling in his limbs until the ache was a physical pain. My God, it had been so long.

"Stay."

Her voice was so soft, longing so profound etched into that one simple word that it tugged at every part of his soul. He looked over his shoulder at her. She was right behind him, her breaths still panted out in sharp little bursts, and the look in her eyes was his undoing.

For some unfathomable reason, Keri wanted him.

She proved it the next instant by reaching for the buttons of her dress, unhooking each one clean to her navel. The ribbon on her chemise was pulled, the material gaping wide before she slid it all over her shoulders, the mound of fabric catching on her hips. Naked from the waist up, all that creamy flesh exposed, the question he'd been asking himself since first seeing her was answered when he took in the sight of her breasts. Her nipples were pink.

What little sense he had left fled in a rush of need so powerful, he barely remembered turning away from the door. He grabbed her, wrapping his arms around her waist and lifted her from the floor, his mouth latching on to her left breast while he walked to the bed. His legs hit the mattress and he raised a knee, leaned down and lowered her, letting go of her breast just long enough to jerk her skirt to her waist. He was pulling her underwear down when she unfastened his pants and reached inside, wrapping her hand around his cock. He clenched his eyes tight as she stroked him, her soft fingers playing over his skin until he thought he'd spill himself before ever getting inside of her.

Pushing her hand away, he slid between her legs and plunged inside of her damp passage with one quick, smooth tilt of his hips.

He nearly lost it at the feel of her. He groaned, bit back a curse when she gasped, her muscles clamping tight around him. He kissed her again, trying to think of anything other than how good she felt. How he was about to embarrass himself by finding his release before even getting started.

Sliding one arm around her waist, he slid her up the bed, settling between her pale thighs before pulling out of her, then sliding back in. Small moans, deep in the back of her throat, raised the hairs on his arms. He reached under her, cupped her buttocks in both hands, his fingers tightening and squeezing her flesh as he stroked back and forth.

She captured his tongue, sucked on it until he couldn't think straight. Her legs wound tightly around his waist, trapping him against her as she rocked her hips, writhing under him in a dance so erotic, every nerve in his body tightened, the force of his thrusts getting harder while he clung to her. The pain from her short nails digging into his back and her slick heat drew his balls tight. It had definitely been too long.

She clenched around him moments later and stiffened, broke their kiss and threw her head back, a sound so guttural escaping her throat it grabbed every part of him and forced his own release. He emptied himself inside of her as his own yells mingled with hers.

The tide of pleasure rode his body until he was drained, collapsing against her as every ounce of strength he had fled. Keri was shaking beneath him. Or was it him who was shaking? He was too disoriented to tell.

Lying with her under him, Noah breathed in the floral scent

of her skin, buried his face in her curly hair and tried to remember everything he could about her. One small taste would never be enough. He should have taken his time, stripped her naked and kissed every inch of her skin. Tasted her properly, drawing her pleasure out until she was unable to move.

Then doing it all over again.

Instead, he'd jumped on top of her and finished his business in an embarrassingly short amount of time. He sighed. He'd definitely been too long without a woman. He was surprised he lasted as long as he had, truth be known. He'd been ready to spill in his pants the moment she kissed him. The fact he didn't do so when he entered her was a small miracle.

Their bodies cooled and his common sense returned by small degrees. When he was able to think clearly, he realized he'd not pulled out of her when he climaxed, their flesh still one. His heart thumped against his chest at the thought. How could he have been so stupid? What if….

He disentangled himself from her and stood, turning his back to tuck himself into his pants. The bed ropes squeaked when she moved. He knew he should say something but he couldn't turn around and look at her. Fear of what he'd see shining in her eyes when he did held him frozen.

He glanced at the clock, relief nearly staggering him. It was time to go. He headed to the door and slipped his coat and hat on. "I'll hitch up the wagon and wait for you outside."

CHAPTER TWENTY-ONE

K eri watched him leave, the small ache pulsing in her chest at his hasty retreat enough to make her throat and eyes burn.

Had it been so terrible he couldn't even look at her? She stared at the closed door for long moments, swallowed repeatedly to dislodge the lump in her throat, and told herself she'd not cry. He'd at least been kind enough to leave instead of listing her every fault as Robert always did.

The pain from Noah's quick dismissal still choked her, though, still felt as if he'd taken a fist to her instead of walking away as if she didn't matter. As if giving herself to him didn't matter.

"You asked for this," she whispered. "You practically begged him for it." And she had. She'd wanted him, but she knew before he even touched her that he'd shut himself off from the world and formed no connections or attachments to anyone. Just because she seduced him into bedding her didn't mean he'd sit around staring at her like a love-sick school boy afterwards while professing his undying love. A miserable sob crawled its way up her throat before she could stop it.

Scrubbing her face, refusing to succumb to a crying fit, she inhaled a cleansing breath, then stood, fixed her clothes and walked to the kitchen. She grabbed a bowl of warm water, carried it back behind the blankets around the bed and washed, trying to figure out what exactly had come over her to begin with. One moment she was trying to reassure Noah that the scar on his face meant nothing, that it didn't matter as much as he thought it did, and the next, she was kissing him as if she had a right to.

If you could call such a carnal act a kiss. A shiver raced up her spine just thinking about it.

Noah Lloyd may have lived his life as a hermit for the last twelve years, but sweet heavens could that man kiss. She wasn't sure if it was because it had been so long since he'd done so or if he was just that good at it. Whatever the reason, she'd tingled clean to her toes the moment he slipped his tongue into her mouth, her breasts aching while a wild pulse beat between her legs. She'd wanted to crawl into his lap, strip him bare, and drown in those soul stealing kisses and never come up for air.

But he'd pushed her away and stalked to the door instead.

The loss of contact had been jarring. She hadn't wanted a man's touch in so long, she was amazed her body still responded, but what that one kiss did unhinged her. She'd wanted him so much it hurt to watch him walk away.

But why had he walked away to begin with? Had she been too bold?

Her cheeks heated just thinking about the way she'd bared her breasts to him so he wouldn't leave. Then cringed at the thought. What must he think of her? She'd acted like a shameless wanton, practically threw herself at him, squirming underneath him while trapping him against her with her legs around his waist. And nearly choked on her own screams when she'd come to completion, her release sneaking up on her so fast she was almost embarrassed.

Another delicious tingle raced up her spine when she remembered how complete she'd felt. How alive.

She sighed and finger combed her curls into place, glancing into the small mirror hung by the bed. Her face was flushed. Her eyes seemed too wide and too bright. She looked close to glowing. She snorted a laugh while studying her reflection. Five intense minutes with Noah Lloyd between her thighs and she looked like a different person.

She chalked it up to the fact she hadn't wanted a man so intensely in...well, ever. She'd not minded lying with John. She may not have loved him, but she'd given herself to him without regret and enjoyed it for the most part, but their coupling had never been so... passionate. She'd never ached for more so soon after.

Keri blew out a breath then banked the fire, slipped on her coat and hat and grabbed the box of pies she'd baked for the party. Snow still covered the ground, the clouds threatening to spill more at any moment. She spotted Noah by the wagon, his arm laid along the sideboard with an unreadable look on his face. Just seeing him standing there took her breath. He looked like a completely different person now with his tamed hair and his beard trimmed neatly.

He turned his head to look at her, their eyes locked, and for one brief moment, she thought she saw the same desire she'd seen in his gray eyes earlier. It was gone in a flash, though.

Noah took the box of pies when she reached him and sat them in the back, then held out his hand to help her into the wagon. He didn't lift her in like he'd been doing lately, instead, he held her hand so she wouldn't fall. He almost acted as if he didn't want to touch her now. Her chest clenched tight at the thought. She shouldn't have come on so strong. She regretted doing so now.

Neither said a word on the ride to town and Keri was glad when they pulled to a stop in front of the school. Noah's silence was killing her. The streets were filled with wagons, the sound of children's voices echoing down the street to mingle with the music she could already hear. The entire town was adorned with evergreens, ribbons in red and gold dangling from wreaths and the air seemed to buzz with excitement. The sidewalks were cluttered with people, their happy, laughing voices creating a soft hum that was carried on the breeze. A crisp wind blew in from the mountains, the biting nip stinging her face and as worried as she was about what Noah thought of her, her heart felt light.

She saw Aaron and Sophie, the smiles on their faces bringing one to her own lips. Noah held his hand up to her and she looked over at him. No emotion showed on his face and he barely looked at her. He helped her to the ground without a word.

A barrage of questions were on the tip of her tongue but she couldn't get a single one articulated enough to ask them. When he grabbed the box of pies and started for the stagecoach station, she followed along behind him wondering if her wanton behavior had forever ruined what tentative normalcy they had. If Noah couldn't even look at her, how would they be able to live in the same house together? And where would they go if he asked her to leave?

"What in the world did you do to that man?"

Keri looked up to find Abigail and Laurel Avery next to her but they weren't looking at her, they were staring across the room, their eyes wide and filled with curiosity. She turned her head to see what held their attention and saw nothing unusual. Well, nothing other than Noah leaning against the wall looking bored out of his skin.

The haircut she'd given him, not to mention his trimmed beard, caused more than one head to turn when they'd walked into the building. Keri couldn't blame the residents of Willow

Creek for staring at him, though. She was having a hard time not doing so herself. Regardless of what Noah may think, Keri wasn't the only one to notice how handsome he was despite that scar on his face. The more time she spent looking at him, the more she realized Isabelle must have been the most shallow girl in all of Charleston to give up a man that good looking. A man who obviously cared for her enough that her rejection sent him running to the other side of the country to escape the pain.

Laurel slid a glance her way. "For the past two years, Holden has tried his best to befriend Noah without much luck. He could barely get him to talk to him, truth be known. Noah rarely came to town and when he did, he spoke to no one unless he had to." She grinned. "Now he's taken in you and your children and venturing in to town twice a day, has cut his hair and trimmed that god awful beard. And all of this in a matter of weeks so, I'll repeat my earlier question. What did you do to him?"

The laughter in Laurel's eyes matched Abigail's, she noticed, when the women turned her way. They both wore beaming smiles and looked at her as if she'd performed some magical feat. "I didn't do anything," she said. "He asked me to cut his hair so I did."

A quizzical look drew Laurel's eyebrows high. "Oh really?" She turned to stare back across the room. "Now why do you suppose he wanted to look presentable after all this time?"

"I don't know." And that was the truth. She didn't know why Noah had wanted his hair cut. She'd asked herself that same question a dozen times and she'd yet to come up with a reason other than he just got tired of it. She knew it had to be more than that, though, but it made more sense than the one her heart tried to make. The one where he cut it so she'd look at him as she would any man. So she'd see him as someone she'd want to be with and not some wild, backwoods hermit.

She'd not missed the looks he'd been giving her lately, looks that caused her pulse to leap under her skin and her thoughts to go places they had no business going. Noah had never said anything disrespectful to her, and she had no reason to believe he wanted anything from her, but those looks made *her* think things no decent woman should. And today, she'd acted on them like some wanton harlot who hadn't seen a man in years.

Her neck and face burned hot all of a sudden and she turned, looking back at the table filled with cakes, cookies and pies, trying to get the blush staining her face crimson to disappear.

The chatter beside her grew, more voices joining in with Laurel and Abigail's. Keri finally got her heated face to cool and turned back around. Laurel introduced her to her other sisters-in-law, Sarah and Emmaline, and those four Avery women talked to her as if they'd known her the entirety of her life.

For the first time since leaving home that starless night last spring, Keri felt as if she belonged somewhere. If Peter never sent for her, she'd be content here in Willow Creek with these people. Assuming she had a place she could call home.

She glanced back at Noah. He'd told her she was welcome to stay with him until Peter was found but what would become of them if her brother never turned up? Would Noah expect them to leave? Or would he let them stay on permanently. And if so, in what capacity?

A man she'd never seen before stepped into her line of sight and she blinked up at him. He smiled at her, his kindly eyes wary. When he glanced at the Avery women briefly before looking back at her, Keri realized it was her he wanted to speak with. Why? she had no idea.

An uneasy feeling crept along Noah's spine as one man after another stopped in front of Keri and spent long minutes talking with her. He didn't know who half of them were but he didn't get out much, either.

Those men seemed to linger after they'd said their peace, the Avery women slowly being pushed to the side, and irritation gnawed at him just seeing them with Keri.

He glanced around the room, trying to ignore what was happening, and wished he would have stayed with the wagon. The eyes of nearly everyone in the building were on him. He felt their gazes burning into his flesh like a live thing crawling across his skin.

Asking Keri to cut his hair was a bad decision to begin with but letting her trim his beard was just plain idiotic. What had he been thinking? The answer whispered inside his mind a moment later. He'd been wondering if those smiles Keri gave him meant anything or if she was just being nice.

He got his answer to that one real quick. His body still hummed in remembrance of her kissing him. Of her bearing her breasts and clinging to him as he sank into her warm body.

Pleasant chills shot up his spine just thinking about it. He wondered if anyone could tell by looking at them that they'd been intimate. Not that it mattered. Marshal Avery said he'd spread the rumor of him taking a wife and his coming to town daily with Keri and her kids had to have been noticed by now. Maybe that was why everyone was staring at him. The fact he was at a social event when he never bothered with attending any before.

He glanced around the room again. He was still being watched but the looks thrown his way were more curious than anything. He knew his appearance would cause a stir and draw unwanted attention to himself but at the time, he'd not been thinking straight. He'd only been thinking about what Keri would think, not the people in this dusty little town. They probably thought Keri was the reason for the sudden change. She was, but he wasn't about to make that public knowledge. He wasn't even sure he wanted her to know.

Thinking of her, he glanced back her way. Those men

hovering around her were finally starting to wander off. The unexplained tightness in his chest eased a bit seeing them leave. She smiled, her eyes lighting up the room and he couldn't look away.

Her face was flushed, the same way it had been after their earlier encounter. Remembering it brought the sound of her phantom cries screaming back through his head. He heard her breathy moans until his skin tightened, the collar of his shirt choking him with need to hear them again. But, her silence on the way to town told him he'd never get the chance. Of course, that was probably his fault. He'd ran like a scalded dog the moment the deed was done but damn it all, what was he supposed to say afterwards? Thanks? Sorry it was over before it really began? Can I make it up to you later?

He rolled his eyes at his own idiotic thoughts.

Movement out of the corner of his eye drew his attention. He turned his head and saw Holden Avery heading his way. He should have known one of those Averys would talk to him eventually. He'd seen all four of them huddled in a far corner, engaged in some intense conversation from the look on their faces.

Stopping by his side, Holden gave him a nod of his head in greeting. "Noah, I just about didn't recognize you."

"I barely recognize myself," he said, fixing his gaze back on Keri.

Holden turned, leaned against the wall, and looked across the room. "What do you suppose they're talking about?" he asked, motioning to his wife, sisters-in-law and Keri.

"Hard to say."

"Chances are its nothing good." Holden grinned and shook his head. "Get a gaggle of women together and you've got a recipe for trouble. From the looks of them, they're making a bit of mischief as we speak."

Holden spent the next ten minutes rambling on about this and that. Noah listened, commenting only when he felt the need.

He saw Aaron and Sophie Ann in the far corner with a group of kids close to their age, smiles lighting up their faces. As much as he didn't want to be here, seeing them happy, and knowing Keri was enjoying herself, was worth his discomfort.

Enduring the stares of everyone got easier as the evening wore on. He ignored them for the most part, his gaze locked on Keri. People came and went throughout the night and when a new line of men seemed to grow around Keri again, laughing as they huddled around her, his fists clenched tight the moment one of them raised a hand and touched her hair. His earlier ire returned at the sight, intensifying as thoughts so black and violent filled his head it stole his breath.

CHAPTER TWENTY-TWO

He'd forgotten Holden still leaned against the wall beside him until the man shifted his weight and cleared his throat. "Looks as if the knowledge that Mrs. Hilam is new to town finally made it around to all the single men. If Morgan hadn't been spreading the rumor of her being your wife, I'd be inclined to believe those men were lining up to be suitors." A half smile lifted the corner of his mouth. "Of course, I'm sure most of them don't know the little lie everyone's been telling so I'd not be surprised if she walked away with a dozen marriage proposals by the end of the night."

If Holden said anything after that, Noah didn't hear him. He couldn't hear anything, all the sound in the room dulled to a low hum as the words, "marriage proposals," whispered through his head. Is that what was going on over there? Were those men trying to win Keri's favor in hopes she'd marry them?

Morgan told everyone she was your wife. It doesn't matter what those men say to her, she couldn't accept even if one did.

Could she?

The man next to her said something that caused a pretty smile to light up her face. It was the same smile she gave him most days. A smile he liked to think was his and his alone. Apparently he was a bigger fool than he thought he was.

He turned and left the warmth of the station without a word, the frosty air blowing in from the mountains seeping under his coat and chilling him to the bone. The street was empty, only a few people lingering near the saloon, the tinny piano music drifting from the building a faint echo on the breeze.

Stopping at the edge of the sidewalk, he crossed his arms over his chest, and stared down the street at nothing in particular. The sound from inside the stagecoach station grew once the musicians started playing something other than Christmas carols. He turned his head to look into the window. Couples paired off and walked to the center of the room, a jaunty jig starting about the time he spotted Keri being led to the spot where everyone else was dancing by a man he'd never seen before.

He scowled, turned on his heel, and started down the sidewalk. He made it as far as the mercantile before he stopped. He was doing it again. Letting unpleasant circumstances force him to turn the other way. To run as fast as his feet would carry him. To hide and lick his wounds in private.

"Damn it." He sighed, ran a hand over his face, and stared into the darkened store front window.

The display Mrs. Jenkins had set up was a festive affair filled with evergreen boughs, holly and colorful ribbons and lace. Dolls and small wooden trains sat amongst frilly bonnets and men's hats. A box holding a few pieces of jewelry caught his eye, the gems in one of the rings glistening in the moon-washed street.

He barely remembered the last Christmas he celebrated. It was before the war, that much he knew. Before he ceased to care about warm cider, gifts, or the hopes of catching, and kissing, a girl under a sprig of mistletoe.

Things he'd never missed until now.

Leaning a hand against the window, Noah stared at those small treasures knowing the kids in Willow Creek would wake

Christmas morning to presents tucked beneath a tree decorated with angels and stars. He thought of Aaron and Sophie Ann, wondering what their last Christmas had been like living with the uncle. To hear Keri and Aaron talk, the man was a walking nightmare. For that reason alone, those kids probably hadn't had a happy holiday since their pa died.

"Are you ready to go?"

Noah started at the sound of Keri's voice. He hadn't heard her approach. He straightened and looked behind her, wondering where her admirers were. "Are you?" he asked, turning her question around on her.

She shrugged her shoulder.

Her lack of answer told him she wasn't ready to leave despite her asking if he was.

She glanced back toward the stagecoach station. "I left Aaron and Sophie Ann playing a game with the other children but I shouldn't leave them alone for too long." Catching his eye again, she gave him a smile. The same one she'd given all those men lined up to talk to her. "Are you coming back to the party?"

It was his turn to shrug.

She blew out a soft breath. "We can leave if you'd like. All you have to do is say so."

"I thought you wanted to be here."

"I did." She wrapped her arms around her waist. She'd not put her coat on before coming outside. "I do," she said. "But you looked uncomfortable earlier. When I saw you leave, I thought you were ready to go."

"I'm always uncomfortable around a lot of people or have you been too busy entertaining every man in Willow Creek to notice?" He clenched his jaw the moment the words were out of his mouth, especially when she lowered her lashes and looked away. He regretted saying it. He was irritated and had no right to take his frustrations out on her.

She looked toward the window display, her eyes lingering

over the assortment of items for long moments before she said, "I'll go gather the kids."

When she went to walk away, he grabbed her arm. The moment he touched her, he wished he'd never turned away from her back at the cabin. Wished he'd said something, anything, and stayed a few more minutes. Stayed long enough to make a fool out of himself by spouting god-awful poetry and stealing a few more of her kisses.

Stayed long enough to let her know how much he enjoyed being with her. How in awe he was that she'd even want him.

He loosened his grip on her arm, stared down at her upturned face and wondered, if he kissed her now, would she welcome it like she had earlier or had his actions ruined any chance they may have had. "Let the kids play," he said. "We can stay."

She stared at him for long moments before looking away. He let go of her arm and she crossed them over her body, but she never moved, just stared down the street. He tilted his head, watching her.

"Are you upset with me?" she finally asked.

"Why would I be?"

She shrugged. "You haven't bothered to speak to me all night." She glanced at him then. "I thought…" She stopped speaking mid sentence, shook her head and sighed. "It doesn't matter." She was several steps away when she said, "I'll go see if Aaron and Sophie Ann are ready to go home."

Home. The word held meaning when she said it, and he realized that Keri and the kids had made his tiny cabin just that. The home he'd always thought to have but never did.

He'd thought his life ended the day Isabelle rejected him but looking at Keri, he realized it was just put on hold for a bit. He could still have all those things he once dreamed about.

But could he have them with her?

❄

As late as it was, the kids were still bouncing with energy. Keri should have watched them more closely. They were so sugared up, it would be a miracle if they ever settled down.

She listened to them laugh and tell her everything they did, everyone they talked to and every sweet they put into their mouths. They each had a small sack filled with nuts and fruit, small pieces of hard candies and small spinning tops and whistles. Keri missed seeing them so excited.

As usual, Noah was quiet, listening to the chatter with a blank expression on his face. He'd not bothered to speak to her once all evening except for when she'd sought him out after seeing him leave. He'd watched her from the other side of the room, his gaze on her anytime she looked, but he never tried to talk to her or ask her to dance. Never moved from that wall. Well, not until she'd been asked to dance by a man who wouldn't take no for an answer and started dragging her across the room. Luckily, Morgan Avery had heard her protests and intervened, forcing the ornery man to let her go.

If Noah had been with her, it would have never happened. She'd not have had to stand through countless greetings with men wanting to meet, who they thought, was an available woman. The look of surprise on their faces when she said she had a husband, and who that man was, wasn't missed.

But Noah leaving in the middle of the party just confirmed the growing fear she'd had all night of him purposely avoiding her. She'd foolishly thought things would change between them, and in a way they had, just not the way she'd hoped.

A touch to her shoulder drew her from her thoughts. She turned her head, smiling at Aaron as he leaned over the seat rail and looked at her. The expression on his face was clouded with worry. "What's wrong, Aaron?"

"Are you really gonna marry Ben Atwater?"

Noah stiffened at her side and turned his head to look at

her, an odd expression on his face. She sat frozen as he stared at her, wondering what was going through his head but he looked away before she could figure it out. She turned her attention back to Aaron. "Why would you think I was getting married?"

"Because Betsey and Benjamin said you were going to be their new ma."

"You don't want to be our mommy anymore?" Sophie asked.

Keri's heart slammed against her ribcage. "Oh, Sophie Ann, I'll always want to be your mommy." She reached for her, running a hand over her blond curls. "Don't ever think such a thing."

Sophie smiled, satisfied with her answer, but Aaron was still on his knees waiting. "Who are Betsey and Benjamin?" Keri asked.

Aaron sighed and leaned against the back of the seat. "Kids we go to school with."

"And they told you I was going to marry their pa?"

"Yep. They said he told them they'd have to start minding him cause he was getting them a new ma and he didn't want them embarrassing him. Said you wouldn't want him if you knew his kids were hellions."

Keri's eyes widened a bit at his use of the word, hellions. "Well, I've no clue who Ben Atwater, or Betsey and Benjamin are, so I can tell you that no, I'm not marrying their father."

Aaron let out a breath so deep, it made a small "whooshing" sound. "Thank goodness," he said. "I like Benjamin all right but Betsey dang near drives me crazy. When she ain't looking at me all funny, she's practically standing on my toes." He shook his head, his lip curling in disgust. "I think she's sweet on me."

Keri laughed, the sound so loud and abrupt, the horse shied. "You don't return her feelings, then?"

He looked horrified at the prospect. "Heck no!"

She ruffled his hair and grinned. "Then I don't have to worry about you running off to marry her anytime soon, huh?"

He grimaced. "No. I ain't never getting married," he said. "I ain't being nobody's pa, either. Babies ain't nothing but trouble."

Keri grinned. "Babies aren't trouble. They just need special care until they're big enough to do things for themselves."

He huffed out a breath. "Don't make no difference. I'm gonna live by myself like Noah does. He ain't nobody's pa and he's just fine."

Sophie Ann leaned forward, confusion causing small wrinkles on her forehead as she scrunched her face. "I thought Noah was *our* new pa."

The air was sucked from Keri's lungs at Sophie Ann's words. She heard them repeating over and over again inside her head until Noah glanced at her. His shocked expression probably matched her own. They stared at one another until Sophie Ann leaned toward the seat.

"Ain't that why we live with him now? So we can be a family." Sophie Ann looked between her and Noah as if waiting for an answer.

Keri didn't have one to give her. Not now. Regardless of what she said, someone would get hurt. Telling Sophie Ann that Noah wasn't her new pa might make Noah think he'd be the last man she'd have for the job and nothing could be further from the truth. He'd already done more for them than Robert ever had and he didn't seem bitter for having to do it. But if she led Sophie Ann to believe Noah was, and Peter was found and sent for them, she'd be devastated at having to leave.

She smiled to cover the panic welling up inside of her. "You don't need to worry about that tonight, Sophie. Go lie down and pull those blankets around you. We'll be home soon."

Turning back around, she stared across the prairie, Sophie's words still whispering inside her head. She understood why Sophie was confused. She'd lost her pa and gained what she thought was a new one in Robert, only to be uprooted and thrown into a new life with yet another man who provided for her as John had. It was enough to cause any five year old confusion. And she had no one to blame for that but herself.

When the cabin came into view, she looked back over her shoulder, relieved to see both Aaron and Sophie bundled up in the blankets, asleep. She caught Noah's eye when she turned back around. He never said a word but the expression on his face held as many questions as she herself had.

Duke, that old dog the kids had found, started barking when they were close enough for him to hear the squeak and rattle of the wagon wheels and Noah turned away. It was just as well. She didn't know what to say to him anyway.

Noah pulled the wagon to a stop by the barn, set the brake and climbed down. Keri gathered her things and stood. Noah was by the side of the wagon, ready to help her down and to her surprise, he grabbed her around the waist, lifting her off her feet and setting her on the ground. He didn't let go immediately, just held her close, his gaze roaming her face so long she thought he was going to kiss her.

He turned away without a word, instead.

CHAPTER TWENTY-THREE

It was snowing again. Keri watched the flurries swirl by the kitchen window, Aaron and Sophie Ann's laughter chasing behind on the wind.

She spotted them coming around the side of the barn and smiled. They were running after Duke as he jumped into the air, snapping at the falling snow. For such a homely looking critter when they'd brought him home, he looked as if he'd always belonged here now. He'd filled out, his ribs no longer visible, and he played with the kids as if he were a pup. Love really did change a person. Or a dog, in his case.

The barn door swung open, Noah stepping out leading his horse. The animal was saddled. Was he going somewhere?

Grabbing another plate, Keri dried it off and put it on the shelf above the sink. She kept a watchful eye on what was going on outside, her thoughts still on all that had happened the day before.

Noah avoiding her now a result of that.

He'd sat quietly through breakfast, leaving as soon as he was finished and didn't return. It was the first time in a while that he'd not come back in after tending the animals.

She knew why he was avoiding the house, though. Why he was avoiding her. They hadn't spoken of what happened between them and Noah's silence was telling. It wasn't worth discussing in his eyes. He was dismissing the whole thing as if it never happened.

Disappointment tightened her chest, the dull ache squeezing the breath out of her. She didn't know what to do about it either. Or why it hurt to begin with. She'd been trying to figure that out since he'd left her sitting on the bed with her skirts twisted around her waist.

Examining why she cared so much left her emotions raw. She'd spent a great deal of energy learning to ignore Robert. Telling herself it was okay that he treated her and the kids the way he did, that she didn't care, but deep down in that small space of her heart that thought they deserved better, that she deserved better, something withered and died with every harsh word he uttered. Every bruise and humiliation he heaped on her stung just a little bit more until there was nothing left. She'd been numb by the time she gathered Aaron and Sophie Ann and ran.

But that numbing sensation had begun to fade as of late, small sparks of.... something, caused her breath to catch every time Noah looked at her as if he'd never seen another woman in his life. As if he couldn't look away regardless of how much he tried.

As if she would be enough for him.

She sighed, feeling melancholy, and put the whole business out of her mind, going about her chores instead. She finished cleaning the kitchen, then made the bed, folded the blankets on the cot Noah slept on, and dusted the mantel. The leather journal Noah kept his sketches in lay there on one corner. She lifted it, dusted the spot it had lain in and paused when she went to lay the book back down.

As long as she'd been there, she'd not once snooped in any of Noah's things. The drawer on the small desk along the wall still held items she'd never seen, the trunk at the foot of the bed largely unexplored. She'd only ever pulled a blanket out of it but never looked to see what lay in the bottom. And this book…

She ran her hand over the worn leather, her fingers itching to take a peek. Noah spent every day drawing on these pages and her curiosity about the type of things he drew got the best of her most days. She'd never peeked over his shoulder, regardless of how badly she'd wanted to. If he wanted her to see what he'd drawn, he'd show her, right?

She glanced toward the door and bit her bottom lip. *How long before he came back inside?* Seeing as he'd yet to come back in, she suspected he'd stay out there for a while. It did seem as if he were actively avoiding her at the moment.

Looking back at the book, Keri eased the cover up. The first sketch brought a smile to her face. It was a plantation-style mansion, three stories high. Trees lined a drive leading to the house, a wide porch spanning the length of the front. A second porch hung suspended from the second floor, a row of windows arching high above it. The words *Rosebriar* were scrawled near the bottom, the elegant script curling around the letters.

She knew from stories and paintings that houses like this one were common in the South. Huge, sprawling estates with fancy ladies in gowns so beautiful and extravagant it seemed a shame to wear them. Ladies like Noah's Isabelle.

Imagining Rosebriar in Charleston wasn't hard. This home looked exactly like the ones she pictured when she thought of the coastal town. As rough as Noah seemed, there were times when she glimpsed an honest to goodness Southern gentleman in him, his drawl so deep, she could picture him living in a mansion like this.

She studied the drawing for long minutes, taking in every nuance of it while the question of whether or not Rosebriar was where Noah grew up echoed across her thoughts before she dismissed it as a fanciful notion. If Noah had lived here, then his leaving meant he'd given up everything. Given up his family, wealth she knew whoever lived in this house had to possess, and a society that thrived on the finer things in life. No one would give that up for the middle of nowhere, Montana.

Putting it out of her mind, she flipped the page, thumbing through each one, Noah's memories sketched in shades of black and gray.

She paused when she reached a page with a collection of people's faces, some of the townsfolk of Willow Creek looking back at her. She recognized almost everyone, the Avery's all huddled in small groups. More of them appeared as she flipped the pages again and she gasped softly when she saw her children, their faces lit with laughter as they sat by the fireplace. There were pages of them, Sophie Ann in various poses and Aaron as he tended the horse in the barn and sat on one knee, Duke sitting in front of him as if they were having a conversation.

When she saw herself on one of those yellowed pages, her mouth opened as she inhaled a shaky breath, her fingers pressed to her lips.

Noah had drawn her smiling, the expression on her face showing her glee. Another with sadness etched across her features. Page after page, he'd sketched her likeness with exact detail.

All but one.

A fluttering sensation tickled her stomach as she stared down at the sketch. She was wearing a dress like the ones she pictured those Southern belles in Charleston wore, the sleeves draped in such a way as to leave her shoulders bare, the neckline so low the top of her breasts were visible. Her hair wasn't chopped off as it is now. He'd drawn it long, the way it had once been, the curls falling down the length of her back to settle around her hips. Her pulse beat wildly as she stared at the woman looking back at her. Noah had drawn her as if she were beautiful. As if she were as lovely as his Isabelle.

Was this what Noah saw when he looked at her? Or was it what he wished she was?

She closed the book, squeezed her eyes shut and rubbed them to remove the dampness gathering there. She exhaled a breath, placed the book back on the shelf and wiped her cheeks dry, refusing to acknowledge the tears those drawings pulled from her and turned, her heart skipping a beat when she saw Noah. She hadn't heard him come in. He stared at her, his gray eyes guarded and curious and no matter how hard she tried, she couldn't get a word past her lips. Couldn't apologize for messing with his things. Or tell him how wonderful his drawings were. How beautiful she felt seeing herself reflected in his eyes.

Aaron and Sophie Ann burst through the door, their laughter dispelling the heaviness in the room. Noah glanced down at them when they ran past him to kneel at the chest at the foot of the bed, both of them yanking blankets out before standing back up.

They looked from her to Noah, and back again, Aaron's head tilting to one side. "Well, is she coming or not?"

Noah blinked. "I don't know. I haven't asked her yet."

Aaron sighed dramatically and shook his head. "Well ask her already. I want to go."

"Me too!" Sophie Ann squealed, jumping up and down as she clutched her blanket.

Keri raised an amused eyebrow at them before looking back at Noah, an unreadable expression on his face. "What did you want to ask me?"

Noah's eyes roamed her features before coming to rest on her lips. She saw him swallow, his throat moving with the action before he looked up. "We're going to get a tree."

"We're getting a Christmas tree," Sophie Ann shouted, her excitement infectious.

Keri smiled. Sophie Ann's cheeks were pink, her eyes shining. "A Christmas tree?"

"Yeah and Noah said we can decorate it all by ourselves."

Keri looked back at Noah. He still hadn't said anything but he was as amused at Sophie Ann's outburst as she was. She could see it in his eyes. She glanced back at the kids. "Then I guess I better get my coat."

The chorus of cheers dimmed as Aaron and Sophie Ann headed back outside. Noah turned as well, stopping when he reached the door, taking her coat from one of the pegs on the wall and holding it open for her.

There was that Southern gentleman in him shining again.

Neither said a word as she slipped her arms inside the coat, then buttoned it. When she was ready, Noah was still there, staring at her. He looked as if he wanted to say something, his eyes darting across her face. He sighed and opened the door, holding it open for her instead, then pulled it shut when they were both outside.

The horse stood by the barn, his warm breath fogging the air in front of him. There was some sort of small contraption resembling a sled hooked to him, Aaron and Sophie Ann already sitting on it wrapped in their blankets. They were talking to Duke who paced the yard behind them, his whole body moving side to side as he wagged his tail.

Noah started for the horse and she followed wordlessly. The sled wouldn't hold her, Sophie Ann and Aaron taking up what little space it provided, which meant she was on the horse. Would Noah ride with her or walk as he'd done when he brought them from the woods to his cabin all those weeks ago?

To her surprise, he climbed into the saddle himself. She stopped and stared up at him. When he'd settled, he reached for her. For some reason, butterflies swam in dizzying patterns in her stomach as she looked at his outstretched hand. She ignored them and lifted her arm.

He swooped her from the ground with little effort and set her down on his lap as bold as you please. His arms wound around her, the reins tucked into his hands and with a gentle urging, the horse was walking, the kids' happy squeals as the sled started moving and Duke's exuberant barking echoing across the prairie as he ran and jumped at their side.

They were headed toward the trees, in the same direction as the line shack they'd been hiding out in. It seemed so long ago that Noah had found them. But it hadn't been, just a few short weeks, but they'd settled into such a routine, it felt longer. Long enough Keri had the crazy desire to forget about heading to California and stay right here in Willow Creek instead.

Noah's current mood made that impossible. He was undoubtedly upset. She just wasn't sure what about. Was it her? Or the fact she'd forced their relationship into uncomfortable territory by kissing him? By baring her breasts to him?

Whatever it was, his continued silence was more than she could bear. She had to know one way or the other what was wrong. "Why are you not speaking to me?" she asked, not daring to look up at him.

He was silent so long, she wasn't sure he was going to answer. When he finally said, "I don't have anything to say to you," she wished she'd never asked.

Misery flooded her heart, ached inside her chest until it was a physical pain. "I'm sorry."

"For what?"

"For causing this. I should have never..." She sighed, picking at a loose thread on the front of her coat while shaking her head, loathed to finish the sentence. Truth be known, she wasn't sorry for kissing him. For seducing him into bedding her. Not one bit.

Noah touched her chin, nudged her to turn and look at him. He was so close, his warm breath fanned her face. His gray eyes darkened as he looked at her and he tilted his head a fraction to one side before saying, "Should have never what?"

She felt his words across her mouth, his rumbling voice, for once, soft, the barest of whispers stirring the air between them. She looked into his eyes and saw the same heated desire she'd seen the day before. "Kissed you," she whispered, answering his question.

"Why?"

Keri stared at his mouth, her pulse beating rapidly under her skin as she remembered the feel of his lips against her own. "Because I can't stop thinking about doing it again."

CHAPTER TWENTY-FOUR

N oah heard her as if she'd shouted, but he had a hard time processing what she'd said. She wanted to kiss him again? The knowledge nearly knocked the breath out of him.

He'd run through every emotion he could name trying to figure out what the hell was happening between them and why. As of yet, nothing made sense. They'd been so uncomfortable around each other at the town's Christmas party, his frustration making it hard to say more than three words to her without getting tongue tied. Then every single man in town had sauntered up to her as if she were on display just for their pleasure and that frustration had turned to anger, the fear she'd accept a marriage proposal from one of those prospective husbands despite his pretending to be married to her burning his gut until thoughts of violence ran like moving pictures inside his head.

And the blame for that fell completely on her shoulders.

Living alone for so long, and caring for nothing or no one, had given him a sense of peace. The people of Willow Creek may cross the street to avoid walking on the same side of the sidewalk as he did, but he ventured into town so seldom, he didn't really care. He'd grown complacent. Falling into a routine so mundane, that the moment it was disturbed, he hadn't known what to do.

Being thrust into providing and protecting this slip of a woman and her kids, a job he'd taken on for reasons he hadn't wanted to think about at the time, left him feeling.... exposed. For the first time in years, what he did mattered. Having Keri cast those shy smiles his way made the way he was perceived, matter.

The man he'd transformed into over the years wasn't the man he wanted to be now. He wasn't the man he wanted Keri to see. That man wasn't good enough for her smiles. He didn't deserve the things she did for him. The meals she cooked, or the clothes she washed, just so she'd feel as if she were paying him back for letting them stay with him. She'd softened him. Made him care.

Then she'd kissed him and stirred something he thought long dead. Something that made him vulnerable. And it scared the hell out of him.

He'd had his heart ripped out once and he wasn't in the mood to repeat old mistakes, but looking down at her upturned face, her lips only inches away from his, he thought it might be worth the risk to taste her once again. To take his time, soak in every aspect of her, remember the way she felt against him, and commit to memory the scent lingering on her skin. To never forget the sound of those tiny mewling sounds she made when he'd loved her.

All he had to do was move his head another few inches and he'd be able to taste her lips, to sate the longing he'd been struggling to ignore since he'd walked away from her, too afraid of what he'd see in her eyes if he lingered. But he saw now. He didn't understand why, but Keri still wanted him and even now, waited on him...

"Ma, are you and Noah kissin'?"

Keri jumped, her cheeks blooming bright red in an instant. She jerked away from him, her eyes wide as she peered over his shoulder at Aaron. "I most certainly am not," she told him, hastily. "We were just talking."

"Then why didn't I hear you say anything?"

If possible, her blush increased, her cheeks turning blistering scarlet. Noah smiled, guided the horse into the pines and bit his tongue to keep from laughing. He went as far as he could with the sled and tugged on the reins, getting the horse to stop near a cluster of trees.

"Are we there?" Sophie Ann asked.

Noah looked at Keri, her eyes darting at everything around her but him. "Yes, we're there." He looked over his shoulder at them. "You still got that hatchet, Aaron?"

The boy stood, his shoulders pulled back as if he were ten foot tall and lifted his arm to show him the hatchet. "Got it right here."

"All right then. Go find us a tree."

Sophie and Aaron tossed their blankets aside and took off at a run, Duke following on their heels as they darted between the small pines searching for the perfect tree. Noah watched them for long moments before turning his attention back to Keri. She was still blushing at Aaron thinking she was kissing him, something she'd said she couldn't stop thinking about. Heat surged through his body at the mere thought, images of them together flashing in his mind's eye and he hardened in an instant.

He lifted his hand, curled a finger under her chin so she'd look at him and waited until he knew he had her attention. Then he kissed her, the contact brief and soft, a mere brush of his lips against her own before he pulled away. "When we don't have an audience, I'd like to kiss you properly."

She blinked up at him and nodded her head before he scooted her off his lap and climbed from the horse. When he reached for her, settling his hands on her waist and lifting her from the horses back, the desire he saw shining in her eyes quickened his breath.

✳

A aron and Sophie hadn't been this happy since before John died. Keri watched them scouting the forest, looking for the perfect Christmas tree while snow swirled around them.

She'd found a tree to lean against to watch them. They were meticulous in their search, discarding trees for being too big, or not green enough. Their happy chatter was the perfect distraction. As long as she watched them, she could ignore the fact that she was so uncharacteristically nervous. The fact Noah leaned against the tree beside her only made it worse, those fluttering butterflies in her stomach flitting in ferocious patterns for no other reason than he was so near.

He'd yet to say anything since lifting her from the horse. Since giving her a barely there kiss with the promise of more. Her heart hadn't stopped pounding yet and her confusion at the sudden change in his attitude left her dizzy.

Had she been wrong about why he left so quickly after making love to her? About why he was so quiet and acted as if he didn't want to discuss what had happened?

She'd assumed his silence had been because of her. That he'd not enjoyed being with her. Robert certainly complained enough, being sure to tell her of every fault, then proceeding to instruct her how he wanted her to move and react. She'd never satisfied him and assumed that was the reason Noah left so abruptly, too.

But that soft kiss he'd given her.... It made no sense that he'd kiss her if he'd been disappointed. Would he?

He shifted beside her, crossing his arms over his chest as he watched Aaron and Sophie Ann. She noticed his gloved hands. He'd not removed those gloves when they'd tumbled onto the bed. Nor had he removed his clothes. He hadn't even pushed his pants down that she knew of. Not that unusual since their encounter had been so quick, she was barely undressed herself, but the more she thought about it, the more she began to wonder.

Was Noah hiding more than just his hands? And was that why he'd left so abruptly?

Sophie Ann squealed, her delighted giggles drawing her attention to them. It looked as if they'd found their tree. Aaron was determined to chop it down himself, apparently, and made Sophie Ann stand back until he was satisfied she was out of harm's way. Then he fell to his knees and swung the hatchet. It barely chipped the wood. Keri grinned. They'd be here until dark if Noah didn't eventually help him. "You know he'll never get that cut down by himself, don't you?"

One of those rare smiles of his turned the corners of his mouth. "I know." He glanced down at her. "I'll help him out when he's tired of trying."

Silence once again made her uncomfortable. She shook her head at the irony. She'd spent nearly two years wishing Robert would swallow his own tongue just so she didn't have to hear him talk. The man loved the sound of his own voice so much, he rarely ever shut up. She should be glad Noah was so quiet but, for some strange reason, she wasn't. Him being quiet unnerved her so she tried to think of something to say. Anything to break the silence.

The only thing she could think of caused her to squirm. As uncomfortable as she felt, she knew she needed to say something. She inhaled deeply, then once again, before clearing her throat. "I'm sorry for looking through your journal," she said, crossing her arms over her chest and glancing at her feet. "I had no right to look through your things."

For once, he answered right away. "It's fine." Out of the corner of her eye, she saw him turn his head to look at her. "They're just drawings."

"They're more than that." She recalled every sketch she saw, how perfectly he'd captured the faces of everyone he'd drawn. His life was etched into that book. She knew by looking that the scenes he'd drawn were from his memories. "It's rare for someone to have such talent, especially way out here in the middle of nowhere."

Silence fell again thick enough she thought she could touch it. Noah was still looking at her, his head tilted to one side as usual, but he unfolded his arms, sticking his hands into his coat pockets instead. "You liked them, then?"

Keri turned to look at him and nodded. "I think they're beautiful." The drawing of her flashed in her mind's eye. "All of them."

His gaze touched every feature of her face, the look in his eyes so warm, it felt like a soft caress. "Not nearly as beautiful as the real thing."

Her heart nearly beat out of her chest at his words. She knew he meant her, the play of emotions on his face told her as much.

They saw Aaron at the same time and looked his way. He was standing there staring at them, the hatchet in his hand, his chest rising and falling quickly. He'd worn himself out trying to chop down that tree.

Noah held his hand out, Aaron handing the hatchet over without a word. The tree fell minutes later, Sophie Ann still where Aaron had told her to stand.

The tree was tied to the end of the sled, the kids climbing back on and bundling up in the blankets. When Noah once again lifted her to his lap and started back to the house, the tension she'd felt since the day before was gone, the air around them less heavy.

Snow still fell, blanketing the world in white, and the warmth of the cabin when they made it back home, welcomed. Noah and Aaron built a base for the tree and set it next to the window, Sophie Ann's excitement still shining in her eyes as she watched.

They spent the rest of the evening decorating that little tree with bits of ribbon and hand drawn pictures Aaron and Sophie meticulously cut out with scissors. There wasn't much else to put on it, but they didn't seem to mind. The tree was enough. That and knowing they wouldn't miss Christmas.

It took three days for Willow Creek to thaw, the snow finally melting enough to take Aaron and Sophie back to school. Noah had lived alone for a damn long time and never once went stir crazy. Until now.

He tapped the last nail into the horseshoe and lowered the horse's leg, letting his hoof hit the ground then patted the animal on the neck. Tossing the hammer back into the box, his thoughts once again drifted back to Keri. Of that kiss he said he'd give her. A kiss he'd yet been able to have.

They hadn't had five minutes alone since they'd chopped the tree down and dragged it back to the house, the snow making it impossible to get to school, which meant Aaron and Sophie Ann were underfoot most of the day. They raced out to play for small snatches of time but it wasn't long enough. Noah wanted more than stolen kisses when the kids' backs were turned. He wanted to be able to linger and take his time about it. And the wait was killing him.

The horse throwing a shoe on the way home from town just prolonged his agony. Three days of her smiles, of those secret looks she gave him when she didn't think he noticed. Three days of waiting for a kiss.

He shook his head and guided the horse to his stall, securing the gate behind him. The trip from town took nearly half an hour and he'd had time aplenty then, but kissing her in the open seemed wrong. He checked the other animals, made sure they were settled and left the barn, anticipation thrumming through his veins.

A small fluttering sensation around his heart stopped him at the door, breathing difficult all of a sudden as a case of nerves prevented him from going inside. A dozen questions whispered across his mind just then, the loudest, asking him what he was doing, ringing inside his head. What *was* he doing? He sighed, ran a hand over his face and waited for an answer. One never came.

Thoughts of Keri plagued him daily and he couldn't get her out of his head. Nor did he want to, if he were honest with himself. He'd been alone for so long, it had taken time to get used to being around people again but now he had trouble imagining life without Keri and her kids in it.

And it scared the hell out of him.

The pain of what Isabelle had done to him had lessened over the years but he never wanted to feel the hurt of another loss like that. He knew Keri would never turn her back on him like Isabelle had, but she would leave him. The moment her brother contacted her, she'd leave, and he'd be left with nothing again. The thought caused his chest to ache.

But what if Peter never came?

Believing Keri's brother would never contact her would make things less complicated. He'd be free to explore whatever it was between them without fear of her leaving. Without ever having to give her up, and if he knew nothing else, it was that he didn't want to be without her. Even if she never loved him, having her look at him as if she enjoyed him being there was enough. To see those smiles she always graced him with.

That small fluttering in his chest grew until his heart was pounding, thoughts of keeping Keri always whispering inside his head. Would she stay with him if he asked her to? Would she stop pretending to be married to him and be a true wife instead? Did she want him enough to stay forever?

Ask her and find out.

Sweat broke out on his forehead. Common sense knocked the stupid notion out of his head and he took a cleansing breath and pushed the thought away. At the moment, he had more pleasant things to think about. Like that kiss he'd been waiting three long days for.

He opened the door with one thought whispering inside his

head. Regardless of what happened in the future, he'd be a fool if he didn't at least let Keri know how much he wanted her. Removing his hat and coat, he hung them on the peg by the door and looked around the room.

Then froze, his heart skipping a beat before racing inside his chest.

Keri was in the tub, light from the fireplace bathing her in soft shadows. She looked his way then stood, the water droplets shining on her skin sparkling as if she'd been dipped in diamonds.

When she lifted a leg and stepped out onto the rug, every delicious inch of her was bared for him. He took in every curve, dip and dimple, the swell of each breast, her pink nipples hard and pebbled. His gaze landed on the thatch of curly blond hair at the apex of her thighs and he suddenly forgot how to breathe.

CHAPTER TWENTY-FIVE

The shocked expression on Noah's face was quickly replaced by one so full of heat and longing, Keri's hands were shaking by the time her feet hit the floor.

She wasn't sure who moved first, him or her, but the moment he touched her, his hands cupping either side of her face, her fear of being so bold again vanished. He lowered his head, molding his mouth over hers, his tongue sliding inside in a kiss so ravenous, her knees buckled, gooseflesh dotting her arms as she leaned against him and wrapped her arms around his waist.

She'd thought for days that she'd imagined Noah's kiss much more amazing than it had been, but knew now every tingle she'd felt from nothing more than thinking about it had been earned. Noah's kiss was consuming, her thoughts scattering at the thrust and slide of his tongue licking against her own. Heat pooled between her legs, that incessant throb letting her know she was truly alive and all she could think about was him being inside of her again. Of feeling his warm flesh against her own.

Noah let go of her face, his hands sliding down her body until he cupped both her breasts, giving them a gentle squeeze before letting go, touching her everywhere he could reach while continuing to kiss her as if he'd never get another chance to do so. He wrapped his arms around her waist, lifted her from the floor and guided her legs around his hips, then carried her to the bed.

The blanket was cool against her back, Noah's warmth covering the front of her a shocking contrast. He pulled away from her mouth to pepper kisses along her jaw, over her collarbone to her breasts, and she arched her back when he latched onto her left nipple, his tongue flicking back and forth over the sensitive tip. She gasped at the feel of his teeth grazing her skin, the abrasive rasp of the whiskers on his face stinging her tender flesh.

Keri raised both hands, sliding her fingers into his hair and held him to her, heat surging through her limbs as she watched him suckle her. She closed her legs around him, that throbbing ache pulsing in her center drawing quick breaths from her lungs, her need intensifying until she threw her head back and cried out his name.

Noah let go of her breast, placed lingering kisses on the other, then kissed his way to her stomach, his tongue dipping into her navel before moving on. Her legs were trembling by the time he spread her knees wider, hot, open mouthed kisses leaving behind a trail of fire on her inner thighs.

Then he was there, the warmth of his breath and the velvety slide of his tongue delving into the very center of her, small shocks of pleasure coursing through her limbs as he licked and kissed the wet folds between her legs.

She raised her head, looked down at him and bit her lip when she locked eyes with him. He was watching her, his tongue doing the most delicious things and she couldn't look away. Spreading her knees farther apart, she raised her hips a fraction, sighing when he reached under her, cupping her bottom, and bringing her closer to his mouth.

Keri laid a hand to the back of his head, holding him to her. Coherent thought ceased, her senses heightened to every small touch, the gentle breeze of air blown onto her heated flesh, and the mind-numbing pleasure surging through her body. She dug her fingers into his hair, held him to her and rolled her hips, a moan so low and raw crawling up her throat she felt it to her toes, her trembling limbs shaking moments before she shattered, splintering apart from the erotic sway of his tongue between her legs until she was reformed, whole, and completely his.

He entered her before she'd even caught her breath, her mouth opening on a silent scream, the pleasure rippling through her body sending small spasms rolling through her limbs to leave her trembling.

She lifted her arms, wrapped them around him and held him close, seeking out his lips and sighing into his mouth when he kissed her. His hold on her tightened, his hips rocking back and forth while the hard length of him filled her until she felt consumed.

Noah gasped, the rhythm of his hips faltering before his grip on her tightened. Keri looked up to find him staring at her. Their eyes locked, his heated gaze stealing her breath as his thrusts became harder, her stomach clenching tight as tingles rode her limbs.

Her eyes fluttered, her breath catching. "Noah…" She gripped the material of his shirt in her hands, hooked one foot around his leg and tightened every muscle in her body.

He hissed her name, his lips hovering above her mouth. "Look at me."

The moment she locked eyes with him, saw his intense hunger shining down at her, she shuddered, a harsh cry spilling from her lips as she climaxed again. Waves of pleasure rode her limbs, Noah's hold on her tightening before he buried his face against her neck, his body stiffening, then jerking, their mingled cries muffled against each other's shoulders.

Keri didn't know how long it took for her body to stop shaking, for her heart to resume a normal beat, but she'd still not let go of Noah, her arms and legs tight as she held him against her. His breath was warm against her neck, his weight solid and comforting. When he finally stirred, she mourned the loss of him even though he was still pressed intimately against her. He kissed her neck, the pressure so light it tickled the fine hairs on her skin.

Raising up and propping his weight on his elbows, he looked down at her, some unidentifiable emotion shining in his eyes before he lowered his head and kissed her, the contact soft and sweet, his tongue teasing the tip of hers before he sucked her bottom lip into his mouth.

Then he was gone, rolling to lie beside her. Keri stared up at the ceiling, trying to catch her breath and silently thanking him for not leaving. For staying with her, even if he was just lying by her side.

Neither spoke for a long time, the ticking of the clock and the crack and pop of wood in the fireplace the only sounds in the room. Keri wondered what he was thinking but was too afraid to ask. Her mind was too jumbled with thoughts to form a coherent sentence anyway.

She'd been bedded by John, and taken by Robert more times than she could count and not once had she ever felt anything so exhilarating as what she experienced when she was with Noah. She wasn't even sure how it was possible to feel so much pleasure without it bursting from her skin. Tiny sparks were still firing in her muscles, the jolts left her feeling languid and sated.

Noah turned his head to look at her. She could see him out of the corner of her eye and she inhaled a deep breath, readying herself for whatever it was he was about to say. She feared the worst, past experience conditioning her to expect it, so her body tensed on its own accord.

He rolled to his side to face her and it took every ounce of courage she had to look at him. His eyes were so clear they looked silver in the low light and her pulse leaped for no reason whatsoever.

"What happened to me giving you a kiss once we had a bit of privacy?" He smiled, a genuine, honest to God, smile and Keri felt as if she were melting as he looked at her. "Not that this was in any way a disappointment," he said. "Quite the opposite, in fact."

She laughed and covered her face with her hands as her cheeks heated. He shifted, his body touching her from shoulder to ankle before he kissed her neck.

He pulled her hands from her face, amusement shining in his eyes when she looked up at him. "Seducing me is very unneces-sary." He grinned again, his hand raising to cup her breast, his thumb rasping against her nipple until it hardened and ached. "I've thought of little else but bedding you since the last time you gave yourself to me."

Heat flooded her face again. "It's been three days," she said. "I thought you'd changed your mind about that kiss you promised me. That's why…"

He interrupted her by laughing. "I didn't forget. I just wanted more than stolen kisses when the kids' backs were turned." He leaned in, his lips sliding softly against her own. "I wanted time to enjoy you at my leisure."

Keri sighed against his mouth as he kissed her properly, proving his point by lingering so long, her heart was racing when he pulled slightly away, nibbling on her bottom lip. "We've got hours yet before school is dismissed. Is that enough time for all the kisses you wanted?"

"Not hardly, but it's a start."

She grinned, rolled toward him, and let him have all the kisses he felt like taking. Their breaths were labored, his hands roaming her flesh and a small voice in the back of Keri's mind noted that he was still wearing those gloves, his clothes still fastened and in place while she was as naked as the day she was born.

Reaching for the top button of his shirt, she unhooked it, slid her hand inside the material to touch his skin and was startled when he grabbed her, flipped her to her back and captured her hands, holding them above her head as he rolled on top of her and settled between her legs.

His kisses never stopped, her thoughts scattering with every wet, open mouthed touch, but she knew he was hiding something under all that fabric. His reaction to her touching him had been too quick and she was determined to find out what it was he didn't want her to see.

The Christmas recital had Aaron and Sophie bouncing with excitement. They rehearsed the lines they were supposed to say repeatedly, fidgeted as she combed their hair, the ribbons she'd tried to tie into Sophie Ann's blond curls coming undone twice before she got her to hold still long enough to get them in place, and she'd run herself ragged making sure their best clothes were clean and presentable before she'd even thought about supper.

Noah opened the door, stomping snow off his boots before coming inside. He locked eyes with her, that heated, knowing look in his gaze never failing to quicken her pulse. Aaron ran to him, his nervous energy visible from across the room. "We're going to stay for the whole thing, right, Noah? Until after we've had cake and presents?"

Like he'd done so many times in the past week, Noah smiled, the sight never failing to take Keri's breath. He tore his eyes from her to look down at Aaron. "I said we'd stay until it was over and I meant it."

Aaron's shoulders relaxed as a whoosh of breath left his lungs, the relief on his face evident. Keri grinned, finished tying the sash at the back of Sophie Ann's dress and stood. "Now you two don't get dirty," she said, fixing them with a hard stare as she walked to the kitchen. "I'll get us something to eat on the table as quick as I can, and then we can go."

"Don't," Noah said, reaching out to grab her hand when she neared him.

She stopped. "Don't what?"

He looked as if he'd changed his mind about whatever it was he was going to say, but the uncertain look she'd seen lingering in his gaze was chased away when she squeezed his hand. He inhaled a breath, his eyes roaming her face. "I want to take you into town for supper." He threaded his fingers between hers, his grip tightening. "I had us a table saved over at the hotel."

Keri's eyes widened, shock at his words sending a jolt rushing through her limbs. Noah hated going into town, especially if he had to linger with the townsfolk, and him arranging for them to eat at the hotel was so out of character for him, she wondered who the man in front of her was. "Are you sure you want to do that?"

He nodded, his thumb brushing gently against the back of her hand, the look in his eyes filled with warmth and she suddenly felt like a school girl with her first suitor, her heart started beating so fast. She'd never experienced the exhilaration of being courted, of having someone go out of their way to make her feel special. She was way past the age for such fanciful thoughts, but looking up at Noah, she imagined his quiet invitation to supper as just that. She smiled at him and tightened her hold on his hand. "I've never eaten in a restaurant before."

Noah leaned closer to her, his gaze lingering on her lips. "Then I suggest you get your coat on so we can remedy that."

They were bundled in their coats, Aaron and Sophie running out the door ahead of them, their excited voices sounding farther away as they ran from the house. Noah pulled her to him and left a series of lingering kisses on her mouth, his tongue teasing hers until her skin felt tight and twitchy.

Her eyes remained closed after he pulled away, the bliss she felt causing a contented sigh to escape. *Hmmm....I'll never get tired of you kissing me.*

"Well, that's good to know."

Keri's eyes flew open, then widened. "Good Lord, did I say that out loud?"

Noah threw his head back and laughed, the sound so joyous, Keri's embarrassment was minimal. Her face still heated enough she ducked her head but she grinned in spite of the blurted sentiment when he pulled her against him, his chuckles causing his entire body to shake.

When he calmed and kissed her on the top of her head, his arms closing around her tighter, she sighed, enjoying the feel of him. She may not have meant to say the words out loud, but she'd meant them. And maybe now that he knew how much she enjoyed them, he'd give her more of his kisses with each passing day.

CHAPTER TWENTY-SIX

They hadn't been sitting in the hotel restaurant for five minutes and Keri was ready to leave. Thankfully she'd taken the chair facing the majority of the other diners. Noah didn't have to see the stares directed at them but the look on his face said he already knew.

A thin woman with unfriendly eyes stopped by her side and handed them menus, her gaze darting to Noah every few seconds. The rude woman nearly threw a menu at him which set Keri's pulse to racing so fast she was sure her head would explode, her blood was rushing through her veins so quick.

When the woman left, giving them time to decide what they wanted, Keri reached across the table, grabbing Noah's hand to get his attention, then leaned forward and kept her voice pitched low. "We can leave," she said. "I don't want you to be—"

"It's fine." He cut her off mid-sentence, squeezing her hand. "I'm used to them staring. They'll get tired of it eventually."

Keri sighed. "Are you sure?"

"Yes." He glanced at the kids, who were looking over the menu neither of them could read. "I won't ruin their night by running away because some old biddies can't stop staring at me. Besides," he said, lowering his voice to a whisper, "they're probably just trying to get a good look at the woman brave enough to be my wife."

The way he said, "be my wife," made Keri think he meant it, that it was real, that she had indeed married him. And that secret place in her heart wished it were true.

She had no idea what he felt for her, if he could ever love her, but she knew he cared and that was enough. He protected them and provided everything they needed, and his small cabin felt more like home than her own home ever had, but she had no idea if he wanted them on a permanent basis and was too afraid to ask.

When the woman came back to the table to take their order, Keri kept a hold of his hand, ordered what she wanted and never took her eyes off him. If the people of Willow Creek wanted something to talk about, then she'd give them something. She'd let them see how much Noah's new family loved him.

The moment the thought popped into her head, Keri's heart raced as the truth of it surged through every fiber of her being. She stared at him, his gloved hand held between her own and she understood now what that fluttering feeling was in her chest when he looked at her. Why his kisses caused her entire body to burn, why she missed him when he was only gone a few minutes.

She'd fallen in love with him. A man who at one time had scared the life out of her with his harsh tone of voice and wild, untamed appearance. A man who cared for their well being when no one else in the world had.

His thumb brushed the back of her hand and she looked up to see him staring at her. He looked so different now. The scar was still on his face, and his barbered hair and beard were a notice-able difference, but it was more than that. Something in his eyes made him look less... harsh. As if the anger she'd seen there before had vanished. She'd like to think she was the reason why, but other than those wonderful kisses and intense bed play, Noah had given her no indication he wanted more. And it was the not knowing that kept her nerves on edge. If he ever asked her to leave, she'd be heartbroken.

Their food arrived, Aaron and Sophie Ann's excited ramblings joining in with the chorus of other voices filling the air. The curious stares from the restaurant patrons were stopped when she boldly stared back at anyone looking their way and by the time they'd finished eating and were outside on the sidewalk, Keri had forgotten all about those nosey, rude people she'd had every intention of giving a piece of her mind to.

The street was filled with wagons now, the sidewalks full of bustling families all making their way toward the school. Aaron and Sophie were bouncing, their nervous energy infectious. Keri grinned as she followed them, listening as they both repeated their verses over and over again.

Noah grabbed her arm when they reached the school and stopped her. He stared at the building, a worried expression on his face. "You go on in," he said, not bothering to look at her. "I have something I need to do first."

He gave no other explanation, just turned and walked back down the street. Keri watched him go, her shoulders falling as she sighed. He'd been so quiet through supper. The stares of those in the restaurant caused him to withdraw, the crowd trying to get inside that little school house chasing him away from her and the kids, as well.

"Is Noah coming back?"

Keri looked down at Sophie Ann and smiled. "He said he had something he needed to do." She fixed the ribbon in Sophie Ann's hair, tucking stray curls in around it. "I'm sure he won't chance missing either of you as you get up to recite your lines. He'll be back." She hoped he'd be back, but something told her he wouldn't.

Sophie Ann and Aaron believed he would for they hurried up the sidewalk and in to the school. Keri followed them, stopping to glance back down the street in search of Noah. She couldn't see him. There were too many people on the sidewalks.

The school building was filled with parents, the noise level high as everyone seemed to be talking at once, and the air was filled with the scent of pine and spices. Keri smiled while taking it all in. The room was decorated with greenery and red and gold ribbons. A large tree sat in the far corner, wrapped packages underneath it with colorful ribbons holding the plain brown paper on them. She could hear music but couldn't see where it was coming from and craned her neck to look toward the front of the room.

Movement in the corner of her eye caught her attention and she turned her head to see Dr. Reid coming her way. He smiled, his warm brown eyes shining as he stared down at her.

"Mrs. Lloyd," he said. "It's good to see you. I take it you're feeling better?"

Keri smiled, a tingle of pleasure rippling up her spine at hearing Dr. Reid call her Mrs. Lloyd. He was the only one who did so and even though it wasn't real, it still felt nice to hear.

They talked of nothing in particular until he was pulled away by a group of elderly ladies. Keri stood quietly by herself, wishing Noah had come in with her, melancholy beginning to take hold before Sarah and Emmaline Avery walked into her line of sight.

The women stopped much to Keri's surprise, both of them offering her a friendly smile. Sarah held her young daughter by the hand while Emmaline's infant son was nestled close to her chest. "We saw Sophie Ann a few moments ago," Sarah said. "I don't think I've ever seen anyone as excited as she is."

Keri grinned. "You probably haven't. I can't remember the last time Sophie Ann and Aaron had so much fun. They've been looking forward to the recital for weeks now."

"I think every child in Willow Creek has been." Sarah stared at her, a spark of amusement shining in her eyes. "You look different, Keri."

"Oh?" Keri's brow scrunched as she tried to think of what Sarah could see different. She raised a hand, smoothed down her unruly curls and shrugged. "How so?"

Emmaline glanced at Sarah and grinned. "She's near to glowing, don't you think?"

Sarah nodded. "Yes, that and something in her eyes."

Both women smiled, their gazes locked on Keri so long, she started fidgeting. Someone touched her arm and she turned to see Abigail standing slightly behind her, grinning.

"Leave her alone," Abigail said, shaking her head. "They're teasing you, Keri. We saw you when you got into town and were walking to the hotel restaurant. Laurel noted that you actually looked happy, that's what these two are talking about." She laughed and squeezed Keri's arm. "They like to stir the pot every once in a while."

"We most certainly do not," Sarah said. She sounded offended but the glimmer in her eyes gave her away. "I was just making an observation. She does look happy."

"Glowing," Emmaline said.

Keri's face heated and she wished there were a mirror nearby. She wanted to see what it was these women saw when looking at her but Laurel got everyone's attention and asked them to take a seat. Sarah and Emmaline said their goodbyes and headed toward the front of the room with Abigail following behind them. Keri found a bench halfway up the isle. She perched near the end so she could see Aaron and Sophie when it was their turn to take center stage.

The wicks in the lamps were lowered until the majority of the room was bathed in warm shadows, but the front of the room was bright with light, the kids all standing near the wall seen very clearly. Sophie Ann's head was darting from one side to the other as she rose up on her toes. She finally spotted her and Keri smiled and wiggled her fingers in her direction.

When the children were hushed, Laurel Avery, sitting at the

front of the room, raised a hand, the children all opening their mouths to sing as one. The tune was loud, a few voices screeching above the others, but Keri had never heard anything so wonderful. Aaron and Sophie Ann looked so happy, their beaming smiles lighting their faces from across the room.

One song turned into two, then each child on the stage began to step forward, retelling the story of a babe in a manger. Someone touched her shoulder and she looked up, surprised to see Noah standing there looking down at her. Her delight in seeing him was obscured by the dim lighting in the room. She slid over so he'd have room to sit, the smile on her face widening when Noah reached for her hand, weaving his fingers together with hers.

He'd come back to them after all.

He hadn't missed them. Noah sighed in relief, Keri's grip on his hand tightening as Sophie Ann walked to the front of the make-shift stage and started reciting her verse. She got tongue-tied and had to start over three times before getting it out.

Every child there had a turn until the story was told. There were songs, even one sang by Betsy Atwater, her angelic voice catching the attention of everyone there as she stood alone in the front of the crowd.

By the time the program was over, Noah's hesitation about coming in had vanished, especially when Sophie Ann, her face flushed, ran toward them and slid into the row to stand between him and Keri.

"Did you see me?" she asked, her eyes wide and luminous. She looked back and forth between them. "I got messed up but I said it."

Noah smiled. "I think you were the best one."

Her eyes widened. "You think so?"

"Absolutely."

She grinned and held her arm out, Noah noticing the paper she was holding. "I made you this."

Noah stared at her, then at the paper. It was a drawing. "You made it for me?"

"Yep. And I did it all by myself."

Reaching for the drawing, he turned it and stared down at what Sophie had drawn, his chest tightening the instant he realized what she'd done.

The drawing was nothing more than four stick people with wide smiling faces and what he assumed was a dog. A small structure was off to one side, the cabin, if he had to guess, with a round sun in the top corner, the rays long and pointing down at everything below. It wasn't the clumsy lines that made Noah's eyes sting but the words someone had printed at the top. *My Family*, it said, with each of their names underneath one of those stick figures. Seeing his name there with Keri, Aaron and Sophie Ann's caused something in his chest to tighten and pinch and he had to swallow twice before he could say anything. "You drew this for me?" he asked.

"Yep." She pointed to everyone, telling him who each person was even though their names were there, and smiled the whole time she did. "Everybody had to draw what they wanted for Christmas but I already got what I wanted." She grinned up at him. "Can I have cake now?"

His throat was so tight he couldn't speak. He'd never been so glad when Keri said, "Is that cake all you've been thinking about?"

"It's chocolate," Sophie said, as if that alone was reason enough.

"Oh, well, let's go get in line then." Keri stood and stared down at him. The look on her face told him nothing of what she felt about the drawing but she tightened her hold on his hand briefly before she let go.

He watched her walk away, trying not to think too much about Sophie's drawing and focused on the fact that Keri wasn't afraid to be seen in public with him, or too afraid to boldly hold his hand when anyone looking at them could see. She left him feeling out of sorts and he wasn't sure why.

Keri had never acted unfriendly toward him. Not even when he was bellowing at her like a crazy person and scaring them half to death. She'd tip-toed around him, spoken softly in his presence and somehow broken through that hardened exterior he'd spent years erecting.

And in the privacy of his cabin, she gave him everything else he never thought to have again. A sense of belonging, of being part of a family just as Sophie's drawing suggested.

He stared at her, watched the sway of her hips as Sophie Ann pulled her toward the table of goodies at the front of the room. He still had trouble believing she'd so freely give herself to him, every day if he wanted, and most days he did. He couldn't seem to get enough of her. His pulse leaped just thinking of the times she gave herself to him.

Denying himself the company of a woman for twelve years got easier with time but now that he'd indulged, it was all he seemed to think about. The last few weeks had been so life changing, he'd had a hard time coming to terms with it at first. He still had a hard time believing Keri actually wanted him most days, but every kiss she gave him told him she did. Every time she bared herself for him, stretching across his bed and opening her arms to him so he could love her, left him in awe, his heart near to bursting as she gazed up at him as if he were the only man she'd ever wanted.

He just wished they didn't have to pretend nothing had changed. He wanted to be affectionate toward her and not be afraid to show it. To hold her hand when the lights were bright and not hide his feelings for her.

Telling her goodnight, and watching her slip behind those

blankets he'd hung around the bed left him restless. He wanted to join her there, to hold her close when he closed his eyes. To hear her soft sighs as he drifted off to sleep.

Those thoughts led to the realization that he wanted to be a proper husband to her, to build those extra rooms onto the cabin like he'd imagined doing and let every person in Willow Creek who ever looked down on him know that he wasn't the monster they all thought him to be. That Keri didn't see him as they did. That despite their ridicule, she wanted him.

Movement to his left tore his attention from Keri. Morgan Avery stopped beside him and Noah stood, shaking Morgan's outstretched hand. "I'm really glad to see you here, Noah."

The Avery men had been a burr in his hide for so long, he should have been used to them approaching him, but it still amazed him when they stopped to talk. And for the first time, Noah didn't much mind that they sought him out. "I couldn't miss Sophie Ann's acting debut," he said. "She would have never forgiven me."

The marshal laughed and crossed his arms over his chest, looking across the room to the line of kids waiting on their share of the goodies that had been brought for them. "Those kids look a lot happier than they did when you brought them to me after the blizzard." He slanted a look back at Noah. "Everything's been good at home?" Noah nodded in reply and the inquisitive look on Morgan's face intensified. "That's good." He leaned in, his voice pitched low when he said, "The rumor we spread worked its way through town in a matter of days. You should consider making those fake rumors a reality."

He'd thought about it, but Noah kept the knowledge to himself. He wasn't sure he'd ever get the courage to ask Keri to stay with him but if he did, she'd be the first to hear it, not Morgan Avery.

They finally parted ways, Morgan headed to the front of the room where his wife and girls stood. Noah spotted Keri and

Sophie Ann walking his way, his chest tightening at the very sight of them, and smiled when he saw the chocolate frosting smeared across Sophie Ann's face.

She slid onto the bench beside him and sat down, devouring her cake as if she'd not eaten an hour before. She looked up at him and smiled. Morgan was right. She did look happy. They all did. And he couldn't help but wonder why. Was it because he'd given them a place to call home or was it more than that?

A commotion at the door caught Noah's attention, raised voices, then a shout, people scurrying to look outside. Someone yelled for Dr. Reid and the noise grew until the entire room was in chaos.

Noah looked for Aaron. He didn't see him. "Sophie Ann, where's your brother?"

"He went outside with the big kids."

Outside where the commotion was. Noah looked at Keri. "Stay here. I'll go find him and see what's going on."

Getting out the door took a bit of shoving but he managed to make it to the steps. The crowd on the lawn was nearly as big as the one inside, the voices growing louder as he searched for Aaron in the sea of bodies.

He spotted him near the gate, his heart nearly stopping when he saw blood running down his face.

CHAPTER TWENTY-SEVEN

Noah made his way across the yard, Aaron finally spotting him. Tears shined in his eyes as he drew closer, blood dripping from his nose faster than Dr. Reid could stop it. He was glad Keri had stayed inside.

"What happened?" he asked, when he'd made it to Aaron's side.

"I got caught up in a fight."

"A fight?" Noah looked the kid over, placing a hand on his shoulder and turning him this way and that to see if he was hurt anywhere else. His clothes looked a bit scruffy but other than the bloody nose, he looked fine. "Who were you fighting?"

Aaron's eyes widened. "I wasn't fightin' nobody," he said. "I just got in the way." He turned his head and pointed to his right. "They were the ones fighting."

Noah looked in the direction Aaron pointed, to where the majority of people were standing and saw the culprits, his own eyes widening when he realized who it was. Holden Avery's tomboy daughter was red-faced and fighting mad, her blond hair in a tangle around her head. She was glaring at the same redhead kid Noah had seen when he'd brought Keri and the kids to town to leave them with the marshal. The boy had been trapped in the house with the rest of the school kids. Jesse, the marshal had called him, if he remembered correctly, was sporting a few scratches on his face and his right eye wasn't open all the way. Grace Kingston, the blonde woman Holden had introduced him to in the mercantile two months back stood by the boy's side.

Looking back down at Aaron, Noah raised an eyebrow. "Alexandra Avery was involved in the fight?"

"Alex *was* the fight." Aaron shook his head and took hold of the towel Dr. Reid had put under his nose. "She got mad at Jesse. Him and Alex are always going at it and end up fightin' at least once a week."

Noah stared back across the school yard. "He hits her?"

Aaron laughed. "Gosh no. He just lets her knock him about and laughs at her while she does it. And that's why she always comes up swingin'." He looked back over at them and grinned. "I think they're sweet on each other but just too stubborn to know it yet."

"He'll be fine," Dr. Reid said, getting Noah's attention as he stood. "He just got too close to those wild punches Alex was throwing."

Noah thanked the man before he walked off, watching as he crossed the yard to where Jesse and Alexandra were standing. He turned his attention back to Aaron who was still bleeding into the towel. "You going to be okay?"

He nodded his head. "Yeah." Neither said a word for long minutes, both of them watching Alexandra and Jesse, then Aaron glanced at him before looking away again. "Can I ask you something?"

The tone of Aaron's voice told him whatever it was he wanted to know was serious enough to cause the boy a bit of grief. He was looking at his feet, one leg bouncing. Noah bent his knees, squatting to be eye level with him. "You can ask me anything, Aaron."

He wiped his nose again, pulled the towel away to see if he was still bleeding, then sighed. "Benjamin said his pa told him my ma couldn't be his and Betsey's new ma now cause she'd done went off and married you. He said his pa was spittin' mad about it." He looked up, a hopeful look in his eyes. "Did you really marry my ma? Do we get to stay here with you now?"

Noah inhaled a breath, then let it out slowly, and tried to think of what to say. He stared across the yard, watching as the crowd broke apart and chose his words carefully. "It's a bit complicated, Aaron."

"How so?"

When Noah looked back over at him, that hopeful look was still in his eyes. He would have given anything to tell the kid yes, to lie his ass off to keep that look on the boy's face, but couldn't risk it. If Keri's brother showed up and took them away, Aaron wouldn't understand. He lowered his voice so no one would overhear and said, "Can you keep a secret?" When Aaron nodded his head at him, Noah cleared his throat. "We told everyone that me and your ma got married so no one would speak ill of her. A woman living with a man without marrying him just isn't done, so we said we got married so no one would talk."

That hope shining in Aaron's eyes vanished in an instant. He stared at him long minutes before looking away. Noah saw the glassiness in his eyes, tears forming before he blinked them away. "What is it, Aaron?"

He sighed, then lifted a hand to rub his eyes. "Benjamin said that it was okay he didn't get a new ma cause me and Sophie just got a new pa instead, and that meant one of us at least got something good for Christmas." He looked back over at him, tears still gathering. "But if you and my ma ain't really married…"

He stopped talking when those tears slipped past his lashes and he raised both hand, wiping his face dry. Noah had thought for years he knew what heartache was but looking at Aaron, watching him cry because those innocent lies they'd been telling hadn't given the boy a new pa like he thought, ripped his heart in two. His throat tightened until it was hard to breathe, pressure in his head increasing until he had to inhale a deep breath just to clear it, and the slight sting in his eyes increased until he too was blinking to chase tears away.

Reaching up to run his hand over Aaron's head, Noah leaned in closer to him to try and explain, to take some of the hurt out of his eyes, but Keri's voice interrupted him. Aaron stiffened and said, "Don't let her know I got sucker punched by a girl, okay?"

Noah held back a smile and nodded. "Sure thing," he said, then stood as Keri rushed across the yard toward them. She gasped when she saw Aaron, panic setting in before she even knew what was wrong. "He's fine. He was just in the wrong place at the wrong time."

Keri fussed over the boy like mothers do and Noah couldn't take his eyes off them, Aaron's words playing on repeat inside his head and leaving him in stunned silence.

Sophie Ann stood to his left, the drawing she'd given him inside the school still clutched in her small hand. The family she'd drawn seemed like a given only minutes ago, but now those old doubts and insecurities crept in until it felt like a dream he couldn't quite grab hold of.

A small voice in the back of his head whispered things he'd not dreamed of having since he left Charleston, but the moment Keri and those kids came barreling into his life, they were there for the taking and he knew all he had to do was have enough courage to put his heart on the line again and ask Keri to marry him.

And he would…

If only the thought of her saying no didn't tear a piece of his heart out, he'd ask her tonight. He'd tell Aaron nothing would make him happier than to be his pa, but the fear he felt in taking that step was greater than his desire to make it happen. He'd wallowed in his own despair for so long, it was hard to walk away from it. He wasn't even sure he could.

Regardless of what he wanted, there was no telling if Keri would want to spend her life with him. She may give her body to him, and act as if she enjoyed it when she did, but that wasn't enough to build a relationship on. It wasn't enough for him. He wanted more than her kindness and attention. He wanted her love and he really didn't think that was possible. Isabelle certainly couldn't do it once she'd seen what had been done to him. And Keri wouldn't either.

K eri watched Noah shut the barn door behind him, then sighed. Something about him was off and it was driving her crazy that she couldn't figure out what it was.

Ever since the night of the Christmas program, Noah seemed a bit distracted. He still acted the same, talked no more or less than usual, and still gave her those toe curling kisses when they were alone but something in his eyes told her he was preoccupied. Something that plagued him constantly. She'd see it when he didn't know she was looking and fear coiled in her stomach every time she caught a glimpse of it.

Her overactive imagination conjured all sorts of things that could be bothering him. Things that had to do with her and their situation and that fear she felt when seeing that far off look in his eyes grew until she spent most of her time fretting over something she had no idea if it was even worth fretting over.

Her hands submerged in soapy dish water, she closed her eyes. She was driving herself crazy with worry and the sleep she was losing was going to take a toll sooner or later.

Something brushed her back and a harsh gasp was pulled from her throat. Her eyes snapped open as Noah slid his arms around her waist moments before his warm breath tickled the back of her neck.

"Did I scare you?" he asked, kissing the tender skin along her hairline.

She smiled. "Yes. I didn't hear you come in."

He made a small "hmm" noise. "You did look deep in thought." he said while continuing to kiss his way around her neck. "Were you thinking about me?"

Keri tilted her head, giving him room to place all those kisses he was determined to give her. She leaned back against his chest, closed her eyes as shivers raced up her spine when he started unhooking the buttons on the front of her dress. "I might have been."

She felt him smile against the side of her neck. "Were you thinking we should go mess up those bed covers you just straightened?"

"You're a mind reader now?" She grinned. "What other talents have you been keeping from me?" Her need to touch him grew by the second. She arched her back, his erection pressing into her bottom as he untied her shift, pulling the material apart and cupping her breasts in his gloved hands, pinching her nipples between his thumb and forefinger.

Tingling sparks shot down her spine, her breath catching as she pulled her hands from the dish water, not bothering to dry them before reaching behind her to cup that growing bulge in his pants. He hissed a breath as she turned her head toward him as far as she could and caught his mouth, kissing him as his groping hands caused moisture to pool between her legs.

The odd angle of the kiss made her more desperate for it, her body clenching tight as she strained to keep her mouth locked with his. He slid his tongue along her lips, then slipped in, licking inside her mouth while pulling her skirts up and sliding his hand between her legs.

Keri gasped, Noah taking advantage of her open mouth to

deepen the kiss as he untied her bloomers, then delving inside the material. The moment she felt his gloved fingers touch her, she sucked in a breath and broke the kiss. "Noah, take your gloves off. I want to feel *you* touching me."

He stilled, his very breath halting. When he pulled away, she almost regretted saying anything. He let go of her, dropped her skirt and turned around without a word. She watched him leave the room while her chest ached at his quick retreat.

It took her long minutes to decide what to do. Whatever he didn't want anyone to see bothered him enough to keep it hidden every hour of every day and no one should have to live their life like that. She dried her hands, pulled the front of her dress closed so her breasts weren't exposed, retied her underwear, and followed him into the other room. He was staring into the fireplace, one palm resting on the mantel, his head bowed. She crossed the room and stopped behind him, almost afraid to touch him.

Her hands were shaking when she reached out to him. He didn't pull away. He didn't react at all. Keri closed the distance between them and wrapped her arms around him the same way he'd done to her, then laid her cheek against his back. Neither spoke a word but she could feel his heart pounding in his chest. "What is it, Noah?" When he didn't reply, she tightened her hold on him. "Whatever it is, you can tell me." He still gave no answer. Keri lifted her head, but didn't let go of him. "Why do you never take those gloves off?"

He sighed and was quiet so long, she didn't think he was going to answer. She held her breath and nearly sighed herself when he spoke. "I don't want you to see, Keri."

"See what?"

"Me."

"Why?"

A harsh laugh shook his chest but the sound was so forlorn,

her eyes filled with tears just hearing it. "Because I can't bear to see the look on your face when you do."

Keri stepped around him, made him turn so she could see him. He wouldn't look at her, the expression on his face one she'd never seen. He looked so miserable, as if his whole world had crumbled before his very eyes.

She grabbed his hands, squeezed until he finally looked down at her. "If you can't show me, then tell me. Make me understand, Noah." The misery in his eyes broke her heart. She looked down at his hands, tightened her hold on him. "This happened during the war?" He nodded and kept his gaze averted. "Tell me what happened."

He was silent so long, Keri was afraid he'd never tell her. He finally looked up, his eyes filled with pain and misery. And resignation. "Three days before the war ended, a small regiment of Yankee soldiers set fire to the barn we were bunked down in. Only seven of us made it out."

Keri glanced down at his gloved hands and held her emotions in check, her hold on him never loosening. "Were you burned?"

He nodded. "I was outside when the fire started. I couldn't sleep and needed some air." He locked eyes with her. "When I saw the flames, all I could think of was Dwight. We'd grown up as close as brothers. I'd promised his momma to bring him home safe, so I ran in to get him."

His eyes grew glassy and Keri moved closer. "Were you able to get him out?" she asked, already knowing the answer by the look on his face.

"No." He got a far off look in his eyes as if he was remembering the events as they were happening. "That old barn was filled with dried hay and it didn't take long for it to go up. There was so much smoke, and the screams..." He looked across the room, inhaled a deep breath and kept going. "All I could think about was getting to Dwight and getting him out. When I found him..." He paused again, took a shuddering breath, and closed his eyes. "He was burning. One of the roof timbers had fallen on him. I didn't think. I just grabbed it and tried to pull it off. I didn't notice I was on fire until I realized Dwight wasn't moving, that he wasn't helping me move that beam."

He opened his eyes, those tears still lingering above his lashes. "Its damn near impossible to put out a fire when you're surrounded by dry hay. The more I moved, the more the fire around me grew. The roof started to fall in, pain exploded on my face and the next thing I remember, I was looking up into a starless sky with voices shouting all around me."

"Someone pulled you out?"

"Yes, and there are days I wished they wouldn't have."

He sighed, those tears slipping from his eyes and Keri reached up to wipe them away, not realizing her own were falling until everything around her went blurry. She cupped his face in her hands, leaned up on her toes to kiss him and felt some measure of relief when he wrapped his arms around her. "If they wouldn't have pulled you out, Noah, me and Aaron and Sophie Ann would be dead right now, probably frozen to death out in that old line shack." His arms tightened around her waist, his head lowering until their foreheads touched. "You may not have been able to save your friend, but you saved us."

She kissed him again, kissed him for so long and so thoroughly, a bit of his sorrow was washed away. She could tell by the way he cupped her bottom in his hands, pulled her against him until she could feel his growing erection pressing into her stomach and she didn't let go of him until her lungs were burning for lack of air.

They were both breathing heavily, their arms wound tight around each other and Keri ran her fingers through his hair, rubbing the end of her nose against his cheek. "Let me see what you've been hiding from me, Noah."

He stiffened but didn't pull away. Keri took it as a good sign, lowered her arms, and reached for his hands. She waited, watching his face, every emotion he felt displayed there for her.

His nod was so slight she was afraid she imagined it, but he never protested when she started to tug at those leather gloves she'd never seen him take off.

CHAPTER TWENTY-EIGHT

Keri didn't know what she'd find when she removed that leather, and concentrated on not making a sound. For no emotion to show on her face. She didn't want Noah to make any assumptions about what she thought until she could see exactly what it was he was too afraid for her to see.

When the first glove slipped away, she bit her lip and reached for his other hand. She realized her own were shaking as she pulled that last glove off and dropped the black leather to the floor at her feet.

She held both his hands in hers and just looked.

The discoloration was the first thing she noticed, large patches were the same hue as the rest of his skin, while other areas were much lighter. The flesh was badly wrinkled with raised areas that resembled veins, but every so often, the skin would smooth out, the feel of it slick against her thumb. It wasn't pretty, but it was nowhere near as horrible as she thought it would be.

She turned his hands over and looked at his palms, noticing the burns ran up past his wrists to disappear under his shirt. The single button on the long sleeves popped open with only a slight tug, the material sliding away from his skin. His right arm was mostly clear, the burns stopping slightly past his wrist, but the left was another story.

The burns traveled the length of his arm as far as she could see. "Is it only your hands and arm?" He shook his head, not meeting her eyes. Keri stared at him, seeing his discomfort at having her see him. Her heart ached, her throat growing tight.

She raised her hand, brushed it across his cheek and waited until he looked at her. "Can I see the rest?"

The answer was in his eyes. He didn't want her to see. Regretted having let her see as much as she did but he nodded his head and inhaled deeply.

Keri grabbed his shirt near the waist of his pants and pulled the material loose, then reached for the row of buttons in the front, unhooking them while watching for any sign she should stop. His lips were a harsh slash across his face, his jaw clenched, but he gave no protest. When the last button came undone, she pulled the ends of the material apart, then slid the shirt off of him, letting it drop to the floor to join his discarded gloves.

The first thing she noticed was how well defined his chest and stomach was, his skin bronzed from the sun. As much as he enjoyed staying covered from head to toe, he'd spent time outside without his shirt on. Living so far from town and surrounded by trees was probably why. Who would see him way out here?

She raised a hand, ran it over his stomach, and smiled when the muscles contracted. A thin patch of dark hair covered his chest and ran from his navel to disappear into the waistband of his pants. A small area of skin on his left side looked much like his hands, the ruined flesh circling around to his back and down his hip. The scars on his left arm ended at the elbow. The rest of what she saw was perfect. "This isn't as bad as I thought, Noah." She ran a finger over the imperfect patch of skin and looked up, then lowered her head to catch his eye. Laying both her hands on his chest she stepped closer when he refused to look at her. "It's not nearly as bad as you had me believe."

He met her gaze, his eyes narrowed. "You don't call this bad?"

Keri looked again, taking time to run her hands over the scarred flesh. "No," she said, shaking her head. "They're only imperfections. Everyone has them to some degree." She laid her hand against the ruined flesh on his side. "But it doesn't define you. What people see on the outside isn't what makes you the man you are. Your heart does. You don't ever have to hide from me, Noah. I think you're beautiful just the way you are."

H is heart was going to beat out of his chest. It was all he could do to catch his breath as Keri rubbed her hand over the ruined flesh.

I think you're beautiful just the way you are...

Her words rang inside his head and God, how he wanted to believe them. Ached clean to his soul with the wanting, but looking at his scarred flesh, all he could think of was pulling away from her, to put his shirt and gloves back on and pray she forgot what he looked like.

She lifted her head again, looking up at him. It took effort to meet her eyes, to look and see what was there, but the moment he did, his throat burned, the back of his eyes scalded with tears and the pressure in his head gave way to a pounding headache.

Unlike the day when Isabelle had looked at him, there wasn't any disgust on Keri's face. She looked at him no differently than she had that morning at breakfast. There was compassion in her blue eyes but something else was shining up at him. Some emotion he couldn't identify. She smiled and grabbed his hands, lifting them to lay against her face, and his chest constricted, his breath snatched from his lungs as his heart started pounding.

She let go of his hands, her fingers sliding down his arms to rest near his bent elbows. "There's no such thing as perfection, Noah, but you're about as close as any man I've ever known to being just that."

Noah stared at her, her words slowly penetrating his brain enough to know all the pain and loneliness he'd lived with was a thing of the past. The warmth of her skin, the softness under his palms causing something in his chest to pinch.

He'd wondered countless times what she felt like, dreamed of touching her like this, feeling her skin under his hands, but nothing had prepared him for the feel of her. He moved his thumb, brushing it against her cheek and she turned her head until her lips brushed his skin, her breath warming his hand as she placed a soft kiss against his ruined palm.

When she looked up at him and smiled, the tightness in his chest loosened, the fear she'd reject him vanishing as if it had never been there. She really didn't care. He could see it in the way she looked at him, in the soft smile she gave him. She'd seen the worst of him and hadn't turned away. The realization eased the remaining tension he felt, released the last of his fear and then, he couldn't stop touching her.

He dug his fingers into her hair, felt the texture of those blond curls between her fingers and leaned down to kiss her, covering her mouth and slipping his tongue inside to taste her. She angled her head, deepened the kiss immediately, and leaned against him, her arms circling his waist.

He'd never wanted her as much as he did in that moment. The soft floral fragrance clinging to her skin and the taste of her kiss sent a wave of longing through his body.

Her dress was still unbuttoned from his earlier attention in the kitchen and it took very little to get the material off her shoulders and pushed to her waist. He broke the kiss, looked down at her exposed chest, then touched her, the back of his fingers brushing the underside of each breast. He ran his fingertips lightly over them, circling her areolas until they tightened.

She sighed, her eyes closing as he manipulated her soft flesh, his fingers brushing her nipples until they pebbled.

"That feels nice," she said, opening her eyes back up. "Much better than those gloves."

Noah kissed her again, pinched her nipples between his thumb and forefinger and didn't stop until she moaned and pushed her hips again him. He pushed her dress down until it pooled around her feet, untied her bloomers to join the rest, and cupped his hand between her legs, those tight curls tickling his palm. She shuddered, lifted to her toes and urged him on by tilting her hips toward him again, that noise she always made when he loved her spilling from her lips.

He teased the inside of her thigh until she was squirming before inserting a finger into her slick heat. She gasped and grabbed onto his shoulders as he pulled from her and added another digit, sliding them in and out until she was panting for breath, her short nails digging into his shoulders. She kissed him, hard, quick, bit his lip, the sting chased away when she sucked it into her mouth. His body tightened, his groin drawing tight until he ached.

A slight movement of his thumb on that small pearl of flesh hidden in her slick folds and she moaned, the sound low and ragged, her arms around his neck tightening with every in and out plunge of his hand. "Faster," she whispered against his lips, rocking her hips as he drove her to the point of madness with nothing more than his hand between her legs. When she trembled, her muscles clamping around his fingers, he swallowed her scream and didn't stop manipulating her flesh until she stopped shivering against him, those curls covering her sex, wet with her pleasure.

She blinked up at him sleepily and he reluctantly pulled his hand away. Keri stared at him for long moments, her breaths coming out in shallow puffs, her eyelids drooping. She smiled, bent and unhooked her boots, kicking them, and the dress still pooled at her feet, away.

Then she sank to her knees in front of him.

His heart gave a powerful thump in his chest just seeing her at his feet like that, the light from the fire casting shadows across her naked flesh. She unlaced his boots and pulled them off, along with his socks, then sat up on her knees and unhooked his pants, pulling the material down so he could step out of them.

Standing naked before her had been a terrifying thought an hour before, but now, seeing her look up at him, desire shining so bright in her eyes, he forgot how imperfect he was.

Keri touched him, her hand wrapping around his hardened length, and Noah could do nothing but stare down at her. His heart was pounding, every nerve in his body on edge, and when she leaned forward, her tongue darting out to lick the tip of him, he took a shuddering breath, his eyes rolling back when she took him fully into her mouth.

The moist heat scorched him, drew his balls tight and it was all he could do to stand still, to not grab her head and force her to take all of him, root to tip. Her hands slid up the front of his legs to his stomach, around to his back, her soft fingers gliding over every inch of skin she could reach. The pressure of her mouth increased as she sucked him in, his whole body clenching as she drew him in and out of her mouth.

Noah fought to keep his eyes open, to watch his flesh slide between her pink lips, the wet tip of her tongue burning a trail over his length as she licked him from top to bottom. The way her gaze latched on to his and didn't let go left him feeling wanted. Desired. Capable of being loved.

He reached out, his fingers tunneling into her hair to hold her to him for long moments before finally having to pull her away for fear he'd spill himself into her mouth.

Noah scooped her off the floor, carried her to the bed and kissed her as he laid her down, stretching out beside her, holding himself as far away as he could to give himself time to calm down. Their frantic kisses slowed, the languid slide of her lips against his mouth pulling a moan from his throat before she suddenly pushed at him, tumbling him onto his back and straddling his hips, impaling herself on his erection in one hard, swift, downward motion.

The heat of her fully against his flesh, her inner thighs cradling his hips, caused his stomach to clench tight. He ground his teeth, sucked in a harsh breath as jolts of pleasure raced up his spine. He grabbed her at the waist and held her to him. "Hell's bells, Keri, don't move." She stilled. Noah lay under her, his eyes clenched shut, trying to control his breathing and willed himself not to let go. Not yet. But the feel of her slick heat clenching around him made it nearly impossible. He concentrated on each breath, the feel of her under his hands and long minutes later, his heart rate slowed. He inhaled a breath, then opened his eyes.

And groaned.

She looked like a siren. The firelight shimmered against her skin, the expression on her face as she looked at him kicking his pulse into rapid action again. She smiled and leaned down, bracing her hands on the bed beside his head. The tips of her breasts grazed his chest before she brought one to his mouth, her beaded nipple teasing his lips. He licked the pink flesh, sucked it into his mouth, her sigh of pleasure echoing in his head. He gripped her bottom in both hands, squeezing, and he took his time touching every inch of her he could reach.

Desire rolled through his limbs, hot burning need gripping him until he knew there was no use trying to take things slow. Not today. Not now that he was finally able to touch her. To feel her warm skin against his own. He wanted her too much to take things slow now, his whole body vibrated with his need to claim her. He raised his hands to cup her bottom again and tilted his hips upward before urging her into moving.

The moment she sat up, bracing her hands on his chest and

started to move, her hips rotating to dance against his lap, he held his breath, watched her stare down at him and finally recognized what that tightness in his chest was whenever she touched him, that small flutter he felt whenever he caught her looking at him. That crazy, obsessive desire to lock her away from the world and keep her forever.

He loved her. Craved her more than air. Needed her to feel whole.

A part of him scoffed at the very idea of opening himself up to such a powerful emotion as love again, but every soft caress her hand left behind a longing so intense it ached in his chest and left him feeling alive for the first time in twelve years.

Keri leaned down and left small kisses on his chest before working her way up his neck, her tongue lapping at the soft skin behind his ear. The tingles those tiny kisses produced drove his need for her, increased the urgency he felt.

She sucked his earlobe into her mouth, the moist heat raising gooseflesh across his body. When she finally slipped her tongue inside his mouth, a chill raced up the length of his spine. Her undulating hips rocked against him in time with the thrust and parry of her tongue, causing a new urgency. He threaded his fingers into her hair, those springy curls wrapping around his hands as if to hold him against her and he tilted his hips as she increased the speed of her thrusts.

He inhaled the flowery scent of her skin, tasted the sweetness of her mouth and knew he never wanted to feel as dead inside as he had before he found her that snowy night in the line shack. Never wanted to spend a day without her. As she rode him, their sweat-slicked skin sliding together, his thoughts centered on one repetitive desire. He wanted her forever and he kissed her more deeply to keep from screaming it like some love sick fool.

Keri lifted her head and gasped, her body clenching around him and Noah's hold on her tightened. She stared down at him, her gasps like music when he felt his own release nearing, her hips moved faster, the mind-numbing pleasure stealing their breath as she closed her eyes, threw her head back and gasped out his name. She tightened around him, her body clamping down hard against his length, and he followed her, their bodies writhing as their mingled cries filled the stillness in the cabin.

She collapsed against him, her breaths panted out as her body trembled. "Don't let go."

Noah held her tight, one arm clenched around her waist, the other across her back to tangle his fingers into her hair while burying his face against her neck. "I'll never let you go." He whispered the words against her skin and wasn't sure she heard him. They lay like that, Keri draped across his chest until their skin cooled, until he softened and slipped from her body while the ticking of the clock marked off the minutes.

The air grew cold around them and Noah grabbed the blanket, pulling it over them both and sighed, content for the first time in longer than he could remember.

CHAPTER TWENTY-NINE

For years, Christmas had been another day on the calendar, but this year was different. Keri and the kids obviously made it so, but for the first time since moving to Willow Creek two years past, Noah didn't dread it.

He remembered the excitement that always hung in the air when he was Aaron's age and he knew it was still there. The look on those kids' faces said as much. They were happy. With nothing more than they had, they were happy.

And so was Keri.

She smiled at him as she set one of the kitchen chairs down near him and sat down. Aaron and Sophie Ann were on the other side of the room, playing a board game he'd picked up for them at the mercantile. Other than their soft voices, there wasn't a sound in the room besides the crackle and pop of the fire and that old clock.

Noah leaned forward, grabbed Keri's hand and raised it, kissing the back of her knuckles. "So, what do you want to do with the rest of the day?"

She smiled. "Things that aren't appropriate with small kids in the room."

His blood heated at the look in her eyes, those things she was talking about filling his head with images of her naked, her warm skin touching every inch of him. "I should have built that bedroom onto the back of this cabin like I planned to when I moved in here. I regret not ever getting around to doing so now."

She smiled and turned her body toward him. "That is a shame," she said. "But sitting here with you is enough."

She squeezed his hand and it was odd seeing his scarred flesh while she was in the room. It would take a while to get used to taking those gloves off when he came in the house but knew, once the initial shock wore off, it would feel as if he'd always done so. Aaron and Sophie Ann had questions when they'd seen his hands and he'd answered every one of them. Luckily, nothing held a kid's attention long and their questions finally stopped.

Keri stood, grabbed his journal before taking her seat again and flipped the book open to the sketch of Rosebriar. When she asked about it, his heart pinched. "I grew up there," he said.

She smiled. "I thought as much." She looked back down at the drawing, her finger tracing the lines of the house. "Is your family still there?"

He didn't answer right away, memories he'd tried to bury bombarding him too fast to form a coherent sentence, but when he could, he nodded. "I think so." He stared at the drawing, memories flooding his mind. "Rosebriar has been in our family close to a hundred years. It doesn't look much like this now, though. The Yankees destroyed a good bit of it. They set fire to the east wing but it wasn't a total loss. My mother and sister stayed on." He shifted in his seat. "Well, they were there when I left."

"When you left?" Keri turned to look at him, confusion marring her features. "You don't know if they're still there?"

"No."

"Have you not spoken to them since you left home?"

He shook his head and her eyes widened. She looked stunned by the admission. "Why?" she asked. "They're your family."

Noah leaned back in the rocker and stared at the fire. Why hadn't he contacted them? He glanced at his hand and gripped the arm of the chair tight. "I said some awful things to them when I left. I don't much think they'd want to hear from me."

Keri was silent for long minutes. She closed the journal with a snap and turned to look at him. "You've not spoken to your family in twelve years?" She made a small sound, a strangled gasp before shaking her head. "Noah, how could you do that? Your mother must be beside herself wondering what happened to you!"

She stood, put the journal on the mantel and walked off, entering the kitchen without another word. Noah stared at the spot she'd been sitting in stunned silence. What the hell had just happened?

He stood, motioning for Aaron to stay where he was when the boy climbed to his feet and looked his way. Keri's outburst had drawn the kids' attention. When Aaron sat back down, distracting Sophie Ann again, Noah walked into the kitchen and stopped by the table. Keri was fussing about the stove, scrubbing the top even though he'd never seen it cleaner. "Keri?"

She stopped and stared at the wall, her shoulders lifting as she heaved a large breath. "You've no idea how it feels to be waiting for word from a loved one and never receive it." Turning, she looked at him, sadness filling her eyes. "It causes a small part of you to die. To think you're not loved enough to matter to them." Tears gathered in her eyes before she blinked them away. "I've not heard from Peter since Sophie Ann was born. I don't even know if he's still alive." She laughed, but there was no humor in the sound. "Can you imagine? Dragging my children halfway across the territory to find a man who might very well be dead. What kind of irresponsible person does that?" Her eyes filled with tears again. "I'm the worst mother in the world."

Noah crossed the room when her tears started sliding down her cheeks. She wiped them away and sighed. "You can't leave your family to wonder forever, Noah. It's cruel to do so. Regardless of what happened when you left, a simple note telling them you're still here, that you're thinking about them, is all it would take to ease their mind. I'm sure they're worried about you."

He'd thought the same thing a time or two but dismissed the notion as quickly as it came. He'd left his old life behind and had no intentions of revisiting it but looking at Keri's stricken face, he knew she was right. Hell, for all he knew, his mother and sister could be long dead. The thought caused his chest to tighten. "I'll write them," he said, reaching out to wrap his arms around her. "You're right. I shouldn't have been so thoughtless."

She leaned against him, tucking her head under his chin and heaved a breath, sinking further into him while raising her arms to wrap around his waist. "I'm sorry I yelled at you."

Noah smiled into her hair. "I'm sorry I gave you a reason to." They stood for long minutes, neither saying a word. A gust of wind blew past the house, snow flurries dancing past the window as the frigid air whistled through the glass panes. The sun was setting, the day almost over.

A noise drew their attention and they shuffled away from each other as if they were about to get caught doing something they weren't supposed to. Sophie Ann walked into the room asking for a drink of water and just like that, the intimacy they'd been sharing was gone.

"What'cha doin'?"

Noah glanced down at Sophie Ann and smiled at the way her face was scrunched as she stared up at him. "Looking."

Sophie Ann stared at the wall, her forehead wrinkling. "At what?"

"The mirror."

"Oh." She narrowed her eyes. "What ya see in there?"

"Me." Noah turned his attention back to the mirror. It had been a long time since he'd spent any time looking into it but he found himself glancing at it every day now. Every time he walked past it, his attention was drawn to the man staring back at him.

That man wasn't the same one who left Charleston twelve years ago and drifted across the country, lost, alone and broken hearted. He wasn't even the same man he was after settling down in Willow Creek. He'd changed since Keri and her kids came into his life and he knew letting go of the past was the only way to enjoy his future.

He'd done pretty good so far doing just that but looking in the mirror told him one thing still remained. He raised his hand and rubbed his palm against his bearded jaw. He hadn't seen the whole of his face in so long, he could barely remember what he looked like anymore. Allowing Keri to trim it had taken every ounce of courage he had. He'd done it for no other reason than he could tell she wanted him to. And as much as it had terrified him at the time, her kissing him afterwards had been worth it. That one kiss had altered every aspect of his life.

The last bit of the old him was still lingering, though. It was there on his face. His gaze was drawn to the scar. It had changed his life in so many ways, but now as he looked at it, he had to ask why. Keri was right when she said the scar didn't define him, that it shouldn't be a reason to hide forever. He needed to put his past behind him once and for all but that old fear still lived inside his head. The need to hide and stay secluded from everything and everyone had enough hold he was almost scared to let it go.

Sophie Ann shifted at his side and he looked back down at her. She was staring at him inquisitively, the expression on her face telling him she had no idea what he found so fascinating.

When she met his eyes, her eyebrows rose. "You forget what you look like?" she asked.

"I think maybe I have."

She smiled, her blue eyes wide and bright. "You could see better if you shaved." She shifted and leaned her head to one side. "My other pa never had hair on his face. My ma said it made her nose itch when he kissed her so she always made him cut his whiskers off."

"Is that right?" Noah looked back at the mirror. Keri had never said anything that indicated she didn't like the beard. She'd not hesitated to cut it, seemed eager to do it now that he thought about it, but he assumed it was because it was so long and bushy. Was it because she didn't like it at all?

He looked back down at Sophie Ann, her head still tilted to one side as she stared at him. "Think I should get rid of it, then?"

She nodded her head, her curls bouncing around her shoulders. "Yeah." She straightened her back, the look on her face turning serious. "Want me to help you do it?"

Noah laughed. "Depends on what you plan to do to help." He found out a second later when she turned her head toward the kitchen and yelled, "Ma! Noah needs help shaving off his whiskers."

He heard something fall in the kitchen, a muttered string of words, then Keri poked her head around the doorway. "Everything all right in there?" he asked, smiling when he saw how pink her cheeks were. She stepped into the room wiping her hands on that sorry excuse for an apron she liked to wear and said, "I dropped a pot."

She took two steps toward him, a questioning look in her eyes. "What's Sophie Ann yelling about?"

"She thinks I should shave."

Her eyes widened a bit. "Does she?"

"You don't like whiskers," Sophie Ann said. "Remember?"

Keri's cheeks turned from pink to red. "I'm gonna help him shave. What do I do?"

Keri chuckled. "Draw some water. That's the safest thing."

When Sophie Ann ran toward the kitchen, Keri crossed the room to him. "What brought all this on?"

Noah shrugged, unwilling to tell her where his mind had been wandering lately. "It's been a while since I've shaved. How steady is your hand?"

"You trust me with a razor that close to your neck?"

Noah nodded. "I trust you."

Sophie Ann walked back into the room, each step slow and measured, water sloshing to the floor every time she moved. Keri laughed and took the cup she was holding from her. "I think we'll need more than this," she said. "Let's go find something a bit bigger."

Aaron laid the book in his hand down and stood, shaking his head while looking at him. "She cut my pa once when she shaved him."

Noah raised an eyebrow. "Bad?"

"He bled a bit."

He smiled. "Well, as long as your ma doesn't cut too deep, I may be all right."

Sophie ran back into the room. "Ma said for me to come get ya. You gotta sit at the table."

Noah grabbed his old shaving kit from the chest at the foot of the bed and followed her back into the kitchen. Keri set a bowl of water on the table and glanced his way. "You have a razor?"

He showed her the kit, then set it on the table.

"Are you sure you want to do this?"

"As sure as I was the day I let you trim it."

She smiled. "Well let's do it before you change your mind."

There wasn't time to protest even if he had wanted to. Once Keri started preparing to shave him, there was no way to stop her. Sophie Ann must have been right. Keri apparently didn't like the beard at all if her haste to get him shaved was any indication. She had him in a chair, his straight razor sharpened, a cloth tucked over his shoulders and a good lather going in a cup before it fully sunk in what he was about to do. He met her gaze once she picked the razor back up. She looked as nervous as he felt. He winked at her and leaned his head back. "Don't cut off anything I might need later on."

He closed his eyes the moment she touched him. Memories from the past twelve years played inside his head like moving pictures as Keri slowly scraped away what remained of the man he'd let himself become. He let go of the pain Isabelle had caused and knew the only reason it still hurt was because he let it hurt and every taunt and odd look he received over the years was forgotten as if they'd never been. Keri and those kids made the hurt seem trivial now.

When Keri finally said, "I'm done," long minutes later he opened his eyes and looked up at her. She was smiling, her wet hands running across the smooth skin along his jaw line. Aaron stepped up beside him and handed him the mirror from the wall. He was almost scared to look but took the mirror, held it in front of him, and saw his entire bare face for the first time in twelve years.

He should have left the beard on.

The scar was the only thing he saw. It would be the only thing anyone else saw, too. He'd forgotten how crooked it was, how wide toward his jaw. The jagged white line slashed across his cheek as noticeable now as it had been when the cut had been fresh.

Keri touched him, the back of her fingers sliding across the scar until he lowered the mirror. Aaron and Sophie Ann were gone, their voices a soft whisper from the other room. "I'll add the decision to shave to the others I've regretted in my life."

"It'll grow back."

She was still touching him, her fingers a gentle caress against his face. The look in her eyes showed him nothing more than he was used to seeing when he looked at her. "Not quick enough."

"That's what I'm hoping." She smiled and leaned down, kissed him so tenderly his heart raced as if she'd been in his arms and he'd taken his time kissing her. She nuzzled the side of his face, the softness of her skin and the warmth of her breath heating his flesh before she left whisper soft kisses along his jaw. "For what its worth, you're still as handsome a man as you were twenty minutes ago, but if you want to grow the beard back, I'll suffer through the nose tickling."

He smiled, then turned his head to look at her. "Well, I guess I better give you as many tickle free kisses as I can before it grows back."

"You can start now," she said, her smile lighting up her eyes. "And make it quick before Aaron or Sophie Ann decide to come back."

He chuckled and reached out to cup the side of her face. "If you insist."

The morning was cold, the ground frozen, but for once, the sky was blue. A few patches of snow still lingered under the trees but other than that, and the frigid temperature, it looked as sunny as any spring day.

Keri smiled at Noah when he helped her down from the wagon, his hands lingering on her waist longer than usual. "Hurry back," he whispered, the smile on his face letting her know immediately he had plans for her today. Thoughts of what those plans might be heated her blood. They only had one more day to themselves before school let out for the month long Christmas break and from the look on Noah's face it would be one neither of them would ever forget.

"I'll be back in a second." She hurriedly ushered Aaron and

Sophie Ann to the school house, stumbling once before making it to the steps. She could hear Noah's laughter long after Laurel greeted them at the door. "Good morning, Laurel."

Laurel ushered them inside and waved at Noah before closing the door. "To be so pretty out, I don't think I've felt it so cold."

"Me either." Keri helped Sophie Ann remove her coat and stuffed her small gloves into the pockets, then hung it on one of the pegs by the door. The kids were already rambunctious. Knowing it was their last day of school for a while left them all a bit wild.

Laurel tried to get them to settle down and turned to look back at Keri when they paid her no mind. She shook her head while laughing. "Looks as if I'm in for a hair raising day."

The sound of shattering glass and the report of a fired gun echoing in the street nearly stopped Keri's heart and pulled a startled scream from everyone inside the school building. Everyone but Laurel. The look on the school teacher's face was one Keri would remember until her last breath. The horror and disbelief shining in Laurel's amber eyes caused Keri's heart to slam against her ribcage, her breath to leave her lungs in a swoosh that left her dizzy and her knees wobbly.

And the sight of Laurel's blood staining her pretty yellow dress caused Keri's screams to ring out the loudest.

CHAPTER THIRTY

Noah ran toward the school, the gun shots coming from inside the saloon ignored. His heart was in his throat, bile churning in his stomach as he reached the steps, the screams coming from inside nearly deafening him. The fear of what he'd see once he made it inside the little building made his limbs so weak he could barely climb the stairs.

He flung open the door, his heart stopping for a brief moment as he saw Laurel and Keri both on the ground. It took long seconds to realize Keri was moving. That the blood on her hands wasn't her own. The relief he felt didn't last. Laurel was gasping for air, the front of her dress stained a ruddy brown. The bullet that shattered the window had hit her.

"Noah! What do I do?"

Keri's frantic question snapped him out of his daze and he crossed to where they were and sank to his knees. He grabbed Keri's hands and placed them over Laurel's wound. "Hold your hands here. Don't let go." He stood, his gaze darting to those looking back at him, their tear-streaked faces causing his heart to pinch inside his chest.

Broken glass littered the floor in front of the window. Fate had a way of reminding you how precious life really was and that stray bullet from the saloon was a major wake up call.

Noah spotted Holden's daughter, Alexandra, Laurel's step-daughter, at the front of the small group of school kids, the redhead boy she was always fighting with had his arms wrapped around her while he tried to hold her still.

Searching the faces looking up at him, he finally saw Aaron and Sophie Ann, both of them huddled against the wall with three more kids. He sighed in relief and met Aaron's eyes. "Keep Sophie Ann with you," he said. "And stay right where you are. I'll be back in a minute."

He waited for Aaron to acknowledge him before leaning back down and placing a hand on Keri's shoulder. "I'm going after Dr. Reid. I'll be right back."

She threw him a look so full of fear it tightened his chest. He didn't even think when he leaned over and kissed her. It was quick, brief, but enough to ease his mind a bit. Leaving her and the kids behind as the sound of gunshots still echoed through the streets was the hardest thing he'd ever had to do.

Stepping out of the school with the occasional wild shots still pinging across town had his nerves on edge. He could hear the marshal yelling and searched him out, finally catching a glimpse of him tucked in between two buildings, his rifle raised and pointed toward the saloon.

Noah hurried down the steps, keeping his head low and made it back to his wagon just as another shot flew across the street, the sound of breaking glass once again causing screams to ring out in town. Whoever was in that saloon shooting into the street deserved an ass kicking and he hoped Morgan gave it to him.

He waited for a lull, then raced across the road and ducked into the doctor's office. Dr. Reid was stuffing things into a black bag and turned wide eyes his way when he slammed the door shut behind him.

"A stray bullet hit the school teacher," he said. "Looked pretty bad to me."

The doctor nodded, snapped the bag shut and lifted it from the table and crossed the room. "Lead the way."

They were crossing the street when all hell broke loose. Shots rang out nonstop, yelling echoing off the buildings. Noah turned, saw two men run from the saloon still shooting, and he felt his blood heat as rage clawed at his chest. He knew those two, his gaze landing on the wiry, brown haired fellow in front. It was the same bastard who'd broke into his cabin, the man who'd attacked Keri. A man he'd wished he'd killed the day the son of a bitch dared to touch her.

It looked as if fate was going to give him a chance to rectify that mistake. Turning away from the school, he hurried down the sidewalk toward the saloon.

Keri wiped her eyes against her sleeve, her hands still pressed against Laurel's shoulder like Noah had told her to do. Gun shots were still popping in the street and every second Noah was gone, the fear she felt increased.

Laurel made a funny wheezing sound and Keri's heart kicked against her ribs. "Don't go to sleep, Laurel. Noah went to get Dr. Reid. He'll have you fixed up in no time."

The school teacher blinked, her eyelids drooping a bit before she looked up at her. "Seeing a doctor twice in one day. Doesn't sound like I'll be okay." She smiled but there was despair shining in her eyes. "I'm pregnant."

The words were whispered so softly, Keri barely heard them. Fear was etched on every tense inch of her face. "You'll be fine," she told her again. "And so will your baby." She tried to reassure her and knew she failed by the look on Laurel's face.

Laurel's smile waned. "No one knows. I didn't even tell

Holden I thought I was." Her eyes grew glassy. "I wanted to surprise him." She licked her lips, her eyelids fluttering again. "Don't let Dr. Reid tell him."

"I won't."

"Promise?" Laurel said. "He'll have a hard enough time dealing with me gone."

Keri's eyes filled with tears again. "You're not going anywhere, Laurel. Dr. Reid will fix you right up. You and your baby will be just fine."

The door opened the moment the words were out of her mouth and Keri sucked back a sob of relief at seeing the doctor walk through the door. He sank to his knees and pulled her hands away from the wound and all Keri could do was sit there and wonder why Noah hadn't come back inside.

The minutes ticked by, the gunshots in the street finally stopping and Keri felt as if she were in a daze by the time Dr. Reid stood and peeked out the door. He turned and picked Laurel up, then said, "Hand me my bag." Keri did as he asked and stood, her legs cramping from sitting on them so long. "Thank you," he said. "I'll take her over to my office." He glanced around the room. "Are you okay here with the children?"

Keri nodded and felt a languorous sort of numbness steal into her limbs when he left. The children were still crying, Alexandra Avery still fighting to be let loose and Keri knew the last thing Evan needed was a hysterical girl in his office.

She crossed the room, gave a brief look to the redhead boy trying to hold Alexandra still, and didn't miss the anguish in his eyes as he held the crying blonde in his arms. For all the fighting the two did, he cared about this girl. It was written all over his face.

Stopping in front of them, Keri smiled and reached out to try and comfort her but stopped when she noticed the blood on her hands. She lowered her arm. "She'll be all right," she said. "Dr. Reid will take care of her."

"She can't die. My pa...." She cried harder, her blue eyes red and puffy.

"Shhh..." Keri tried to soothe her and knew nothing would. Not until she knew her stepmother was all right. Keri gave the boy a look, knowing he'd try to calm Alexandra and finally stepped away from them to look at the others in the room. They were all huddled together in a small group and Keri's heart broke for them all.

She crossed the room, sank to her knees again and felt the first bit of relief since the first shot was fired when Aaron and Sophie Ann flew into her arms. The others gathered close, their crying finally giving way to sniffles.

The door flew open and Keri turned, her pulse leaping until she saw Abigail. The woman's face was etched in the same fear Keri knew her own showed.

Abigail looked around the room, spotted Alexandra and crossed to her, folding her arms around her as the girl started crying harder. "Jesse, I need you to go get your horse and ride out to the Avery ranch and get Holden. Can you do that?"

The boy stood and nodded. "Yes, ma'am. I'll be quick about it, too." He gave another look at Alexandra, his mouth opening as if he wanted to say something, but turned instead and left the school at a run.

Long minutes ticked by, the noise in the street growing. Men were shouting but thankfully the gun shots had ceased. Keri waited for Noah to come back but when the shouting stopped and the sound of horses racing through the town grew distant, her fear grew. Where had he gone? Was he hurt as well?

Laying a kiss on Aaron and Sophie Ann's head, Keri stood and turned to face Abigail. "Is it over?"

Abigail cut a look across the room at her. "Not yet." She sighed and closed her eyes as a shudder wracked her body. "They stole horses that were tethered in front of the saloon and headed across the valley. Morgan and a few other men went after them."

Keri glanced at the still open door. She could hear voices, people talking, some shouting, and that fear she'd felt when Noah didn't come back grew. She turned to Abigail, met her eyes and said, "Did you see Noah outside?"

Abigail nodded. "He went with Morgan and the others."

The air left Keri's lungs in a rush as her pulse leaped. Why did he go and leave them all alone? They needed him here. She glanced at Abigail again and guilt caused her stomach to clench. Abigail probably thought the same about Morgan, but it was his job to go after those men. She couldn't imagine the fear the woman felt. It made her own seem trivial knowing Abigail probably spent many nights worried for her husband as he hunted down men hell bent on raising a ruckus.

Her husband. The moment she thought it, Keri knew she had no right to feel abandoned. Noah may provide for them but he owed her nothing. Not even his time, if truth be known.

Noah had cut himself off from everyone for so long, it would be selfish of her to refuse to let him finally be an active member of this small community. If helping Morgan and whoever else went with them was what he thought he needed to do, then who was she to say otherwise?

Knowing there was nothing to do but wait until Noah returned, she turned to Aaron. "I need to walk outside and wash my hands. Will you be all right until I get back?" He nodded but she could still see fear shining brightly in his eyes. "I'll be back before you can count to twenty."

Keri hurried outside to the well, pulled up a bucket of water and washed her hands, drying them on her skirt and rushed back inside. Aaron looked relieved when she came in and shut the door. She smiled in his direction then searched every corner until she found a broom. She swept up the glass, straightened the desks and benches and finally settled into a corner of the room to sit with the school kids until Noah came back.

Abigail eventually took Alexandra to her house, telling Keri she'd send word once she knew how Laurel was. It was near noon when the sound of horses running caught her attention. Keri stood and crossed to the broken window. Jesse and Holden Avery came barreling into town. Holden barely slowed his horse before he jumped from the saddle and rushed into the doctor's office. Her heart pinched. She imagined she knew exactly how Holden felt when Jesse told him the news that Laurel had been shot.

John's death replayed in her mind's eye and the anguish she'd felt hearing he was dead was as fresh as if it happened only yesterday. There may not have been any love between them but she'd cared about him. Had felt the blow of his death like a punch to the gut. The fear and confusion she'd lived with hearing the news left her knees weak.

She turned to the bench closest to her and sank onto it, her heart pounding as images raced across her mind. The temporary relief Robert had brought when he showed up after John's death was dulled by the horror of him moving in as if he owned the place. As if he owned her. His cruelty and harsh words were burned into her memory to the point she'd never forget a moment of it. Never forget the night it all went so wrong.

She stifled a sob as the memories surfaced again and she stared at the floor as the past two years played like moving pictures inside her head. She'd felt true fear when she grabbed Aaron and Sophie Ann and ran from the farm that night, but nothing compared to the terror she felt a month later when she realized they were starving. The obstacles they'd faced, the uncomfortable nights trying to sleep on the ground littered with rocks while things scurried in the grass by their heads.

And the apprehension when a wild, untamed man tossed them out into the snow, then came back and rescued them.

As if only thinking about him had conjured him into life, Keri lifted her head to find Noah standing a few feet away, the look in his eyes full of an emotion she was too scared to try and read.

Her heart knew what she wanted to see, what she wanted to believe, but Noah had yet to say anything to make her think he cared deeply for her. That he loved her. But the look in his eyes as he stared at her made her wonder, and her heart skipped a beat just thinking about it. Thinking of how much she loved him.

Sophie Ann's voice forced them to turn and look across the room. She was running toward them and Keri stood, ready to hug away any fears she had but her baby girl bypassed her and ran to Noah. He looked as shocked as she felt but it didn't last long. He knelt, wrapped Sophie Ann in his arms and let her cling to him.

Sophie Ann's voice was barely a whisper when she said, "Can we go home now?"

Noah glanced up, locking eyes with her for a brief second before turning his attention back to Sophie Ann. "Yes, we can go home now."

Keri glanced back across the room and saw Aaron and the other children. "I can't leave yet," she said. "Someone has to be here for the children."

"Percy Goins over at the livery stable is getting a wagon hitched up. He's going to take them all home."

It took nearly an hour but with the help of Jesse Samuels, they finally got the remaining school kids loaded into a wagon and headed out of town. Keri's nerves were still on edge when she stepped out of the school.

The townsfolk were in the street, some of them inspecting windows of nearby storefronts, and a small congregation had gathered near Evan Reid's door. Abigail and Alexandra were there, along with others she didn't recognize. "Do you know how Laurel is?"

"Still alive," he said, his hand on her back. "The doctor said she'd survive the bullet wound. It missed everything important. She may lose some function of her right arm, though. Evan's worried about infection more. If anything gets her, it'll be that."

Keri nodded. She knew all too well what an infection could do. Her uncle had died from nothing more than a cut to his leg. The wound festered and he was dead before anyone even knew it wasn't healing.

Noah helped her and the kids into his wagon then crossed the street. He spoke to Abigail for a brief moment then came back, crawled up into the wagon and took the reins. "Still no change," he said before turning them toward home.

Keri's gaze lingered over that small crowd. "I saw Holden ride into town earlier and go inside. I'm surprised he's calm enough to help Dr. Reid much."

"He wasn't." Noah readjusted his hat. "Morgan locked him inside the jail."

"He locked him up?" Keri's eyes flew wide. "Why?"

"To keep him from killing the man who shot his wife." Noah turned and gave her a strange look. There was anger there, but she saw fear, hopelessness and desperation. She wasn't sure what was going through his head. Questions about what happened when they chased down those men shooting up the town filled her thoughts, but she held her tongue. Aaron and Sophie Ann still had a look of shock about their face and bringing it all up again would just cause their fear to return.

The ride home was made in silence, no one saying a word. Supper was a somber affair, the tension in the air thick and choking. It wasn't until she'd tucked Aaron and Sophie Ann into bed that she dared ask Noah what happened.

He was still at the kitchen table, a single candle burning. His face was cast in shadow, the candle light flickering across his features. He raised his head to look at her when she sat down across from him, his voice pitched low when he said, "The men who shot up the town were the same ones who broke in here."

It took long moments for his words to sink in. When they did, Keri's heart started racing. The man who attacked her, and the one who tried to shoot Noah, had shot Laurel? Keri tensed, her body flushing hot. "Did the marshal catch them?"

Noah nodded. "Yes." His voice was bland, no emotion shining in his eyes. "The one who attacked you is dead."

Keri's heart thumped harder against her ribs. The same look she'd seen in Noah's eyes when they left town was there again. Some unnamed emotion she couldn't quite figure out. She waited for him to say more but when he sat there, silent, she finally asked, "What about the other one?"

"In jail." He shook his head, a far off look in his eye. "Holden came after him the minute we got back into town. It's why Morgan locked him up. Although, I'm not sure how well that's going. I can't imagine Holden sitting quietly knowing what the bastard in the cell beside him did."

Noah sighed and raised his hand, pushing his hair away from his face. He didn't have his gloves on and even though the light was dim, Keri could see the skin around his knuckles was busted and splattered with dried blood.

She reached out and took his right hand. "What happened?" He made no attempt to answer and Keri sighed before standing and turning to the sink. She wet a towel then retook her seat and spent long minutes seeing to his busted knuckles.

He never said a word as she tended to him, just sat rigidly as she cleaned the abrasions on his hands and by the time she'd finished, a sense of dread filled her, especially when she saw the look on his face. It was distant, as if she were looking into the face of a stranger. "What's wrong?"

Noah refocused his gaze on her and shook his head. "Nothing," he said. "It's been a long day. Go to bed. I'll be back in once I see to the animals."

He blew out the candle before she could say a word and left her in the dark kitchen alone. The front door opened, then closed, and the waft of cool air tickling the back of her neck sent shivers down her spine.

Noah said he had to check on the animals but a small voice in the back of her mind whispered it was more than that. Something had happened when Noah went with Morgan to chase after those men. Something he didn't feel like sharing.

Her mind flashed back to his busted knuckles, to the distant look on his face, and she remembered the anger she'd witnessed that nearly drove him to shoot a man right in front of her when she'd been attacked. A man she now knew was dead.

Dread settled in her stomach like a rock. How did the man die? And who killed him?

CHAPTER THIRTY-ONE

The images wouldn't go away. Noah paced the length of the barn, his harsh breaths crystallizing in the cold air as he crossed the dirt floor, turned, then started back the other way.

His hands ached, his busted knuckles cracked open again from clenching and unclenching his fists and the suffocating tightness in his chest damn near took his breath.

He'd rode back into town with Morgan and the others resigned to his fate but no one had said a word. He'd been waiting for Morgan to arrest him, but the marshal had walked into the jail as if he wasn't even standing there. As if he hadn't killed a man with his bare hands right in front of him and six other witnesses.

A sickening wave of nausea caused his stomach to roll. Killing the bastard who attacked Keri had left him feeling numb—until he saw her face. Then the reality of what he'd done hit him. He'd killed a man without remorse and a small twisted part of him relished the man's shocked gasp when his neck snapped, the loud pop of breaking bone still ringing in his ears. The hard thud of his body hitting the frozen ground caused a satisfied warmth to spread through his limbs... then he saw Keri's face in his mind's eye and realized those taunts the people in Willow Creek always made about him were finally true. He really was a monster. Anyone who could kill a man and be glad he did it, had to be.

He stopped pacing and stared at the barn door. The wind whistled past the walls, the night quiet and cold. That small place in his heart that Keri had warmed started to chill as the day's events kept playing inside his head. He'd made plans enough to last the whole of his life and Keri and those kids had been in every one of them but now...

Noah closed his eyes, the tightness in his chest stealing his breath. How could he ask Keri to stay with him after what he'd done? He'd killed a man for no other reason than he'd wanted to. Because he didn't think the man deserved to live. Because he'd hurt and terrified a woman he loved more than he loved himself.

Reaching into his coat, he closed his fingers around the ring he'd bought for Keri and pulled it from his pocket. The gold and emerald ring cost him a bundle, Mrs. Jenkins charging him extra for the special rush order. It was too extravagant, much too fancy for life in a dusty little town like Willow Creek, but no more so than the coat he'd bought her. The look on her face when he'd held that fur lined coat open for her so she could slip it on told him it was worth every penny he spent on it. He imagined that look of awe would fill her eyes again when she saw the ring. When he asked her to marry him. Something he knew now, he had no right to do.

What woman would want a man who could kill without remorse? Who still had no feelings of guilt for doing it. A man who would kill that sorry bastard all over again given the chance.

A man Morgan Avery would eventually arrest for murder.

K eri couldn't shake the feelings of dread. They'd been plaguing her body since the day of the shooting in town. Noah had withdrawn again, kept to himself most of the day and spoke very little when they all sat down together in the evenings.

She smiled at him when he walked into the kitchen. As he'd done for the past three days, he barely spared her a glance. He poured a mug of coffee and left again without a word. Her heart ached at his quick retreat. She wasn't sure what was wrong but she'd lived with the silence too long.

Drying the last dinner plate, she placed it on the shelf and removed the old flour sack she used for an apron and stepped to the kitchen doorway. Noah was in the rocker by the fire, staring into the flames with a blank look on his face. Grabbing one of the chairs from the table, Keri made her way into the other room and stopped when she'd reached Noah's side. He never spared her a glance when she set her chair down and slid into it. Nor when she turned to face him.

His coffee mug was perched on his leg but it looked untouched. She sighed, then shook her head. "Noah, what's wrong?"

"Nothing."

The dull tone of his voice told her he was lying. "Don't lie to me."

Long minutes passed, the crack and pop of firewood the only sound in the room. He finally turned his head to her and the look in his eyes nearly did her in. Such sadness. More so than she'd seen when they first came to be with him. Her chest tightened before she leaned over and grabbed his hand. "Please tell me what's bothering you."

He sighed and pulled his hand away. "Nothing's wrong, Keri. I just have a lot on my mind is all." He turned back to the fire. "I didn't realize I was required to tell you my every thought."

"You're not."

"No?" He shot her an accusing glare. "Then stop badgering me with all your stupid questions and go to bed. It's late. Those kids will be up before the sun as usual and I have better things to do tomorrow than tend them while you sleep in."

He stood and walked back toward the kitchen, dismissing her yet again. Keri watched him walk away, her heart aching as his cross words replayed inside her head. He was angry and she didn't know why. Had she done something to upset him? Had the kids?

Or was he finally getting tired of them being there all the time?

She thought back to the day of the shooting, to how happy he'd been when they'd dropped the kids off at school. He'd had plans for them that day. Plans, she was sure, which consisted of them being naked and in his bed. One last blissful day alone before school was dismissed for the Christmas break.

He wasn't happy now. The very sight of her seemed to anger him and not knowing why was eating away at her until fear started to creep into her heart.

Standing, she walked behind the blankets that still hung from the ceiling. She undressed, put her nightshirt on and slid under the covers, careful not to disturb Aaron and Sophie Ann. Her thoughts were a tangle of questions, fears she'd not had to worry about since Noah had found them that snowy day in the line shack once again making her stomach cramp with dread.

Had Noah grown tired of them? Of her? She dismissed the notion as soon as she thought it. He'd been eager to have her three days ago. He couldn't have tired of her in such a short period of time. Could he?

The doubts lingered, grew until her heart was racing, and it wasn't until she realized Noah hadn't attempted to kiss her, to touch her in any way since the day of the shooting, that real worry started to sink in. What if he *was* tired of her? Tired of taking care of, and having them, in his house.

She felt sick, anxiety making it hard to breathe. Was this his way of letting her know he was through with her? That whatever had been between them was now over?

Tears clouded her eyes as the very real possibility whispered inside her head. She'd known since the day Noah took them in that their current situation was temporary, but not once had she realized how much it would hurt when it was all over. To walk away from a man she'd do anything for would be the hardest thing she'd ever had to do, but something told her she'd have no choice.

"D o you think it'll snow again before Christmas? Can we take another ride on that sled you rigged up if it does? If Sophie Ann gets better, I mean. You think she'll be sick long?"

Noah blew out a breath and tried again, unsuccessfully, to ignore Aaron and his questions. The kid hadn't stopped talking since breakfast.

He opened the stall door and spoke softly to his horse when he nickered at him, then grabbed the brush and spent the next ten minutes ignoring Aaron's constant chatter and thinking of anything other than what had happened over the past week.

It seemed to work and the moment he noticed the silence, he breathed a sigh of relief. Until he looked toward the stall door. Aaron stood there staring at him, his eyebrows raised as if he were waiting on him to say something. He tried to remember the last thing he'd said but couldn't. Lowering his arm, he tossed the brush aside and turned to face him. "What?"

Aaron smiled but there was a bit of apprehension shining in his eyes. "I said my pa promised to teach me how to ride a horse but he never got around to it. Just wondering if you'd teach me."

The kid swiped at his nose with his coat sleeve. His eyes, Noah noticed, were the same brilliant blue as Keri's, his hair a darker shade of blond, and just looking at him made him think of her. Made him think of how he'd spoken to her the night before. He wasn't sure she'd ever forgive him for it.

Aaron was still staring at him, waiting for an answer to his question, he supposed. Noah walked out of the stall and across the barn to the hay bales and bent to cut the string off the one on top. "Ever been on a horse before?" he asked, turning his head to keep Aaron in his line of sight.

"Lots of times," he said, grinning. "Only with my pa holding the reins, though, but that's the easy part. I want to learn how to saddle one up and ride clean to town all by myself if I had to. Then I could help out more. Well, if I had my own horse...."

Listening to Aaron talk brought his thoughts right back to Keri and the past three days started replaying in his mind again. It had been the closest thing to torture he could imagine pushing her away when she desperately tried to talk to him and it tore a piece of his heart out every time he walked away from her.

He'd hurt her last night with his harsh response to her questions. He'd been irritated and had taken it out on her, but his irritation had nothing to do with her. Not really. She was still in his every thought and the fact he hadn't been able to touch her, or taste her lips, was killing him. His need for her burned through his veins and he'd come so close to telling her so, but always pulled back at the last moment.

Aaron stepped into his line of sight and Noah blinked, chasing his thoughts away.

"Think the Averys will let me ride some of their ponies? Alex said they'd have a bunch of 'em come spring."

Something in Aaron's face made Noah really focus on the kid. He'd been dogging his every step since the sun came up and as he stood there staring up at him, he noticed a strange look in his eyes, one he hadn't seen before. He straightened to his full height and looked down at him. "Why are you out here pestering me, Aaron?"

He looked surprised, his eyes widening just a fraction. "No reason."

"You're lying."

Aaron looked toward his feet, scuffed the toe of his boot across the ground and sighed. "Are you getting tired of us?"

The question shocked him. "No. Why would you think that?"

He shrugged. "You ain't been talking to any of us much and my ma's all sad 'cause of it." Aaron glanced up at him and frowned. "I heard her crying last night after we all went to bed and I ain't heard her cry in a long time. She was trying to be real quiet about it but I could hear her."

Noah wasn't sure how he walked across the barn to dump the hay in the horses stall, each step he took was slow and agonizing. His chest ached until he couldn't breathe as his mind's eye flashed pictures of Keri inside his head, pictures of her crying because he'd been such a horse's ass to her over the last several days.

All because of what he *thought* she may think of him.

He sighed and leaned against the stall wall and closed his eyes. What was he doing? Why was he pushing her away when he'd never needed her more? When he didn't even know if Morgan was going to arrest him for killing that drifter.

Aaron touched his arm. "Did we do something wrong?"

The look in Aaron's eyes nearly brought him to his knees. He'd never seen the kid look so vulnerable. "No, you didn't do anything wrong, Aaron. None of you did. I've just had a lot on my mind lately. That's all. Now stop worrying. You'll get wrinkles frowning so much."

He wasn't sure if Aaron believed him or not but the kid nodded his head, turned and left the barn at a dead run. Running to tell Keri he wasn't tired of them, he supposed, and Noah's chest ached knowing he should have been the one to tell her. That she shouldn't have felt like he was tired of them at all. None of them should have.

The horse nickered and stomped one foot. Noah stared at him

as thoughts of Aaron asking him if he'd teach him how to take care of and ride a horse whispered inside his head. Of seeing that Sophie Ann's Christmas wish for a family came true.

Thoughts of making Keri his legal wife instead of just pretending she was.

He needed to talk to Morgan. He couldn't wait around to see what the marshal was going to do. Christmas was three days away. He couldn't wait any longer. His plans for the future depended on what Morgan would say and he couldn't keep pushing Keri away like he'd been doing.

Saddling his horse, he led him outside, secured the barn door and lifted himself up onto the beast's back. He clicked his tongue, gave the reins a snap and raced out of the yard toward town.

CHAPTER THIRTY-TWO

Duke's deep-toned bark drew Keri from her thoughts. The old hound rarely barked unless he had a reason to. He must have seen something. She hoped it was Noah coming back.

Watching him climb onto his horse and leave after spending the morning talking to Aaron had puzzled her. She'd questioned Aaron until he was near tears but neither of them could figure out why Noah left without saying a word to any of them. According to Aaron, he seemed fine when he left the barn.

She finally stood to go peek out the kitchen window when Duke didn't stop barking. She heard the squeak of wagon wheels in the distance, her heart racing as she looked out to see who it was.

The wagon looked like any other but it was too far away to tell who was driving it. A man on horseback rode beside the wagon and when they pulled off the main road and started down the drive to the cabin, fear caused her pulse to race. It wasn't Noah on that horse. She could tell by the man's slight build.

Which meant they were home alone while two strangers approached the house.

As the wagon and horseman drew near, she could see it was

two men, the outline of their hats and the cut of their coats giving them away. She still couldn't tell who either of them were.

Visions of the last uninvited visitors flashed inside her head and she turned, running back into the main room to throw the latch on the door, securing it so no one could enter. Her heart was racing as she walked to the fireplace and reached up, grabbing Noah's gun and checking to see if it was loaded.

"Ma?"

Aaron stepped into her line of sight, his eyes wide. She nodded to the other side of the room with her head. "Take Sophie Ann and get behind the bed. Stay low to the floor and don't come out until I tell you to."

He didn't question her, just turned and grabbed Sophie Ann's hand and did as asked. She was probably overreacting but she'd learned first hand what letting your guard down got you.

A fist to the door caused her heart to leap into her throat. She lifted the gun and aimed the barrel at the door and prayed she wouldn't have to pull the trigger.

"Mrs. Lloyd? It's Percy Goins from over at the livery stable. You in there?"

"Percy?" Keri whispered the name, picturing Percy inside her mind's eye. She'd met him the night of the Christmas party in town. He was a small fellow with a kind smile. She breathed a sigh of relief. She knew him.

She swallowed the lump in her throat and tried to calm her racing heart. Her knees were shaking so bad, she could barely stand. "Just a minute, Mr. Goins."

"No worries ma'am," he said, before laughing softly. "I'm in no hurry, but your brother looks ready to jump out of his skin. He dang near broke the wheels off his wagon racing out here."

Percy was still talking but Keri hadn't heard a word since he'd said, "your brother." She stared at the door, the gun still raised while her mind raced. *Peter was here?* Her heart skipped a beat. Is that who the other man was?

Tears filled her eyes as she placed the gun back on the hooks above the fireplace, then turned and ran across the room, throwing the latch and swinging the door open wide. Percy's smiling face greeted her. She looked past him, searching for Peter as she stepped out into the cold morning air.

A figure moved off to her left. She wiped the tears from her eyes and smiled as he shifted, putting the sun to his back and allowing her to finally see him after five years.

The moment she saw his face, her heart slammed against her ribcage so hard, it took her breath. She shouldn't have put the gun away. The man with Percy Goins wasn't Peter.

He was stalling again. He'd taken his time riding into town, stopped twice to mull things over in his head and after not finding Morgan inside the jail, had spent a good ten minutes standing outside the building, thinking things through before venturing to the man's house, only to be told he was at the saloon.

He'd taken even more time walking across town and stood on the sidewalk looking up at the wooden building for long minutes before finally deciding to go inside.

In the two years he'd lived in Willow Creek, Noah had never stepped foot inside the saloon. He'd lost himself in enough drink after the war to last him a lifetime and the need to numb his brain until nothing remained, thankfully, hadn't hit him in years.

According to Abigail Avery, Morgan spent a good hour every Saturday over in the saloon leaning against the bar, swilling enough foul whiskey to make him think he didn't have a predetermined limit on the stuff while telling lies with the other men inside. If Morgan hadn't been in there, Noah wouldn't have even entertained the thought of entering the building but since he was, he crossed the sidewalk and walked through the swinging doors as if he'd done it hundreds of times.

A few curious gazes turned his way as he stepped inside. He ignored them and let the doors swing closed at his back.

Morgan spotted him before he made it across the room and waved him over, downing the whiskey in his glass and motioning for another. "Noah, you shock me more with every passing day."

"How so?" He leaned against the bar and shook his head when the bartender tried to slide a glass his way.

"Well, you took in Keri and her kids," Morgan said, his voice pitched low so no one else could hear him. "Then you start coming into town everyday to drop those little ones off at the school house, cut your hair, shaved off that beard, start attending social functions and now you're frequenting the local watering hole. I'm just surprised at how much you've changed over the past few weeks."

Noah didn't reply. There wasn't a need to. Morgan was right on all accounts. He had changed. And Keri was the reason. She was also the reason he'd tracked Morgan down and it wasn't to socialize over whiskey in the saloon.

He turned and glanced over his shoulder, looking at the men scattered across the room and realized this is where all his trouble had started. Where those two drifters had caused a fuss and started shooting up the town.

Noah turned back to Morgan, almost hating the fact he was about to bring it all up again. But regardless of what happened, he still didn't regret that old bastard was dead. "I know the day of the shooting things got a bit chaotic, and normally I wouldn't be so eager to seal my fate, but I can't wait any longer, Morgan. I need to know, if for no other reason than I have to see that Keri and the kids are taken care of." He inhaled a deep breath and blew it out, Keri, Aaron and Sophie Ann's faces appearing in his mind's eye. "Are you going to arrest me or not?"

Morgan raised an eyebrow at him. "Arrest you? What for?"

"I killed a man three days ago right in front of you."

Morgan stared at him for so long, Noah wasn't sure he even heard what he said. The look on his face told him he did though. He finally turned and motioned for the bartender to pour him another drink and waited until the man had done so and walked away before saying, "There were so many of us out there that day, Noah, so much chaos, that I'm not sure anyone who rode out with me will remember the details in exactly the same way as the man who rode next to him does." He downed his drink and pushed the glass away. "From the way I remember it, you and Percy both had a time getting hold of that man and the minute he pulled a knife on you, anything you did from that point on was self-defense." He shrugged his shoulders and tilted his head a fraction to one side. "It could have easily been Percy who got a hold of him instead of you. Do you think Percy would have let himself get gutted or do you think he'd have fought that old coot off, just like you did, possibly killing him in the process?"

"It wasn't self-defense, Morgan. I'd do it again given the chance, only this time I'd make it hurt a hell of a lot worse."

Morgan nodded. "Understandable given the circumstance, but from what I saw, it *was* self-defense." He looked toward the door when someone came in. "Speak of the devil and he shows up," he said before smiling. "We were just talking about you, Percy."

"All good, I'm sure," he said, smiling as he walked to the bar.

Noah looked over at him and nodded a greeting. The man was panting for breath as he leaned against the bar. He accepted the glass the bartender gave him, slung it back and shivered after swallowing the bitter liquid. When he set the glass down, he motioned for another.

Percy watched the bartender pour him another drink, then said, "I knew my ears were burning for a reason. What was you saying about me, Marshal?"

Morgan grinned. "Nothing that wasn't true."

"Which would be?"

"Noah thinks I need to arrest him for killing the drifter you two tangled with the other day."

Percy grinned as the bartender poured him another shot. "A man who thinks you should arrest him. That's a new one." He downed his drink and glanced his way. "You gonna do it?"

"I should just because he asked for it." Morgan laughed and readjusted his hat. "But the jail's had enough visitors as of late." He looked at Noah. "I'm not going to arrest you. You've nothing to worry about."

The relief Noah felt nearly buckled his knees. He held on to the bar and listened to the two men talk while trying to get strength enough to walk back out and climb on his horse.

All the plans he'd made for Keri and those kids weren't just a dream anymore. He could make them happen. All he had to do was ask Keri to marry him and make it all legal.

He started to make an excuse to leave when Morgan mentioned Laurel's name. He'd almost forgotten about the school teacher. He'd been too caught up in his own problems to think of her. Noah looked his way, then asked, "Is she going to be all right?"

Morgan nodded. "Well, I guess that depends on if Holden will stop coddling her long enough for her to actually recover. She's doing fine, although, Holden will probably keep her in bed for the next seven months." Noah raised an eyebrow and Morgan's smile widened. "She's pregnant. Add in the fact she was shot and Holden's damn near smothering her. I think she's ready to come back to town and sleep in Evan's office just to get a break from his constant attention."

Noah smiled. "I can't say I blame him." He'd probably have reacted the same way had Keri been the one to take that bullet. He understood completely what Holden must be feeling. Just thinking of Keri being the one that bullet found made him eager to see her, to make sure she was all right. He pushed away from the bar. "I need to get back to the house. I left Keri and the kids alone out there and I shouldn't have." He turned and started for the door, but stopped when Percy said, "I was just out there. They're fine."

He turned and faced the man. "You were out at my place?"

"Yep. Everything seemed all right when I left." He motioned the bartender for another drink before looking back over at him. "I didn't know your wife had a brother."

Noah straightened as his pulse started to race. What was Percy doing out at his place? "She does," he said, eyeing the man as questions started firing off inside his head. "Lives out in California."

"Yeah, that's what he said." Percy tilted his glass and downed his shot. "They don't look nothing alike. Their coloring is all different."

Look alike? How did Percy know what Peter looked like? Alarm caused his whole body to jolt. Had Percy seen Keri's brother? Was he here in Willow Creek? Everything he felt must have shown on his face for Percy raised an eyebrow at him before glancing briefly at Morgan. "Why are you two looking at me like that?"

Noah saw Morgan move out of the corner of his eye before he asked, "How do you know what Keri's brother looks like, Percy?"

"I showed him how to get out to Noah's place." Percy eyed them both, looking from one to the other. "I ran across him on my way in to town. He was sitting out on the road like he was lost so I stopped to talk to him, told him how close he was to Willow Creek, and that I was headed this way and he could follow me if he wanted." He leaned back against the bar and propped his elbows up. "He wasn't much interested in town though but asked if I'd ever heard of Keri and her kids." He scratched the side of his neck, and narrowed his eyes. "He said her last name was Hilam, not Lloyd, so I assumed he didn't know she married you, Noah, so I set him straight."

Keri's brother was here? Noah barely heard what Percy was

saying his heart was pounding so hard. How? Why? He closed his eyes and blew out a breath.

Why now? Why, when he finally had the courage to ask her to marry him did her brother have to show up? His timing couldn't have been worse.

Keri had been waiting for her brother, had risked everything by taking off in the middle of the night to find him, and now after months of waiting and searching, he'd found her. Morgan's contact must have come through. He almost wished he wouldn't have.

Percy's voice was a soft hum in the background. He could see the man's mouth moving but nothing he said registered. All he could think of was the fact he'd wasted three days with Keri by distancing himself and now he wouldn't even get a chance to tell her why.

Would she wait to tell him she was leaving or would she be gone by the time he got back home? The way he'd been acting, he wouldn't blame her if she took off without a word.

He looked at Percy and Morgan and nodded his head to both of them. "I've got to go." He turned and pushed through the swinging doors. He was halfway across the wooden sidewalk when he realized he might already be too late. Keri and the kids may already be gone.

CHAPTER THIRTY-THREE

Watching Robert tear through Noah's things as if he had a right to do so left Keri in a state of shock and scalded the back of her eyes with tears.

How was he here?

Memories of the night they ran raced through her mind. The sound of Robert choking, the sickly pallor of his face and the sickening thud of his body hitting the floor slammed into her all at once. She'd been sure she'd killed him. She'd only meant to put him to sleep, to immobilize him long enough so they could get away, but something had gone wrong. She'd known it the moment his lips turned blue. The moment he looked at her, his eyes bulging in his head before he slumped over and fell at her feet.

She held back a sob at the memory and tucked Aaron and Sophie Ann closer to her body. Fear stole her voice, her gaze following Robert around the room as she wondered what he was going to do. Would he take what he found and leave? Or would he get his revenge first? Was that why he was here?

He kicked the trunk that sat at the foot of the bed, the noise the lid made as it slammed down echoing in the stillness. "Where the hell does he keep his money, Keri?"

She opened her mouth three times before finally getting the words, "He doesn't have any," out.

"You're lying!" He braced both hands on his hips and glared at her. "There's enough food in the kitchen to feed a small army and those coats hanging by the door are made of good wool and fur. A poor man don't buy expensive things like that unless he has money enough to do it with so I'll ask you one more time, and by God you better answer me. Where does he keep his money?"

She blinked, forcing the tears away. "If I knew I would tell you, Robert. I've never seen any money or anything of value. What you see is all there is."

He sneered at her and gritted his teeth, his jaw clenching several times before he searched the room again. He stopped in front of the fireplace and reached up, grabbing Noah's journal and thumbing through the pages. His back went stiff moments before he shook his head. "Well, would you look at that," he said before turning and looking at her. The sneer on his face told her he'd seen the drawings of her and the kids.

Robert grabbed one of the pages and ripped it from the book. She flinched at the sound of ripping paper and stared at the drawing of Aaron and Duke before he crumpled the page and tossed it behind him into the fire.

Her heart broke watching that drawing burn. "Please, Robert, just take what you want and go."

He kept thumbing through the drawings and paused at the one of her. "Look at you," he said. "He turned you into a real fancy lady." He stared at the drawing for long minutes before closing the book with a loud snap and looking up at her. The expression in his eyes was cold and distant and she pulled Aaron and Sophie Ann closer. "You like posing for pictures?" he asked, his voice deceptively calm. She didn't answer him. He shook his head again, ran his gaze over her from head to toe before smiling so cruelly, her skin crawled. "You like being married to him more than me?"

The words, "we were never married," hung on the tip of her tongue but she knew better than to voice them. When she didn't reply to his question, he narrowed his eyes, hatred burning brightly. "I want everything that isn't nailed down put into the back of the wagon. Take the food stuff first. Pack it in tight so we can get it all." His gaze ran the length of her from head to toe before he sneered. "You're still a sniveling, pathetic woman, Keri. I can't for the life of me figure out what my brother ever saw in you." He glanced down at Noah's journal. "Nor this man." He looked back up and smiled, the curve of his lips making the gesture look cruel. "We both know you ain't worth nothin'." With a simple flick of his wrist, Robert tossed Noah's journal into the fire behind him and walked off.

"No!" Keri made a move to retrieve the book. Flames caught on the leather cover and the pages inside within seconds. She stood stunned, tears filling her eyes as she watched the book burn, and tried to swallow past the lump in her throat. Sophie Ann sniffled at her side. She pulled her tight against her again and hoped she didn't say anything.

When they just stood there staring into the fire, Robert bellowed, "Get moving! I want this place cleaned out before he gets back."

Keri knew she had no choice but do as he demanded. She'd not been completely honest with Noah when he asked about Robert. She'd lied and said Robert only slapped her when he felt the need, but the beatings she'd taken from him in order to protect her children were still fresh in her mind. She knew he'd use her kids to get what he wanted and right now, he wanted everything Noah had.

She ushered Aaron and Sophie into the kitchen, her heart slamming against her ribcage so hard, she could barely breathe.

She reached up to the first shelf, grabbed a few of the smaller bags and handed them down.

The fear on her children's faces would be etched inside her brain for years to come. The shock at seeing Robert at the door instead of Peter had taken her longer to recover from than it should have. She still regretted not being able to tell Percy that the man he'd brought to their front door wasn't who he said he was, but fear had stolen her breath and taken her ability to speak.

She'd not made a sound as she stood there staring at what she thought was a dead man. She'd killed him. Poisoned him on purpose but killed him by accident. She'd watched his body fall, heard his breath ease past his lips and left him on the floor without a single drop of remorse.

Another crash echoed in the main room. They all jumped, Sophie Ann's eyes filling with tears again. "Don't cry, love," she whispered. "I'll not let him hurt you."

Aaron shook his head. "Then he'll just hurt you instead."

Keri smiled at him. "If I can handle Noah bellowing the way he did when he first found us, then I'm strong enough now to handle Robert." She glanced into the other room where he stood, her lip curling in distaste. "You just do as he says and don't say a word. Got it?"

When they both nodded, she filled her arms with Noah's dry goods and ushered the kids outside, stowing the bags in the back of Robert's wagon. Every trip they made tore a chunk out of Keri's heart. When Noah returned to find his things gone, he would think the worst of her. She could live with a lot of things, and had, but knowing Noah would think she cared so little for him that she'd take everything he had burned in her soul.

She'd spent months scared Robert would lash out and hurt one of them and she'd let him terrorize them until she'd done something drastic. She knew in her heart she'd let her children down. It was her job to protect them, and she realized in the many trips in and out of Noah's small cabin, that she had a chance to rectify that mistake.

When the house was cleaned to Robert's satisfaction, she pushed the kids back into the kitchen and stepped into the main room to face him. "That's everything," she said. "And I covered it all like you said."

Robert reached up and took Noah's gun from the hooks above the fireplace. "Then grab your things and wait for me outside."

Keri swallowed back the fear she felt, her eyes on the gun, and hoped he didn't shoot her. "We're not going with you."

He was slow to turn and look at her but when he did, her heart skipped a beat. His steps were slow, his eyes locking on hers as he crossed the room. "You are going with me," he said, his voice pitched low and harsh. "I didn't spend the last seven months wandering around the territory looking for you to leave you here. Now get what you want to take with you or you'll go home with nothing but the clothes on your back. Your choice."

His black eyes had never looked so dead. Keri swallowed the lump in her throat while looking at the barrel of the gun. She didn't have a doubt in her mind that he'd shoot her.

Robert had changed since that night all those months ago. His dark hair hung limply to his shoulders, the stubble on his face at least a few weeks long. He was unkempt, stank to high heaven and something in his eyes chilled her to the bone. As hateful and mean spirited as he'd been, something told her she was staring into the eyes of the devil himself. Something wasn't right about him and she didn't know what it was. Nor did she want to ask. Her confidence waned and the old fear she'd thought she'd let go of began creeping back in until she wasn't sure what to do.

She needed time to think. She turned to the bed and bundled what few items of clothing they had, then helped Aaron and Sophie slip on their coats. She fastened the last of the buttons on her own coat when Duke started barking. Robert lifted his head, then darted into the kitchen. He muttered a few curses and came back into the main room. "Someone's coming down the road."

The glee Keri felt was short lived. Robert grabbed her by the arm and pulled her close. "If you make so much as a twitch to alert whoever it is out there that I'm not really your brother, they'll be dead before they hit the ground." He looked to Aaron and Sophie Ann. "The same goes for you two. Not a word. I'll put a bullet between your mamma's eyes if you do."

Sophie Ann started crying the moment Robert shoved them toward the door. Keri pulled her close and tried to shush her and nearly succeeded. When they reached the wagon, Robert laid the gun under the seat but kept his hand on the wooden stock.

"Remember what I said," he told them, then grabbed Keri's arm in a grip so tight, she knew her skin would be bruised.

She looked toward Aaron and Sophie Ann. "Don't utter a sound. Do you hear?" They nodded but she wasn't sure they even heard her. "No matter who it is, don't say anything." Her attention shifted back to the person riding down the long drive toward them. As much as she wanted it to be Noah, she hoped wherever he'd gone, he was still there.

The closer the horse and rider drew near, the quicker her pulse raced. It was Noah, she could tell by the set of his shoulders. By how tall he sat his horse. When he was close enough to see his face clearly, tears once again filled her eyes. How would she ever get through the next few moments and manage to stay sane?

She was too afraid to let Noah know who Robert was but too terrified not to. They couldn't leave with him. They'd never escape again.

Noah slowed when he reached the house, his gaze locking on hers as he pulled the horses reins and brought the animal to a stop. He stared at her for long moments before dismounting, letting the reins dangle as the horse roamed, and crossed the yard to where they all stood by the wagon.

When he stopped, Keri's heart lodged in her throat when Robert draped an arm around her shoulder and pulled her close. "You're just in time. We were about to leave."

She looked at Noah and willed him to see that something was wrong. When he tilted his head to one side and stared at Robert, his eyes narrowing, she prayed the look on his face meant she was about to get her wish.

Percy was right. Peter Hilam looked nothing like Keri. Where she was blonde with fair skin and bright-blue eyes, Peter was dark, his hair black as night, the same as his eyes. He also looked much older than her.

Noah stopped at the back of the wagon, glanced at it briefly, then turned his attention to Keri and the kids, noticing their coats were buttoned up tight and no one would look him in the eye.

He'd been right. They were leaving.

The plans he'd made for them were for nothing now. Keri had done the one thing he always suspected she'd do regardless of what they shared. She was leaving with her brother and would forget he even existed.

Since the day he'd found them, he'd known their time together was only temporary and he'd been foolish enough to think she cared about him. He realized now how wrong he'd been and anger settled into his bones quicker than he could control it. He narrowed his eyes, looked at Keri and said, "Were you not even going to tell me you were leaving?"

·She flinched moments before Peter smiled again and said, "I tried to get her to wait but you know how Keri is. Impatient as any woman can be." He laughed and shook his head. "Besides, little Sophie Ann don't like the dark much. The sooner we get going, the sooner we can get settled in before the sun goes down."

Noah glanced at Sophie Ann. Her eyes were glassy. He'd almost say tears lingered in her blue eyes but he knew she'd been feeling poorly the past couple of days. It was probably fever set in again regardless of what his heart wanted to believe.

A thousand memories assaulted him, every second of every day he'd spent with this rag-tag little family beating against his heart until the anger he felt was washed away, replaced with bone deep grief he knew he'd never get over. The pain he'd lived with the last twelve years was nothing compared to the aching hole widening inside his chest as he looked at Keri and those kids.

And he knew the pain was his own fault.

He'd vowed to never let anyone get close enough to make him care again and Keri's shy smiles made him forget. They made him forget what he was, what he looked like, and he let the attention of a woman who was probably just doing what she had to do to keep a roof over her kids' heads fill his heart with something that just wasn't there.

Noah stared at Aaron and Sophie Ann, trying unsuccessfully to catch their eye but neither one of them would look at him. Keri did, though. Her gaze bore into him as if there wasn't anything else in the world for her to look at. It tore that hole in his heart open just a little bit more to see her looking at him so intently.

He looked away and saw Duke sitting near the side of the house. He'd brought that old hound home for them. To keep the kids company and to alert him if anyone was on his property and now the reason that old dog was there was leaving. He tried to harden his heart again and looked Keri in the eye. "Once the sun hits the top of that mountain, it'll get dark pretty quick so I guess you better get a move on." Turning, he walked back to the horse, grabbed the dangling reins and started off toward the barn.

And with each step, it took every ounce of courage he had to not beg Keri to stay.

His steps were sure, each booted foot hitting the frozen

ground just a little bit harder than necessary and once he'd yanked the barn door open and ushered the horse inside, then closed the door behind him, it was all he could do to keep standing. His legs felt weak, as if he'd run all the way home from town.

Unsaddling the horse and getting him bedded in for the night was done in a daze. Sounds from outside broke through the silence every once in a while and he tuned them out and tried not to imagine them getting into that wagon and leaving.

When the animals were seen to, he sighed, looked toward the small loft on the far end of the barn and laughed, the sound bitter to his own ears. The Christmas gifts he'd bought for Aaron, Sophie Ann and Keri the night of the Christmas recital were stacked in one corner, an old horse blanket covering the heap to help hide them from the family he'd thought to keep forever. What was he supposed to do with all that stuff now?

The sounds from outside grew and the pain he'd felt after the fire paled in comparison to the agony ripping through his body. His entire future was being ripped from him and he didn't say a word. He couldn't. His throat felt tight, his chest aching when he heard the squeak of the wagon wheels as it started to move.

As the sounds grew distant, he heard Sophie Ann start calling his name, her sobs loud and anguished, and he suddenly couldn't breathe. He bent at the waist, propped his hands on his knees, and tried to tune her out, to not care, but failed miserably.

The happiness he'd lived with for the past two months slowly drained away to leave him hollow. His family left him and he hadn't even tried to stop them.

CHAPTER THIRTY-FOUR

T he desire to turn and look back was great but Keri couldn't make herself do it. She was too afraid of what she'd see. Her heart was ripping in two and Sophie Ann screaming Noah's name only made the pain worse. She'd not wanted to cry in front of Robert, but she wasn't able to hold back the pain as her children cried for a man who made them fall in love with him regardless of his surly ways.

A man who apparently didn't want them in return.

"Shut her up, Keri!"

Keri wiped her face dry and turned in the seat, looking at Aaron and Sophie Ann where they sat near the back of the wagon. "Hush, love." Sophie Ann's tear-streaked face was red and puffy but she stopped yelling for Noah. Her snuffles lasted for long minutes but she quieted enough that Robert didn't say anything else.

She looked over at him as they neared the main road. "Where are you taking us?"

"Home."

Images of the farm she'd shared with John flashed in her

memory. "Why?" she asked. "It's yours if you want it. You don't want or need us."

Robert laughed. "That's where you're wrong." He glanced her way. "That no good brother of mine went and done somethin' stupid." He looked back at the road. "He had some fancy lawyer draw up papers saying everything he owned belonged to you and you alone if he died." They rounded the curve and neared the fork in the road that would lead into town. Robert went right, and headed toward the Avery Ranch instead. "I need you to sign those property deeds over to me, Keri. That farm belonged to my pa's family for generations and I ain't letting some piss-poor dirt farmer's daughter take it from me."

"Fine. We don't need to go back with you for that."

"Yes, you do." He scowled and shook his head. "That lawyer won't do it unless you're there and he sees you sign the papers himself."

A bit of hope made her sit up straight. All Robert wanted was the farm? She swallowed to moisten her throat and hoped she didn't sound too eager. "Does that mean once I've signed everything over to you, that we're free to go?"

Robert turned his head to look at her and started laughing, throwing his head back and howling with unrestrained glee. When he finally quieted, he shook his head. "You're a dumb-ass woman, Keri." He chuckled again. "You poisoned me! Left me to choke on my own vomit and I'm gonna make you pay for that until the day you die."

Keri's heart lodged itself in her throat. "What do you mean?"

The look in his eye chilled her to the bone. She didn't want to think about how he'd make them pay but knew whatever he had in mind would be painful and last until she wished he'd just kill them to end their misery.

She saw Aaron out of the corner of her eye and turned her head to look back at him when she saw him moving. Her eyes widened when he stood and jumped from the back of the wagon. "Aaron!"

Everything happened so fast then. The moment Aaron hit the ground, Sophie Ann jumped, her small body rolling as Aaron ran to grab her. They both stood and started running back down the road toward Noah's. Tears clogged her throat but she managed to turn, leaning across the back of the seat as she yelled for them both.

The wagon jerked to a stop and Robert moving barely registered until she saw the barrel of Noah's shotgun appear beside her face. Her eyes widened when he aimed the gun at her children and she reached out, pushing the barrel away just as the gun went off, the kick-back from the shot flinging her backwards.

Robert jerked her away, his face a mask of fury. He swung his arm, the blow to her head dazing her enough all she could do was sit there and stare up at him until her anger boiled hot and ugly, all the fear she'd felt from him since John's death exploding into a fury so hot, her blood felt ready to boil in her veins.

Keri screeched, screaming until her throat hurt. She curled her fingers and launched herself at him, her nails digging into the skin on his face and she pushed until they both toppled out of the wagon, the breath knocked from her lungs the moment she hit the ground.

Staring at the sky above her, she gasped, trying to fill her lungs again and barely managed to do so before Robert appeared in her line of sight. He was on her in a second.

The first blow was enough to kill the pain she felt from the fall out of the wagon. She curled herself into a ball and hoped he didn't kill her this time. Long minutes later, the weight of him was gone, the ringing inside her head starting to dim and the sound of grunts finally registered. She opened her eyes, blinking to clear her vision, and wondered if the scene before her was real or if she was imagining it.

Noah had Robert slammed into the side of the wagon, his

hand fisted into the front of his shirt. Blood oozed from Robert's lip and his head hung to one side, his eyes closed. When Noah dropped him, Robert's body hit the ground with a loud thud. Keri blinked and tried to lift her head.

Aaron's voice reached her long moments before she saw him. He was staring down at Robert, his shoulders held at an angle that made him look much older than he was. The shotgun clamped between his hands did too. He aimed it at Robert and never took his eyes off him.

Noah turned to her, the look on his face confusing. He looked angry, but she saw fear shining in his eyes. When he bent to one knee and put an arm under her shoulder, lifting her from the ground, she didn't care what sort of mood he was in. She flung herself at him, wrapping her arms around his neck and squeezed until he grunted. "I didn't want to leave," she said, her eyes burning as her throat grew tight. "He said he'd shoot you if we said anything..."

She didn't get another word out, tears making it impossible to speak. Noah held her, his grip on her tightening as he buried his face into the curve of her neck and it wasn't until her tears had dried that she realized he was talking, the soft, whispered words muffled against her neck.

When she finally understood what he was saying, the tears were once again burning her eyes and falling down her face faster than she could stop them. Pulling back, she met his gaze, her heart thundering inside her chest. "Say it again."

Noah raised his head. "I love you. I should have told you the moment I realized it." He pushed her hair away from her face with one hand. "I can't let you go, Keri. I'll follow you all the way back to Great Falls if I have to. I'm nothing without you. Without those kids. You're my family. I need you. All three of you."

He leaned in to kiss her and Keri whispered, "I love you, too," against his lips.

His eyes brightened. "Does that mean you'll stay with me?"

Her smile widened before nodding her head.

"As my wife?" He grinned. "For real this time. Not just because Morgan Avery said it was so."

Sophie Ann stepped into her line of sight. She glanced at her, saw her smiling face and looked toward Aaron. He nodded his head once before turning his attention back to Robert.

Looking back at Noah, Keri laid her forehead against his own and sighed. "Nothing would make me happier than to be your wife, Noah."

Robert didn't realize how lucky he was. Colt and Tristan Avery showing up was the only reason the man wasn't facedown in the dirt, gagging on his own blood.

The Avery men had been headed into town when they heard the gunshot and set their horses into a run. Noah had been grateful to see them, especially after finding out everything that wasn't nailed down inside his cabin was in the back of Robert's wagon. He'd wanted to kill him, especially when Sophie Ann told him they'd had to carry everything themselves. Seeing his stolen property was reason enough to send for Morgan. Tristan rode into town to fetch him while Colt stayed behind and made sure Robert wasn't going to be a problem.

It took close to an hour before the marshal showed up and he seemed a bit eager to escort Robert to jail when the day's events were related to him. The circuit court judge was due in any day now and Noah hoped the man threw Robert under the jail to rot.

When they got home, Duke barking his usual greeting, the kids jumped from the wagon, excitedly telling the mutt that they were there to stay. Noah helped Keri to the ground, his hands tight around her waist and was reluctant to let go. "Are you sure you want to marry me?"

Her face lit up, her eyes sparkling as she looked up at him.

"More than sure." She wrapped her arms around his neck. "The sooner the better."

The relief he felt weakened his knees. "Tomorrow good for you?"

Keri grinned. "Tomorrow is perfect."

"Tomorrow it is then."

It was snowing. Keri watched fat flakes of it swirl in the breeze as Duke jumped, his jaws snapping open and closed as he tried to catch them. The noise from the other room was a riot of laughter, squeals and the occasional shout.

Putting the last breakfast plate on the shelf, she untied her apron and hurried into the other room. Aaron and Sophie Ann were by the tree, nervous energy causing them both to bounce on their feet as Noah shook his head at their repeated demands to open the gifts. The moment he saw her, he smiled and stood.

"Thank goodness. They were about to drive me to drinking."

Keri laughed and settled into one of the kitchen chairs Noah had sat by his rocker. He kissed her forehead and turned to Aaron and Sophie Ann. "All right," he said. "Now you can open them."

The excitement grew with every opened gift. Keri sat stunned as Aaron and Sophie Ann carefully opened every package, their happy faces lighting up more with each new find.

A hat similar to the one Noah wore now graced Aaron's head. She could tell by the grin on Aaron's face that they'd have a hard time getting the thing off his head. There were books and games, more clothes than either would have time to wear and the blank journal Sophie Ann received for her own drawings held one special picture. A drawing of her, surrounded by flowers, kittens and ponies.

Keri had received her most precious gift the day before in

Missoula. A promise of love and a lifetime of happiness from a man she knew would never harm them. Noah had recited his vows, and threw in a few extra of his own, making their make-believe marriage a reality.

The wedding ring he'd given her rivaled any she'd ever seen, and their single night in a hotel, the kids tucked away in a room right beside their own, was the closest to heaven as she'd ever been.

Her heart felt so full, she wasn't sure she could take much more joy, but seeing Noah sitting beside her, she knew her life would be filled with happiness. With a man as loving as Noah, how could it not be?

EPILOGUE

K eri fluffed the pillows again, rearranged them on the sofa for the third time and stepped back, turning in a full circle to take in the whole room and sighed.

It was perfect.

Duke's deep-toned bark caused the nervous butterflies she'd been fighting all day to roar back to life. She looked to the door as it swung open, Sophie Ann's excited squeals echoing off the walls as she ran inside.

"They're here!" she said, her blond curls bouncing on her shoulders. "They just turned onto the road to the house."

Keri nodded and walked the entire house again. The new kitchen was large enough for a whole army of women to cook in. The new stove and table gleaming as bright as the day they'd been bought.

The main room, which was the original cabin, housed furniture to sit on, a large sofa, chairs that sat near the fire, small tables and oil lamps and woven rugs large enough to cover the entire floor. The bed now stood in one of the three bedrooms Noah had built, the privacy those rooms afforded being the best improvement they'd made to the little cabin. It wasn't so little now. It was a proper home, furnished modestly despite the money she now knew Noah had. After spending the majority of her life just barely getting by, they'd never want for anything the rest of their lives.

"Do you think they'll like me?"

Keri turned her attention back to Sophie Ann and smiled. "They're going to love you," she said. "Go on out and wait for them. I'll be there in a moment."

Noah set the brake on the wagon and jumped to the ground, looking to Aaron as he pulled his pony to a stop near the barn. He smiled at the boy, then rounded the front of the wagon and walked to the side, offering a hand up to help his mother climb down.

His stomach had been in knots since the day he'd gotten a response to his letter. Keri had been right. His family had been worried. The guilt he felt for causing them grief would weigh on him for a while but he hoped to ease a bit of their pain now.

Marcus Cooper, his new brother-in-law helped Noah's sister, Judith, to the ground. He barely recognized her. The young girl he'd left behind was a grown woman now.

His mother looked very much like she had last time he'd seen her. Her hair was peppered with streaks of gray and small line bracketed her eyes, but she was still as lovely as he remembered.

And eager to meet his new family.

He smiled at her, taking her arm and walking with her to the house. Mary Lloyd was a small woman, her limbs thin, but her regal posture made her look as fit as women half her age. She'd talked nonstop on the ride from town, but now that they'd arrived home, she'd not said a word.

Sophie Ann bounded around the corner of the house, the smile on her face as bright as always. Her eyes lit up the moment she saw them and he knew it was taking every ounce of self control the girl had not to jump up and down with excitement.

When they reached her, his mother stopped and smiled. "You must be Sophie Ann," she said.

"Yes, ma'am."

"You're every bit as pretty as Noah said you were."

Sophie flushed, her cheeks turning pink as she beamed. "That's only 'cause I look like my ma."

The moment Sophie mentioned Keri, she rounded the corner of the house, his heart skipping a beat the moment he saw her. She was smiling, her steps quick, but he could see the uncertainty in her eyes.

"Mother, I'd like you to meet Keri, my wife."

Mary Lloyd barely gave Keri a passing glance, her gaze riveted to the squirming bundle in Keri's arms. Noah smiled and reached out to her. "And this," he said, "Is Nathaniel, our son."

He heard his mother's soft intake of breath, tears filling her eyes as she looked at the baby. "You named him for your father."

Noah nodded. "He was the greatest man I've ever known."

The blustery wind was sharp enough to force them all inside. Noah watched from his spot near the fire as his mother and sister showered his children, all three of them, with enough love to last them a lifetime.

Watching his family filled his heart to near bursting. Keri and the kids had given him a purpose, a reason to get out of bed every day, and a will to live life as he was meant to. Surrounded by friends, family and love.

Dear Reader,

Noah and Keri are one of my favorite couples. I heard them talking to me long after their story was finished and I knew one day, we'd see them again and we do, in book 8 of the series. Nightingale is Aaron Hilam's story and takes place quite a few year in the future. Noah and Keri play key roles in the book and it was nice to revisit them and see where life had taken them.

If you're new to the Willow Creek Series, this small close knit community has taken on a life of its on and the people who dwell there have become very real to me. Although each story stands alone and the books can be read in any order, its always nice to start from the beginning so, I invite you to meet the characters who make up Willow Creek by reading The Lawman, book 1 in this series. It is FREE at all ebook retailers. Head back to the store you purchase your ebooks to grab your copy of The Lawman or find links on My Website.

WANT MORE?

For information about upcoming books in the Prison Moon, Willow Creek or Silver Falls Series, and any other books by Lily Graison, subscribe to her Newsletter or find her around the web at the following locations.

Website: http://lilygraison.com/
FaceBook: http://www.facebook.com/authorLilyGraison
Reader Group: http://bit.ly/LilyGraisonReaderGroup
Instagram: https://www.instagram.com/authorlilygraison/

Email: lily@lilygraison.com

Subscribe to email notifications of new releases here:
Newsletter: http://bit.ly/LilyNewsletter

Also by Lily Graison

HISTORICAL WESTERN ROMANCE

The Lawman (Willow Creek #1)
The Outlaw (Willow Creek #2)
The Gambler (Willow Creek #3)
The Rancher (Willow Creek #4)
His Brother's Wife (Willow Creek #5)
A Willow Creek Christmas (Willow Creek #6)
Wild Horses (Willow Creek #7)
Lullaby (A Willow Creek Short Story)
Nightingale (Willow Creek #8)
Heartstrings (Willow Creek #8.5)
The Angel Tree (Willow Creek Stand Alone)

The Avery's of Willow Creek:
Boxset Vol.1 - Books 1 - 4

Willow Creek Boxset Vol. 2
Books 5,6 & 7

A Soft Kiss in Winter (Silver Falls #1)
A Soft Kiss in Spring (Coming Soon)

SCIENCE FICTION ROMANCE

PRISON MOON SERIES
Dragon Fire
Warlord's Mate

CONTEMPORARY ROMANCE
Wicked: Temp Me Not (Wicked Series #1)

Wicked: Leather and Lace (Wicked Series #2)
Wicked: Jade Butterfly (Wicked Series #3)
Wicked: Sweet Temptation (Wicked Series #4)
Wicked: The Complete Series (Books #1 - 4)

SWEET (NO SEX) ROMANCE

Anna: Bride of Alabama (historical romance)

Angel Creek Christmas Brides Series
Julia (historical romance)
Caroline (historical romance)

ABOUT THE AUTHOR

Lily Graison is a USA TODAY bestselling author of historical western romances who has been known to dabble in sci-fi, contemporary and paranormals when the mood strikes. The author of over twenty novels, her stories all lean heavily toward the spicy side with strong female characters and heroes who tend to always get their way. She writes full time and lives in Hickory, NC with her husband and a house full of Yorkies

Website: http://lilygraison.com/
Or Email Lily at: lily@lilygraison.com

Made in the USA
Las Vegas, NV
17 January 2024

84525612R00173